業有限公司
ing Ltd.

U0057194

⋯⋯⋯⋯⋯⋯⋯⋯⋯⋯⋯⋯⋯⋯⋯⋯⋯⋯⋯⋯⋯⋯⋯⋯⋯⋯⋯⋯⋯⋯⋯⋯⋯俱樂部 ◎著

Let's Talk about Gourmet in English!

美食英語

美食永遠是最好的話題

打破語言疆界 分享飲食文化
從平價小吃到高檔料理　無論觀光客還是在地人

餐飲／觀光／旅遊專業從業人員 自我提升必備
沙發衝浪／背包客／出國旅行者 文化交流必備
接待國外友人／電梯巧遇客戶 聊天哈拉必備

特別規劃：
4大 美食主題館：
主食、甜點、飲料、點心

精心準備：
6大 異國經典美食：
美式、中式、日式、義式、港式、泰式

各館導覽：

【實用對話】聊天必備
● 帶老外吃挫冰要點「粉粿加愛玉」你會嗎？
● 手搖茶飲點珍珠奶茶「半糖少冰」怎麼説？

【好用句型】點餐必會
● 咖啡可以續杯嗎？ 用refill很到位。
● 飲料不用了，直接上甜點! 用skip不囉嗦。

【飲食百科】文化大不同
● 在義大利要點拿鐵説Lette卻送來一杯鮮奶?!

【菜餚故事】不說你不知道
● 原來日本有名的傳統甜點「宇治金時」其實是抹茶和紅豆!!

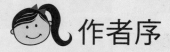

作者序
Preface

　　吃，不僅是為了填飽肚子，人人都嚮往的美食可以滌淨一個人的身心，更是人際交流的最佳管道。你知道嗎？其實從一個國家的飲食習慣可以窺見該國的歷史背景、人文風情、氣候水土，飲食甚至可以跨越國界與種族，經過文化間的彼此融合後呈現出不同風味的多變樣貌。

　　《美食英語》透過無人能抗拒的經典美食一窺六個國家的文化，除了能更加瞭解我們平日喜愛的美食，最重要的是可以從中學到相關的實用英語。《美食英語》不只讓你食指大動，動動食指翻開書頁就能提升英文能力，還有比這更誘人的語言學習方式嗎？

　　《美食英語》讓你不再煩惱周末要吃甚麼美食犒賞自己，再也不必擔心點餐英語老是卡卡。能吃就是福，祝福大家永遠好口福！

伍羚芝

編者序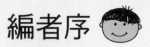

Words from Editor

冷場王還是話題王？「美食」永遠是最好的話題！

　　與上司等電梯時的空檔，與客戶開會時的中場休息，與外籍朋友路邊的閒聊，太多機會展現 您的哈拉功力了，此時 您是話題王，還是冷場王？聊天氣太乾，聊政治太敏感，聊工作又太無趣。「美食」永遠是最好的話題，隨便聊起一道昨天吃的夜市小吃，讓 您與不熟的人也能瞬間破冰。

學的英文都沒用？ 老外在場就失靈！

　　尤其在這全民瘋上傳美食照的年代，半日吃遍各地料理，說得一口美食經，但遇到老外在場就得了失語症？其實是因為很多中式烹調方法與食材英文裡面沒有，要用老外懂的字去解釋。課本沒有，老師沒教，自己平時沒有準備，當然沒辦法在關鍵時刻把美食變成話題讓自己加分。不但不能破冰，反而瞬間結冰。

從平價小吃到高檔料理 分享飲食文化 打破語言疆界

　　《美食英語》特別規劃了四個美食主題館：主食、甜點、飲料和點心，每個館都精心準備了各國不論是觀光客還是在地人都流口水的經典料理。還有聊天必備、點餐必會【實用對話】和【好用句型】，讓 您在這裡盡情【用英文聊美食】，讀【飲食小百科】領略各國飲食文化的精微奧妙，還有不說 您不知道的【菜餚故事】，從此談論各國美食再也難不倒 您，不但破冰，更後味無窮！

倍斯特編輯部

1 號 美食館：主食
Cuisine Gallery 1: Main Courses

目 次
C O N T E N T S

2 號 美食館：甜點
Cuisine Gallery 2: Desserts

3號 美食館：飲料
Cuisine Gallery 3: Beverages

4 號 美食館：點心
Cuisine Gallery 4: Snacks

1號

美食館：主食

Cuisine Gallery 1: Main Courses

料理是極具包容性的人類智慧結晶，原因就在於來自世界各地的外來移民紛紛將祖國的文化及習慣帶至世界各地，再與他國文化互相融合，漸漸演變出我們今日所謂的各國特色料理。加以創新並將料理發揚光大的不一定是料理的起源國家，這使得一樣料理不只侷限於發現初始的狀態，而是持續不斷進化的飲食文化演進。以下就讓我們來看看各國代表性的主食及特色吧！

　　Cuisine is a gemstone wisdom of human civilization. The reason is that emigrants from all over the world have their own country's culture and brought their customs to other countries and integrated them together, creating specialty cuisines in every country. To enhance and glorify cuisine innovation, cuisines do not necessarily have to be originated in that country, which make cuisines not only limited by tradition, but also keeping in constant evolution. Let's take a look at the main courses and characteristics of each country.

1.1
美式主食大集合
American Main Courses

服務生 A： 先生午安，請問需要點些甚麼呢？

Good afternoon sir, What would you like to order?

服務生 B： 我是第一次到美國來玩，想嘗嘗看道地的美國食物，請問有甚麼好推薦的嗎？

It's my first time in America. I want to try some typical American food. What do you recommend?

服務生 A： 烤豬肋排是美式燒烤飲食的精華，最具代表性的就是「紐奧良碳烤豬肋排」。其中一種叫做 Cajun 的調味粉是以十多種香料混合而成，其特殊的風味不僅是美國人的最愛，也受到吃重口味的亞洲人所喜愛喔。

Roasted pork ribs are the quintessence of American BBQ cuisine, and "New Orleans style pork roast" is the most representative. It adds a special flavor known as "Cajun cause," which is a mixture of more than ten spices. It is not only Americans' favorite, but also attracts Asians who enjoy heavy taste.

服務生 B： 聽起來很棒，不過現在還沒到中午，我怕光吃肉類難以消化。

Sounds great, but it's not lunch time yet. I'm afraid that if I just eat meat, it will cause me an indigestion.

服務生 A： 那真是太可惜了，不然我還想推薦您品嘗美國人最愛的肉類料理——牛排呢！那麼您覺得漢堡如何呢？一般美式漢堡除了漢堡排（Hamburger steak）以外，還可以改成魚排、雞排或豬排等，也可以搭配不同的配料和調味料，讓口感更豐富、更美味。

What a pity, or else I'd recommend you American's favorite meat cuisine, steaks! Would you like to have a burger then? In general, American style burgers, except for hamburger steaks, can be switched to fish, chicken, pork, etc. We can also put other ingredients or sauces into the burger, making it rich and tasty.

服務生 B： 我聽說來到美國南部一定要吃當地的美式炸雞，不過炸雞和漢堡在台灣的速食店就吃的到了，我想吃一些比較少見的特色料理。

I heard that if I come to southern America, I should try the local fried chickens. Since there are already fried chickens and burgers at fast food restaurants in Taiwan, I would like to try something rare and special.

服務生 A： 那麼墨西哥捲餅怎麼樣呢？墨西哥捲餅是用一張墨西哥薄餅（tortilla）將肉餡、蔬菜等捲成 U 字型。餡料從烤牛肉、雞肉、豬肉、魚蝦、乳酪都有，搭配的醬料則有莎莎醬（salsa sauce）、酪梨醬（guacamole）、碎番茄粒（pico de gallo）等。

How about burritos? Burritos are made by folded tortilla with meat stuffing and vegetables. The stuffing can be beef, chicken, pork, seafood or cheese. You may also choose

various sauces such as salsa sauce, guacamole, or crushed tomatoes (pico de gallo).

服務生 B： 墨西哥捲餅！？那不是墨西哥的料理嗎？

Burrito? Isn't it Mexican cuisine?

服務生 A： 墨西哥捲餅是墨西哥的傳統家庭料理沒錯，不過現在墨西哥式的烹飪方法已普及到一般美國家庭，對美國的飲食文化影響非常深，因此墨西哥捲餅也可被視為美式料理之一。

Burrito is a traditional Mexican dish for sure, but Mexican food is common in American families. Mexican food deeply influenced American's dining culture, and it is considered part of American cuisine.

服務生 B： 聽說墨西哥料理被譽為世界名菜，與法國菜和中國菜並駕齊驅，看來果真不假，那我就來一份烤牛肉的墨西哥捲餅吧！謝謝你。

I heard that Mexican cuisine is one of the most famous cuisines in the world, like French and Chinese ones. I would like to have a roast beef burrito. Thank you.

服務生 A： 好的，烤牛肉墨西哥捲餅一份馬上來。

Alright, one roast beef burrito. It will be served right the way.

飲食小百科 文化大不同
Differences in Cultures

 牛在各國文化中的定位
Cows Around the World

印度 Cattle In India

印度有「牛的王國」之稱，印度人將牛視為神聖不可侵犯的動物，在路上開車千萬要小心不可撞到牛，更不可配戴牛製品進入廟宇，最好也能盡量避免以牛為攝影拍照的對象，想當然耳印度人更是將食用牛肉視為大忌。

India, also known as "the Cattle Kingdom," treats cattle as sacred animal. In India, people drive carefully to avoid cattle, and cattle hide products are forbidden in temples. They avoid taking pictures of cows, and of course, beef is out of their diet.

美國 Cattle In America

牛肉是美國飲食文化中最為廣泛使用的食材之一。亞洲人偏好將肉類烹調至全熟，因為怕看到肉中帶血，而美國人則是認為帶血才能吃出牛肉的美味，並攝取到豐富的營養。美國人希望儘量保持食物的原汁原味和營養，不會特別著重調味及烹調法，食用牛排時通常只是將整塊牛排燒烤後再切片品嘗。

Beef is the most widely used ingredient in American diet culture. Asians try to avoid bloody meat, so they prefer to cook it; Americans prefer to eat it with blood to preserve its original taste and nutrition. They usually just roast the whole piece of steak and cut it in slices to keep its original taste.

13

日本 Cattle in Japan

日本曾經實施過超過千年的禁食肉類政策,直到近代這項禁令解除,加上日本深受西方飲食文化的影響,牛肉才逐漸成為日本人心中肉類的主要選擇,也成了日本人除了魚類以外最喜愛的動物性食材。

Japan had implemented a policy of abstention from meat for more than a thousand year, and the ban was lifted only in modern era. Beef became the main choice of meat under Western influence, and it also became the favorite animal ingredient, except for fish.

西班牙 Cattle in Spain

西班牙人盛行吃牛肚、牛尾,據説在鬥牛場上陣亡的牛最後都進了廚房,但其實鬥牛場上的牛不一定都會被人吃下肚。有些地方對於鬥牛士刺殺牛的時間和次數有所限制,如果超過限制,主席便會宣告鬥牛士停止刺殺,並將這頭牛視為神牛,直到其自然老死後再將其下葬,且不可食用其肉。

It's very popular in Spain to eat beef tripe and tails. It is said that after bullfighting, all bulls died in the battle are sent into the kitchen. However, not all fighting bulls become their food. In some cases, bullfighters have limited time and frequency to take down the bulls. If the bullfighter fail to take down the bull within the limit, the host will order the bullfighter to stop the event. People consider the survived bull as divine animal, and allow it to die naturally. It will also be buried, instead of being sent into kitchens.

中國 Cattle in China

在字典中,以「牛」為首的詞彙多達三百多個,許多語言學家認為這是牛與中國文化密不可分的象徵。中國古代可以用牛來祭祀、骨頭則用來占卜,牛的力氣大,因此可用來作為坐騎、拉車搬運。不僅牛肉可食用、牛皮可製造器具,更重要的是可以幫助農民用來耕田。在中國社會中也可看到許多與牛相關的典故，在民間社會更有各種敘述牛隻的傳奇故事，足以說明牛在中國人心中的重要性。

In Chinese dictionary, there are over three hundred words starting with "cattle." Many philologists believe that it is a symbol of the close relationship between cattle and Chinese culture. In Ancient China, cattle can be sacrificed to gods, and its bones can be used for divination. Cattle is strong, and it can be used for transportation. Cattle is also sources for food and clothing. More importantly, Chinese use cattle for cultivation. There are many folk legends based on cattle, which illustrate the importance of cattle in Chinese culture.

菜餚的故事 你知道嗎？
Stories About Food

漢堡的起源
The Origin of Hamburgers

最常聽到的說法是，漢堡源自於德國一個名叫「漢堡」(Hamburg)的海港城市，當地的人們把牛肉剁碎之後做成肉餅來食用。十九世紀中期，牛肉餅的作法隨著德國移民傳入美國本土，並逐漸在街頭巷尾流行了起來。另一個說法則是出自大航海時代，因為當時儲存在船艙內的肉塊乾硬不好食用，一艘從歐洲將移民載往北美洲的船隻「漢堡—阿美利加號」（Hamburg America）上的廚師為了能吃到柔嫩的肉塊，因此在船上發明了把碎牛肉剁成末加入洋蔥做成肉餅，並搭配麵包食用。當船上的移民抵達北美之後覺得這種肉餅麵包經濟又實惠，便普遍成為人們的日常三餐。

It is said that the origin of hamburgers was from a harbor city named Hamburg, Germany, where people made patty with smashed beef. In the mid-19th century, German immigrants introduce it to America and it

became popular. Others said that in the Age of Exploration, meat stored inside ship cabin often became too dry and too tough to eat. A chef who served in "Hamburg America," a ship carrying immigrants from Europe to America, invented the method of meat patty to keep the tenderness. The patty was also served with onions and breads. This affordable food item got popular when the immigrants arrived in America, and eventually became American's daily meals.

實用會話 聊天必備
Useful Phrases

 電話訂位
Making a Reservation by Phone

 午安，食神餐廳您好，很高興為您服務。
Good afternoon. Shi Shen Restaurant. How may I help you?

我想訂今天晚上的位子。
I'd like to reserve a table for this evening.

 請問一共幾位呢？
For how many people?

一共六位，我們想訂晚上 7 點。
For 6 people. We will come at 7:00.

很抱歉，目前 7 點的晚餐時段都已經客滿了。請問您願意提前或是晚一點用餐嗎？

I'm so sorry, but we're fully booked this evening at 7:00. Would you be willing to dine earlier or perhaps a little latter?

提早可能沒有辦法，請問晚一點的話，要到幾點才有空位呢？

Earlier might not be possible. If we come later, when will a table be available?

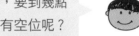

依目前的訂位狀況來看，可能要到 7 點 40 分以後才有空位喔。

As of right now, you might have to wait until 7:40 pm for a table.

那就 7 點 40 吧。那時候你們的招牌厚切牛排會不會都賣完了？

7:40 then. Will you still have the classic thick-cut steak by that time?

不會的，您一定能享用得到，請放心。

Yes, you will definitely enjoy it. Don't worry.

那真是太好了，我可是專程帶朋友過去吃的。

That's great. I am visiting with friends.

感謝您選擇食神餐廳，可以請您留下訂位姓名和連絡電話嗎？

Thank you for choosing Shi Shen Restaurant. May I have your name and phone number for the reservation?

沒問題。我叫 Tom Handerson。電話是 1800-333-0276。

No problem. My name is Tom Handerson and my phone number is 1800-333-0276.

謝謝您，Mr. Handerson。食神餐廳恭候您與您的朋友於今晚 7 點 40 分蒞臨。

Thank you, Mr. Handerson. Shi Shen Restaurant awaits you and your friends tonight at 7:40.

好用句型 點餐必會
Sentence Patterns

1. Can I sit here?／Can I take this seat?

   我可以坐這個位置嗎？

   seat：座位

   👍 會這句更加分 Excuse me, is this seat taken ?

   不好意思，請問這個座位有人坐嗎？

2. I'll have a burger, and one large order of French fries.

我要一個漢堡跟大份薯條。

order：訂購、叫（餐點或飲料）

👍 **會這句更加分** Are you ready to order?

請問您準備點餐了嗎？

3. Will you be eating here or is this to go (take out)?

For here or to go?

請問您要內用還是外帶？

外帶: Take out, please.

內用: I'll eat here.

4. May I have some more ketchup, please?

我可不可以多要一點蕃茄醬？

ketchup：蕃茄醬

👍 **會這句更加分** He spotted his shirt with ketchup.

他的衣服被番茄醬弄髒了。

5. Q: How about onions or mustard？ 要加洋蔥或芥末嗎？

A: Yes, please. 好的，謝謝。

mustard：芥末

👍 **會這句更加分** This mustard does not bite much.

這種芥末不會很嗆。

6. How do you like your steak cooked?／How would you like it cooked?

請問你的牛排要幾分熟？

Medium well, please.

七分熟，謝謝。

👍 **會這句更加分** 牛排的熟度：全熟 well done／七分熟 medium well／五分熟 medium／三分熟 medium rare／一分熟 rare

牛排只有 1、3、5、7 以及全熟，切記不要講出其他的熟度以免鬧笑話。多數高級餐廳在客人沒有特別指示的情況下，至少會將牛排烹調至三分熟。

主食 Main Course

甜點 Desserts

飲料 Beverages

點心 Snacks

19

1.2
中式主食大集合
Chinese Main Courses

用英文聊美食 聊天必備
Talking About Food In English

孫女： 外婆，老師要我們寫出可以代表中式餐飲的經典主食當回家作業，可是我不知道有那些耶。

Grandmother, the teacher wants us to write down main courses that can represent Chinese food as homework, but I don't know any of them.

外婆： 老師出這樣的作業很有意義啊！妳可以回想自己曾經在餐桌上吃過哪些主食。

This assignment is very meaningful. You can collect what you had as main courses on the dining table.

孫女： 可是除了媽媽平常煮的飯、麵以外，我就想不起來了。

But I can't think of any, except for the rice and noodles that mom usually cooks.

外婆： 傻孩子，妳忘了外婆的炒米粉（rice noodles）和端午節包的粽子了嗎？

Silly girl, did you forget grandma's rice noodles and the sticky rice dumplings of the Dragon Boat Festival?

孫女： 對耶！我記得外婆除了包南部粽，還會準備北部粽給我們吃，不過我一直分不出兩者間的差異。

Yeah, besides grandma's southern sticky rice dumplings, I also remember the northern sticky rice dumplings, but I always can't figure out the difference between them.

外婆： 相較於南部粽，北部粽的體積小巧，油較多、味道也較鹹。米粉則是因攜帶、食用方便而在魏晉南北朝時廣為流行，有湯米粉及炒米粉等吃法。

Compared with the southern sticky rice dumplings, the northern ones are much smaller, oily, and salty. Rice noodles are very convenient, and they became popular in the Wei, Jin, Southern and Northern Dynasties. You also can make rice noodles soup or fried rice noodles.

孫女： 原來是這樣，老師還要我們附上簡短介紹，剛好可以把外婆說的話寫進去。

I see. Our teacher also wants us to enclose a brief introduction. I guess I can just write down your words.

外婆： 那讓外婆再想想⋯ 在古代，食用油是相當珍貴的物品，因為必須消耗大量的穀物榨油或宰殺牲畜才能取得。少量的油脂就足以產生飽足感，而燒餅與油條這類的麵食因為可以完全吸收珍貴的食用油，所以十分受到庶民的歡迎。

Let me think... In ancient times, oil was a valuable item. It takes a considerable amount of grains or animal fats to produce cooking oil. A small amount of cooking oil would induce satiety, and seasame-coated flatbreads and fried bread sticks became very popular among the common people because they can completely absorb the precious cooking oil.

孫女： 那這樣的話，餃子跟餛飩算不算呢？

If that's so, how about dumplings and wontons?

21

外婆： 妳很會舉一反三喔，沒錯，餃子和餛飩除了內餡與外皮的搭配組合，沾醬的選擇也可依個人喜好加以變化，可說是集中國麵食烹調技術為一身的主食。最後還有地瓜和玉米喔。以前的農家最多的農作物就是地瓜，因此大家都會想辦法加以運用。吃不完的地瓜可以刨成絲、曬乾做成地瓜簽保存起來；也可以把多餘的地瓜請人磨成實用的地瓜粉。玉米不脫粒就可以直接蒸、煮、烤食用，也可加工製成麵粉、提煉成玉米油等。

You are very good at making examples. That's right. Besides the matching of dumplings' and wontons' fillings and flour wrappers, the dipping sauces may also vary according to personal preferences. You may say they are essences of Chinese food. There were also sweet potatoes and corns. Years ago, the largest farming crops were sweet potatoes, and everyone tried to make the best uses of them. Leftover sweet potatoes could be made into dried stripes. People also grind them into useful sweet potato powders. Corns can be steamed, boiled, and baked. They can also be grined into corn powders or be refined into corn oil.

孫女： 外婆懂好多喔！謝謝外婆。

Grandma really knows a lot! Thank you, grandma.

外婆： 要用自己的話寫，不可以照抄喔

Use your own words. Don't just copy what I said, please.

飲食小百科 文化大不同
Differences in Cultures

主食

麵食的靈魂 The Essence of Wheat Products

　　依考古得知，小麥發源於中亞地區，再分向東西二邊擴散到歐、亞，而後和各地獨特的文化相結合，逐漸出現不同的麵食文化。歐洲發展出以「麵包」為主的飲食文化；亞洲則發展出以「煮麵」為主的飲食方式。麵食有著共同的源頭，卻發展出相異的飲食樣貌。據說小麥首先到達的中國地區為陝西一帶，在這氣候與中亞較為接近的地方，小麥的栽培很快地就開始發達起來。起初因為能收成的小麥量和種下種子的相對比率過低，加上工藝技術不發達，磨製速度緩慢等因素，所以將小麥加工成麵粉在當時被視為一種浪費的行為，因此起初人們仍是以杵樁將小麥脫殼後混入其它的穀物中蒸食或煮食。直到小麥能夠大量製成粉，才是代表著小麥產量已提高、工藝技術進步的現象。

According to archeologists, wheat originated in central Asia and then spread to both Europe and Asia. The East and the west then developed different food cultures. Europeans came with a dining culture based on breads, while the Chinese largely enjoyed noodles. Different cultures create different wheat products. To the East, it is said that wheat first came to China at the province of Shanxi. The climate there is similar to central Asia, and wheat cultivation developed quickly. At the beginning, because the production and farming technology were low, people considered processing wheat into flour as a waste. The common population would just mix wheat with other grains and cook them. Flour can be produced in large scale only when the production of wheat increased and the related technology advanced.

中國的米食文化　Rice Culture of China

　　米不僅是中國人的主食，每逢歲時節慶還能製成各式各樣的米食、糕餅和點心。如春節的「發糕」象徵發財；年糕寓意年年高陞、四季平安。清明節祭祖的艾草粿、紅龜粿據説可保佑子孫做生意賺大錢。端午節的肉粽除了紀念愛國詩人屈原外又可祭拜祖先。中元節的桃形紅龜粿、芋粿巧、鹹粽、油飯等，都是祭拜諸鬼神及普渡眾生的必備祭品。中秋節的麻糬含有祈求人生的圓滿光輝之意。冬至是歲首，湯圓象徵添新歲、祈福與團圓和事事圓滿。臘月則以臘八粥、八寶飯來甜甜灶王爺的嘴巴，以祈求來年四季平安、好豐收。因此米食在我國不僅代表飲食的涵意，更象徵中華文化的傳承。

　　Rice is not only the staple diet for Chinese people, but also can be manufactured into a variety of grain products, pastries and snacks for different festivals. In Chinese New Year, "steamed sponge cake" is a symbol of enrichment. Chinese New Year's cake (Nian gao) represents peace and safety in the four seasons of the year. Mugwort rice cake, red tortoise cake for ancestor worship in the Tomb Sweeping Day (Qingming Festival) are said to bless the descendants earning lots of money from doing business. Apart from commemorate the patriotic poet Qu Yuan, sticky rice dumplings in the Dragon Boat Festival are also used to worship ancestors. Red tortoise cake, steamed taro cake, akumaki, glutinous oil rice, etc. are used for worship various gods and make sacrifices for salvation during the Ghost Festival. In the Moon Festival (Mid-Autumn Festival), mochi are used for praying for the glorious consummation of life. In the Winter Solstice (Midwinter), the beginning of the year, rice balls (tangyuan) symbolize growing to another age and are used for praying for reunion and ensure that things run out smoothly. In the twelfth lunar month, laba rice porridge and Chinese rice pudding are used to make kitchen god's mouth sweet and for praying for safety in the four seasons and for good harvest in the coming year. Therefore, grains are not only representative in our diet, but also a symbol of Chinese cultural heritage.

菜餚的故事 你知道嗎？
Stories About Food

番薯文化 Sweet Potatoe Culture

　　早期民家多將地瓜儲存於床底，時間一久就會腐化，因此衍生出一句諺語：「臭番薯黷過間」，字面解釋為局部腐化而蔓延全部，用來諷喻一個人做了不當之事而壞了全體的聲譽。另有句話為：「拿番薯不準五穀」，指人們沒東西吃時以番薯充當主食，等到豐收時卻對番薯不屑一顧，後用來諷喻「欲利用之時奉為上賓，失去價值時則視如敝屣。」

Early in commoner's houses, people usually stored sweet potatoes under the beds, and sometimes sweet potatoes became rotten after a period of time. The proverb "tshàu han-tsî pháinn kui king" comes from this experience, and the literal interpretation is that partially corruption spread all through, allegory of a man that use to do inappropriate things and destroy all the crew's reputation. Another phrase is: "thê han-tsî bô-tsʻun ngʻoo-kok." It means that people serve sweet potato as a main course in famine year but not during harvest periods. It is later used as the allegory "treat guests in a distinguish way when they are useful, treat them as worn-out shoes when they are useless."

粽子的由來 The Story of Sticky Rice Dumplings

　　最普遍的說法為，楚國愛國詩人屈原投汨羅江自盡後，人們將煮熟的米飯投入江中，藉此懷念屈原的情懷。另有一說為，將粽子投入江中是希望魚蝦吃飽後就不會再去啃食屈原的屍體，好讓屈原能保全屍。除了紀念屈原之外，粽子在江蘇等地則被認為跟伍子胥信仰有關，當地記載：「鄉俗午日以粽奉伍大夫，非屈原也。」

The most common story is that after the patriotic poet Qu Yuan suicided in the Miluo River, people threw cooked rice into the river to

commenorate Qu Yuan. There is another story saying that by throwing sticky rice dumplings in the river, fishes and shrimps would not consume the body of Qu Yuan, thus the body of Qu Yuan can be preserved. Apart from commemorate Qu Yuan, people from Jiangsu and other areas considered that sticky rice dumplings were related to the worship of Wu Zixu. Local records: "The sticky rice in lunch is consecrated to Wu master as rural folk, not to Qu Yuan."

實用會話 聊天必備
Useful Phrases

一位台灣人帶第一次來台灣旅遊的外國友人前往館子用餐。

A Taiwanese invites a foreign friend, who visits Taiwan for the first time, for lunch.

你剛下飛機一定很餓吧？我先帶你去吃個簡單的晚餐！

You just get off the plane. You must be hungry. Let's first go for a casual dinner!

謝謝你，方便的話可以帶我去吃牛肉麵嗎？我在美國老早就想嘗嘗道地的台灣牛肉麵了！

Thank you. If it is ok with you, can you take me to try beef noodles? I've wanted to try authentic Taiwanese beef noodles since I was in America long time ago!

沒問題，這附近就有幾家不錯的牛肉麵店，走，我開車載你去。

No problem. There are several pretty good beef noodle shops around this neighborhood. Let's go! I drive you there.

哇，一走進店門就聞到一股好香的味道！

Wow. Once we walked in the shop, it smells so good!

這裡的牛肉麵湯頭是加了中藥熬煮的，有股獨特的香氣，喝起來更是美味，我們一人點一碗招牌牛肉麵吧！

In this place, beef noodle's soup is based with Chinese herbal medicine, which adds a unique aroma and taste. We shall have classic beef noodles for each of us!

好啊！我等不及要開動了！不過…其實我不太會用筷子…。

Sure! I can't wait to eat! But....actually I don't really know how to use chopsticks...

呵呵，其實筷子的用法很簡單，只要掌握幾個訣竅就可以了，來我教你。

Hehe. Actually once you grasp a few tricks on it, it will be very easy to use. Let me show you.

27

看起來好像很難，我試試看…咦，成功了！
It looks so difficult. Let me try... Huh, I did it!

呵呵，你慢慢吃、慢慢練習，過不久就會習慣了！
Hehe. You will get used to it after practicing!

台灣的牛肉麵真的好好吃喔！麵條有嚼勁、牛肉又香嫩，我還可以再吃上好幾碗！
Taiwanese beef noodles are really tasty. Noodles are quite chewing. The beef is also tender. I can still eat a couple more of bowls!

如果你還吃得下的話，我們再點份炒飯吧！
We can order fried rice if you want to eat more!

好啊！一下飛機就能吃到兩樣台灣經典的美食，讓我越來越期待接下來的旅程了。
Sure! I just get off the plane and I can have two kinds of classic Taiwanese food. It makes me look forward to the following trip.

好用句型 點餐必會
Sentence Patterns

1. I am a vegan. 我吃全素

    vegan：素食主義者

    👍 會這句更加分　What do vegans eat? 素食主義者都吃些甚麼？

    I'm a vegetarian. What do you recommend? 我吃素，請問你們有甚麼推薦嗎？

    vegetarian：素食的、素食者

    👍 會這句更加分　Do you have vegetarian food? 請問你們有素食餐點嗎？

    recommend：推薦、建議

    👍 會這句更加分　Can you recommend me some new movies? 你可以推薦一些新電影給我嗎？

2. Waiter: What kind of food can't you eat? 請問有甚麼是您不吃的？

    Customer: I'm allergic to seafood. 我對海鮮過敏。

    allergic：對…過敏的

    👍 會這句更加分　My mother is allergic to cat fur. 我媽媽對貓毛過敏。

3. This meat is tender. 這道肉很嫩。

    tender：嫩的

    👍 會這句更加分　The meat tastes very tender. 這塊肉吃起來很嫩。

4. This meat is too tough. 這塊肉太老了。

    tough：韌的

    👍 會這句更加分　The alloy cuts tough. 這種合金切起來比較韌。

5. This meat is still raw/not cooked yet. 這塊肉還沒熟。

    raw：生的

    👍 會這句更加分　Most sashimi are eaten raw. 大部分的生魚片是生吃的。

甜點　Desserts

飲料　Beverages

點心　Snacks

6. This dish is too salty. 這道菜太鹹了。

salty：鹹的

👍會這句更加分 We have a bowl of very salty corn soup. 我們喝了一碗非常鹹的玉米濃湯。

7. This dish is practically tasteless. 這道菜幾乎沒味道。

practically：幾乎、差不多

👍會這句更加分 It snowed practically all week. 雪下了差不多一個星期。

tasteless：沒味道的

👍會這句更加分 Did you actually feel that water is tasteless? 你真的認為水是沒味道的嗎？

NOTES

1.3
日式主食大集合
Japanese Main Courses

Talking About Food In English

日本料理店師傅：你到這邊學習已經三個月了，還習慣嗎？

You have been here for three months now. How's everything?

日本料理店學徒：雖然還只能做些打雜工作，但我最期待的就是每天打烊後跟著前輩在廚房修業。日本料理真是博大精深啊，就拿壽司來說好了，僅是醋飯加上魚肉、海鮮等配料，我看師傅們不論是在魚的選用或刀工、捏法上都相當講究呢！

Although all I do is fetch and carry so far, but I'm looking forward to everyday's learning from seniors in the kitchen after closing. Japanese cuisine is extensive and profound. Taking sushi as an example, it's only vinegared rice combining with fish, seafood and other ingredients, but chefs are quite fastidious on choosing fish, cutting and squeezing.

日本料理店師傅: 看你對日本料理這麼有興趣，我就破例先跟你介紹日後會學到的各種日式主食吧！正宗日式壽司用的是稍帶甜味的日本珍珠米。米飯煮熟後加入適量的壽司醋、糖、鹽等調味，待降溫後才用來製作壽司。除了從日本江戶時代興起的握壽司以外，還有以海苔捲成的捲壽司、用小木箱壓製的笹壽司、用油豆皮包的稻荷壽司，還有將配料灑在米飯上的散壽司。

除此之外，還有其他日式的代表米食與麵食。

Seeing you are so interested in Japanese cuisine, I'll make an exception introduce you a variety of Japanese staple that you will learn in the future! Authentic Japanese sushi is made with a slightly sweet Japanese pearl millet. After the rice is cooked, add the right amount of sushi vinegar, sugar, salt and other seasonings, and wait until it cool down before making sushi. Besides the Nigiri Sushi from the Edo period in Japan, there are the Temaki Sushi which is rolled in laver, the Oshisushi pressed in a box, the Inari Sushi stuffed in a pouch of fried tofu and the Chirshi Sushi topped with a variety of ingredients. Apart from these, there are more typital Japanese rice and noodles dishes.

日本料理店學徒：您盡量說，我會一邊做筆記。

You can tell me as much as you want. I will take notes.

日本料理店師傅：咖哩在明治時代由英國傳進日本後深受日本人喜愛，與日本米食文化結合後又演化出各式特色料理。日式咖哩因為加入了濃縮果泥所以甜味較重、不太辣。傳統的蛋包飯是將飯或炒飯倒入以蛋汁煎成的半熟蛋皮。另一種作法是在炒好的飯上放一個鬆軟的蛋包再劃開。日本的丼飯（蓋飯）相傳是在幕府室町時代出現，在米飯上放入菜餚、做成一人份的飯以供迅速進食、省去挾菜的麻煩。如牛丼、勝丼（豬排蓋飯）、親子丼等。日本拉麵自中國引進後，由於日本地形的關係，呈現個別地區不同的特色口味，如醬油、豚骨和味噌。蕎麥麵是用蕎麥麵粉和水製成的細麵條，可調理成熱湯麵或涼式、拌麵食用。都記起來了嗎？

Curry was introduced to Japan by British in the Meiji period

and it became popular in Japan. After being combined with Japanese rice culture, it evolved a variety of specialties cuisine. Japanese curry is sweeter and not too spicy beceuse of the concentrated fruit puree. Traditional omurice is the rice or friend rice wrapped in a sheet of half-cooked egg. Another method is to put the omelet on fried rice and cut it open. It is said that Donburi (rice with meat and vegetables) appeared in the Muromachi period. All ingredients were cooked and topped on rice. It is served for only one person, and saved the trouble of picking up the food from the plates. There are Gyudon (beef rice bowl), Katsudon (pork cutlet rice bowl), Oyakodon (parent-and-child donburi), etc. Due to Japan's geography, after the introduction of ramen from China to Japan, there was a variety of tastes from different regions, such as soy sauce, spare-rib (pork) and miso. Soba is a thin noodle made with buckwheat flour and water, can be served hot or cool with soy sauce. Do you remember all?

日本料理店學徒：是的，謝謝師傅！

Yes! Thanks, Master!

飲食小百科 文化大不同
Differences in Cultures

 各國咖哩文化
Curry in Different Cultures

中國 China

大多以粉狀出售，似乎來源於馬來西亞和新加坡等地。

Mostly sold in powder form. It seems like importing from Malaysia, Singapore, or other places.

印度 India

印度咖哩是所有咖哩文化的起源，在印度提到咖哩，大多指以肉汁或醬汁搭配米飯或麵包的一種主食。

Indian curry is the origin of all curry cultures. Curry in India is mostly used to indicate a main course of gtavy/sance with rice/bread.

英國 United Kingdom

英國曾經殖民統治過印度，當結束殖民統治後，也一併把印度的料理烹調習慣帶回英國。有人打趣說：全世界除了印度以外，就屬英國的印度料理最為道地了。由此可知印度料理在英國的地位。

India was the United Kingdom's colony before. British brought Indian cooking styles and cuisines back to the United Kingdom after the end of the colonial rule. Someone made fun of it by saying that "The United Kingdom has the most authentic Indian cuisine in the world beside India." Therefore, Indian cuisine has chieved a dominant position in Britain.

35

泰國 Thailand

泰國咖哩分青咖哩、黃咖哩、紅咖哩等，其中以青咖哩最辣。

Thai curry can be divided into green curry, yellow curry, red curry, etc. The green curry is the spiciest among them.

馬來西亞 Malaysia

一般會加入芭蕉葉、椰絲及椰漿等當地特產，味道偏辣。由於馬來西亞語將咖哩麵稱為「laksa」，因此咖哩又稱為「叻沙」。在當地亦是不可或缺的家庭美食，幾乎每天都會出現在餐桌上。

Malaysian curry usually adds banana leaves, shredded coconut, coconut milk and other local specialties. Its taste is relatively spicy. Due to Malaysian name the curry noodle "laksa," the curry is also known as "laksa." Curry is also an integral part of the local family cuisine and it almost appears on the table every day.

日本 Japan

日式咖哩除了可以拌飯吃，還能作為拉麵和烏龍麵等湯麵類食物的湯底，這方面和其他國家的咖哩有較大區別。如在北海道札幌地區的獨特湯咖哩以及白咖哩。

Beside rice, Japanese curry can be used as soup base for ramen, udon and other noodles. In Japan, curry is quite different from other countries, such as the unique curry soup and white curry in Sapporo, Hokkaido.

臺灣 Taiwan

　　臺灣咖哩承襲日本殖民時期遺留下來的風味，這是日本人當年前往英國學習科技等技術時，在船上看見印度籍船員烹調時所習得從而帶回日本的。其特徵為使用大量的薑黃，色澤多為鮮黃色，帶有淡淡的小茴香氣味。在台灣也有人使用咖哩粉直接添加於白米飯中作為炒飯食用。

　　Taiwan curry inherited the flavor from Japan's colonial period. When Japanese went to study science and technology and other skills at the United Kingdom, they learned it while they saw an Indian sailor who was cooking on board. It's characterized by the use of large amounts of turmeric, which mostly appears bright yellow, and smells with a hint of cumin. There are also some people who add curry powder in the rice to make fried rice in Taiwan.

各國蓋飯類食物
Various Kinds of Rice Bowls in Different Countries

　　在香港與澳門，蓋飯常用碟子盛裝，因此多稱為「碟頭飯」，一般會附有飲品或例湯。在日本，蓋飯多以大碗盛裝，日語中稱為「丼物」。蓋飯通常在一些小餐館、路邊攤和中式、日式速食店供應。

　　In Hong Kong and Macau, rice bowls are commonly put in the plate, also named "plate meal," usually with drinks or soup. In Japan, rice bowls are used to be big bowls, called "Donburi" in Japanese. Rice bowls are usually on served in hash houses, street vendors and Chinese, Japanese fast food restaurants.

菜餚的故事 你知道嗎？
Stories About Food

鰻魚丼 Unadon

　　早在江戶時代前就有鰻魚飯的紀錄，在當時屬高級料理。後來演變成大碗裝飯、再蓋上烤鰻魚的鰻魚丼才開始普及。到了今天，夏天吃鰻魚丼已是日本的重要習俗。

　　There are records of grilled eel rice bowls as haute cuisine long time before the Edo period. It later evolved into the grilled eel topped on the rice in a big bowl which is called "Unadon," and it became more and more common. Until today, eating Unadon is an important custom in summer in Japan.

牛丼 Gyūdon

　　據說起源是在明治初年，一位橫濱富商的太太將牛肉火鍋的剩菜拌在飯裡餵狗，友人看到如法炮製後覺得非常美味，便研發成一項產品。

　　Allegedly, it was originated in the early Meiji. There was a wealthy businessman's wife in Yokohama who used the leftovers beef pots and mixed them with rice to feed her dogs. A friend of her saw it and did the same, and he felt that it was very delicious after tasting it. Later it was developed into a product.

親子丼 Oyakodon

　　為明治維新後出現的新丼飯，據說是軍雞（鬥雞）火鍋店發明的。當時雞肉價格昂貴，珍惜食物的客人就把吃剩的湯汁加上白飯一起食用，沒想到相當可口。

It is said that Shamo Hot Pot invented the new rice bowl after Meiji restoration. Chicken was very expensive back then, and customers who cherished food and took the leftover soup with rice. To their surprise, it was quite tasty.

勝丼 Katsudon

炸豬排的日文叫做「とんかつ」，簡稱為「かつ(Katsu)」與勝利的「勝」同音，因此又稱做「勝丼」。據説是在 1921 年，早稻田高等學院的學生突發奇想，將炸豬排放在白飯上淋上醬汁一起食用而成。現在已成為日本人在比賽或考試前必吃的吉利食物。

In Japan, pork cutlot is called "とんかつ," also abbreviated as "かつ (Katsu)," which has the same sound that the first letter of "Victory" in Japanese, so it is also named "Katsudon." It is said that a student from Waseda University put the pork cutlet on the rice and topped it with sauce, becoming a dish in 1921. Now it is one of the Japanese auspicious dishes before games or examinations.

實用會話 聊天必備
Useful Phrases

請給我一份握壽司特餐。
I would like to have a special set of Nigiri Sushi, please.

好的，馬上來。
Ok, just a moment, please.

 兒子，你想吃甚麼？
Son, what would like to eat?

我想吃跟爸爸一樣的。
I want the same that you have, father.

 爸爸的握壽司上面是生魚片，而且還要加芥末喔，來，你先吃一口煙燻鮭魚看看，如果你能接受的話就幫你叫。
There is sashimi on top on my Nigiri sushi, and also wasabi. Here, try a bite of smoked salmon first, I will order it for you if it is ok with you.

好香好好吃，只是咬起來軟軟的有點可怕，還有一定要沾這個嗎？好辣！
Tasty and delicious. Only a little bit scared by the soft mouthfeel, and do I have to dip this? It's spicy!

 生魚片沾芥茉是為了殺菌，不過如果你不敢吃的話，我想只沾醬油應該也沒關係。
Sashimi is dipped with wasabi for sterilization, but if you are afraid of eating it, I think it should be fine to only dip soy sauce.

主食 Main Courses

我們有一些口感較為不生、也不用沾芥茉的壽司可以推薦給你喔。像是鮮蝦、烤鰻魚握壽司、鮭魚卵軍艦捲等，還有小朋友最喜歡的玉子燒、海帶芽。再加上茶碗蒸或味噌湯，你一定可以吃得很飽的。

We have some sushi with mild tastes, and you do not need to dip it with wasabi. For example, fresh shrimps, grilled eels nigiri sushi, salmon roe warship roll, etc., and we also have kids' favorite Tamagoyaki, seaweed sprout salad. Together with savory egg custard or miso soup, you will be full.

哇！聽起來好棒喔，我要吃！
Sounds great. I want to eat that!

謝謝，那就都來 一份吧！
Let's have one of each then. Thank you.

好用句型 點餐必會
Sentence Patterns

1. Does the price come with a drink? 請問這個價格有包括飲料嗎？

   price：價格、費用

   👍 **會這句更加分** The cabinet is good except for its price. 這個櫃子很好，只是價錢有點貴。

甜點 Desserts

飲料 Beverages

點心 Snacks

2. Could you make it spicy? 請問能做成辣的嗎？

   Could you make it small? 請問可以做成小份的嗎？

   spicy：辛辣的

   👍會這句更加分 I'd like something spicy. 我想吃些辛辣的食物。

3. Do you have a combination meal? 請問你們有定食嗎？

   combination：組合

   👍會這句更加分 Eggs and hams make a good combination of breakfast. 蛋和火腿是早餐的好組合。

4. Can I order it with half size? 請問我可以點半份就好了嗎？

   half：一半、二分之一

   👍會這句更加分 He who will success is half way to it. 決心要成功的人已經成功了一半。

5. Can I have a large portion of this? 請問我可以點大碗的嗎？

   portion：一份、（食物等）一客

   👍會這句更加分 Please give me five portions of roast beef. 請給我五份烤牛肉。

6. Could you slice it? 可以幫我切片嗎？

   slice：把...切成薄片

   👍會這句更加分 How to slice an onion without tearing? 該如何切洋蔥才不會流眼淚？

7. What kind of fish do you have? 請問你們有哪些種類的魚料理？

   kind：種類

   👍會這句更加分 There are all kinds of flowers in the garden. 花園裡有各式各樣的花。

NOTES

主食
Main Course

甜點
Desserts

飲料
Beverages

點心
Snacks

1.4
義式主食大集合
Italian Main Courses

Talking About Food In English

餐廳服務生： 您好，請問可以點餐了嗎？

Hello, are you ready to order?

客人： 可以介紹一下你們店裡的主餐嗎？我還拿不定主意。

Can you introduce the main courses of the restaurant? I am still indecisive.

服務生 A： 我們有披薩、義大利麵、義大利餃和義式燉飯，每一種都是由義大利籍廚師使用進口食材，遵循道地做法的料理。

We have pizza, pasta, ravioli and risotto, each of them are cooked by our Italian chef, with imported ingredients and genuine taste.

客人： 喔？那麼你們的口味一定很道地。

Oh? The taste must be very Italian.

餐廳服務生： 是啊，我們的廚師正是從披薩的發源地—義大利的那不勒斯來的，一般披薩所用的起司通常是莫札瑞拉起司（Mozzarella），而我們則是少見地混用了帕馬森起司（Parmesan）、羅馬乳酪（Romano）、義大利鄉村軟酪（Ricotta）和蒙特瑞·傑克起司（Monterey Jack）等。麵條則是特別從義大利中南部訂製，使用小麥品種中最硬質的杜蘭（durum）小麥製成的粗麵條。

Yeah, our chef is from Naples, Italy- the origin of pizza. People usually use Mozzarella cheese for pizza, but we mixed Parmesan, Romano, Ricotta, Monterey Jack and other cheeses together. For our pasta, we ordered it from south central region of Italy, where they use the most rigid wheat, Durum, to make pastas.

客人： 你們對食材很講究呢！那麼義大利餃呢？

You are very meticulous about ingredients! How about ravioli?

餐廳服務牛： 義大利餃（ravioli）的麵皮材料主要是麵粉、雞蛋和水，再加入番茄汁和菠菜汁增添顏色。內餡為火腿、羅勒葉、牛柳和帕馬森起司，有時也會使用雞肉、檸檬皮和蛋黃。義大利餃可以搭配牛肉醬、牛肉丸，或是以橄欖油、洋蔥、大蒜、迷迭香、紅酒或番茄為底的醬汁，內餡的蔬菜比例較高，很受女性客人喜愛。

The main ingredients of ravioli dough are flour, egg, water and add tomato and spinach juice to color. Stuffing includes ham, basil leaves, beef fillet and Parmesan, sometimes with chicken, lemon peel and yolk. Ravioli can match with beef paste, meat balls or the stuffing sauce based on olive oil, onion, garlic, rosemary, red wine or tomato. Many female customers enjoy it because it has higher proportion of vegetables.

客人： 聽起來很棒，不過我擔心會吃不飽，義大利燉飯（Risotto）應該很值得期待。

Sounds great, but I'm worried. That's not enough for me. Risotto should be worth the expectation.

餐廳服務生： 義大利燉飯是用高湯把米煮成奶油般濃郁質地的義大利經典料理，高湯通常以肉、魚、或蔬菜為基底，並會加入奶油、酒、以及洋蔥。燉飯在義大利通常是前菜（**primo**），單獨在主菜之前上桌，起源於盛產稻米的北部義大利，是米蘭地方很有特色的菜餚。正宗的義大利燉飯通常為只有六七成熟的夾生飯，習慣全熟米飯的亞洲客人有時會較難接受。

Risotto uses broth to cook the rice as rich as cream. It is a signature Italian dish. Broth is usually based on meat, fish or vegetable, with cream, wine and onion. In Italy, risotto is characteristic cuisine from Milan, origin of the rice in northern Italy. Generally, it's an appetizer (primo) in Italy, served before main courses alone. The authentic risotto usually gets the rice cooked up to medium (about 60~70%), which sometimes is hard to accept by Asian customers whom used to cook it throughout.

客人： 不吃吃看怎麼會知道呢？給我來一份吧！

How will I know if I don't try it? Please get one for me!

飲食小百科 文化大不同
Differences in Cultures

披薩 Pizza

公元前 3 世紀，羅馬的第一部歷史中：「圓麵餅上加橄欖油、香料和蜂蜜，置於石上烤熟」；以及「薄麵餅上面放起司和蜂蜜，並用香葉加味」。在龐貝城遺址附近，考古學家也發現了類似現今比薩店的房址。儘管上述的食品與今天的披薩很相似，然而現在製做披薩所需的兩種原料─番茄和莫札瑞拉起司都還沒有傳到義大利和地中海地區。番茄是在 16 世紀由美洲傳入歐洲的，到了 18 世紀晚期，這種加有番茄的發酵麵餅已成為那不勒斯地區窮人的家常食品。在 1830 前，披薩都是由攤販或披薩烤房露天販售，這時期的那不勒斯出現了世界上第一家真正的比薩餐館名為「Antica Pizzeria Port Alba」。披薩逐漸為人們所喜歡，甚至吸引外地的遊客專程前往品嘗。

In the 3rd century BC, early Rome mentioned "Put olive oil, spices and honey on pita and grilled on stone." and "Crust with cheese and honey topping also add the flavor by bay." Archaeologists also found a prehistoric site similar to modern pizzerias near the ruins of Pompeii. Although the food mentioned above is very similar to modern pizza, two materials for making pizza, tomato and mmozzarella, haven't reached Italy and the Mediterranean regions yet. Tomato was introduced in Europe from America in the 16th century, and it became homely food for the poor in Naples by the late 18th century. Before 1830, pizzas were selling outdoor in vendors or pizzerias. During this period, the first real pizzeria came to the world, and it was located in Naples, named "Antica Pizzeria Port Alba." Pizza became more and more popular and even attracted foreign visitors who travel to taste it.

義大利麵 Pasta v.s. Spaghetti

據考古學家考證，在義大利中部一個公元前 4 世紀的伊特魯裏亞人的墓穴裡就發現了義大利麵。喜好美食的義大利人對義大利麵的作法投注了包羅萬象的巧思，讓義大利麵成為時至今日做法最多樣化的西式麵食之一。「Spaghetti」首次出現在英語中則是 1874 年，很多人以為義大利麵就是 spaghetti，其實「義大利麵」=「pasta」，可指各種形狀的義大利麵，spaghetti 則是指最常見的長麵條、macaroni 為通心麵、 penne 為筆管麵、lasagna 為千層麵、ravioli 為義大利餃。

According to archaeologists' research, pasta was found in an Etruscan tomb of the 4th century BC. For Italians who love gourmet, they are devoted to the method of pasta in all-embracing ingenuity, making pasta one of the most diverse noodles in Western food today. "Spaghetti" first appeared in English in 1874. Many people think that pasta is a synonymous of spaghetti, but, in fact, pasta may refer to various shapes, like macaroni, penne, lasagna, ravioli, just as spaghetti refers to the most common long noodles.

義大利餃 Ravioli

義大利餃是以麵皮做成袋狀，將肉類或蔬菜包起再放入熱水中煮的傳統義大利麵食。義大利餃通常都是正方形，像一個扁平的枕頭，另外也有圓形、窄卷條狀或闊圓環狀。義大利餃不同地區還有其他別稱，好比說在皮蒙特稱為「小小羊（agnellotto）」，在艾米利亞羅馬涅地區則稱為「小帽子（cappelletto）」。其中應該數熱內亞式做法最為正宗，據說當地的做法最能顯出食材的原味。

Ravioli is a traditional Italian pasta made by dough filling with meat or vegetable inside and cooked in boiled water. Its shape is generally square like a flat pillow, but you can also find round, narrow or ring ravioli. Ravioli has many nicknames in different regions, for example, it is called agnellotto in Piedmont and cappelletto in Emilia-Romagna. The most authentic ravioli reflects the natural ingredients and flavor from Genoa.

菜餚的故事　你知道嗎？
Stories About Food

麻雀變鳳凰的披薩　Legends of Pizza: From Rags to Riches

　　傳說中瑪格麗特王后（Queen Margherita），和國王溫貝多一世（Umberto I）於一八八九年到拿坡里造訪，當時他們吃膩了王宮常吃的法國菜，便決定欽點布蘭迪披薩店的披薩師傅艾斯波希多（Raffaele Esposito）為王后準備幾種披薩，他做了三種：第一種加有豬油、caciocavallo 起司和羅勒，第二種是小魚披薩，第三種披薩則加了番茄、莫札瑞拉起司和羅勒。結果王后吃了以後最愛第三種；這種原本叫做加了莫札瑞拉起司的披薩（pizza alla mozzarella）便因為王后的關係改名叫瑪格麗特披薩。這個故事讓披薩成為撫平社會差異的象徵，就連最挑剔的美食家都覺得披薩美味極了。

　　Queen Margherita and King Umberto I visited Naples in 1889. They were tired of eating French food from palace, so they decided to hand-picked the chef from Pizzeria Brandi, named Raffaele Esposito, to prepare some pizzas for the Queen. He made three kinds of pizza: the first one with lard, caciocavallo and basil, the second with fish and the third by adding tomato, mozzarella and basil. After finishing all the pizzas, the Queen loved the third one the most, and pizza alla mozzarella changed its name into pizza margherita because of the queen. This story has become a symbol to calm down social differences, and even the most picky gourmets love it too.

義大利麵的起源 The Origins of Pasta

　　相傳義大利探險家馬可波羅在中國住了十七年後，於西元 1292 年將麵食料理帶回義大利。另一說法是，中世紀時期統治西西里的阿拉伯人便開始吃義大利麵了。

According to folklore, Italian explorer Marco Polo brought pasta back in 1292 after living in China for 17 years. Another statement is that the Arabians who governed Sicily already had pasta since Middle Ages.

實用會話 聊天必備
Useful Phrases

您好，請問可以點餐了嗎？
Hello, may I take your order please?

你們的主餐裡有哪些是加了起司的？
Which main courses are with cheese?

如果您喜歡吃起司的話，我們的披薩使用了頂級的帕瑪森起司和莫札瑞拉起司，您一定會喜歡。
We use the finest Parmesan and Mozzarella cheese for our pizza. You will love it if you like cheese.

你誤會了，其實我有乳糖不耐症，想盡量避開含有起司和牛奶的料理。

You misunderstood me. Actually, I'm trying to avoid any food with cheese and milk because I'm lactose intolerant.

對不起，我剛才會錯意了。披薩是一定有加起司，義大利餃的內餡也包有起司，就我所知，我們的義大利燉飯也會用上一點點奶油。若要避開起司和牛奶，應該還有幾道義大利麵，我再幫您跟大廚做確認。

Sorry for the misunderstanding. As I know, all pizza and ravioli's filling certainly have cheese, and our risotto has some cream as well. There should be some dishes of pasta if you want to avoid cheese and milk. I will confirm with the chef for you.

好啊，麻煩你了。

Okay, please.

請您稍等，我馬上回來。

Please wait. I will be right back.

謝謝。

Thanks.

小姐，我已經確認過了，我們的海鮮義大利麵本來就沒有添加起司和牛奶，至於其他義大利麵今天也可以為您特別烹調處理。

Miss, I just confirmed that our seafood pasta doesn't have any kind of cheese or milk product. We can also prepare a special pasta dish for you.

那來一份海鮮義大利麵就好，謝謝你們！

A seafood pasta then. Thank you!

好用句型 點餐必會
Sentence Patterns

1. What's the difference between the linguine and the fettuccine? 請問細扁麵和寬扁麵有什麼不一樣？

   difference：差別、差異

   👍會這句更加分　Can you tell the difference between the two pictures? 你能區分這兩張照片的差別嗎？

2. I was going to order the squid ink pasta, but I think I want something more hearty. What would you recommend? 我本來想點墨魚義大利麵，但我又想要吃得豐盛些。你有什麼推薦的嗎？

   hearty：豐盛的；營養豐富的

   👍會這句更加分　Grandmother prepared a hearty dinner for whole family. 祖母為全家人準備了一頓豐盛的晚餐。

3. Do you have anything without meat? 你們有任何不含肉類的餐點嗎？

   meat：肉

   👍 會這句更加分　The meat is served with potato salad. 這道肉端上桌時搭配著馬鈴薯沙拉。

4. Is coffee included in this meal? 請問有咖啡做為附餐嗎？

   included：被包括的

   👍 會這句更加分　The tour included a visit to the Eiffel Tower. 這趟旅遊行程包括去參觀艾菲爾鐵塔。

5. What appetizer do you recommend? 請問你推薦哪些前菜呢？

   appetizer：開胃菜

   👍 會這句更加分　I'd like an appetizer and a glass of wine. 我想要來一份開胃菜和一杯酒。

6. Could you hold the salt, please. 鹽能加少一點嗎，謝謝。

   salt：鹽

   salty: 鹹的

   👍 會這句更加分　The seafood is too salt. 那道海鮮太鹹了。

7. Can I have the same one in this guidebook? 請給我跟這本旅遊書裡一樣的餐點。

   guidebook：旅遊指南

   👍 會這句更加分　This restaurant gets two stars in the guidebook. 這家餐廳在旅遊指南當中得到了兩顆星。

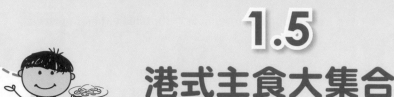

1.5
港式主食大集合
Hong Kong Main Courses

用英文聊美食 聊天必備
Talking About Food In English

朋友 A： 在台灣讀書的這幾年我都是吃這家港式料理一解思鄉之苦。今天特別請你來吃，是為了感謝你這幾年來的照顧。

In the past few years, I have been eating in this Hong Kong cuisine restaurant when I felt homesickness while I was studying in Taiwan. Today I invite you here to thank you for taking care of me in the past few years.

朋友 B： 大家都是同學，互相幫忙是應該的，也多虧你，我才知道學校附近有這麼一家道地的港式料理。

We are classmates. We are supposed to help each other. I also want to thank you that now I know here's an authentic Hong Kong cuisine restaurant near the school.

朋友 A： 這裡的乾炒牛河跟我在香港吃的口味一模一樣喔！

The beef chow fun here tastes exactly the same as I ate in Hong Kong.

朋友 B： 乾炒牛河是甚麼？

What is beef chow fun?

朋友 A： 乾炒牛河又名牛肉炒河粉，主要是以豆芽菜、河粉、牛肉大火快炒，既要炒勻手勢又不能太快，不然粉會碎掉。油的份量也要精準拿捏，不然出油會不好吃，因此這道菜被認為是廣東廚師手藝的一大考驗。

Beef chow fun, also named beef stir fry with rice noodles, is a Hong Kong cuisine mixed with bean sprouts, shahe fen, and beef, stir fried on full flame. You have to stir fry till evetything is well coated but not too rush, or otherwise the shahe fen will be crumbled. Also the accuracy in the amount of oil has to be just right, or it will not be so tasty while it's oily. This dish is also considered as a major test in cantonese cooking.

朋友 B： 這麼厲害？那這裡還有甚麼是必嚐的呢？

That's good! Is there anything I havo to eal?

朋友 A： 你可以吃吃看伊麵，又稱伊府麵、意麵，是一種油炸的雞蛋麵，與現代的速食麵有相似之處，所以又被稱為速食麵的鼻祖。主要材料為菇類、伊麵，用韭菜及蠔油炒成。

You can try yi mein, also named e-fu noodles and yi noodles, It's a kind of fried egg noodles similar to instant noodles in these days. It is also known as the origin of instant noodles. The main materials are mushrooms and yi mein, fried with leeks and oyster oil.

朋友 B： 我今天比較想吃肉耶！

I would prefer to have some meat today.

朋友 A： 那可以點燒味或海南雞飯來吃。

Then we could order the siu mei or Hainanese chicken rice.

朋友 B： 燒味和燒臘一樣嗎？

Are siu mei and cured meat the same?

朋友 A： 燒味有時被稱為燒臘，但兩者其實有別。香港的燒臘店除了賣

燒味之外，秋冬兩季也會兼賣臘味。但這個詞傳到中國其他地方和台灣後，已經失去了臘味的元素，變成與燒味一詞同義。

Barbecurer and curer's shops in Hong Kong mainly sell siu mei, and offer cured meat only in autumn and in winter. However, the phrase of "cured meat" in China and Taiwan has become the synonym of "siu mei" and lost its meaning.

朋友 B： 哪一種你比較推薦？

Which one would you recommend?

朋友 A： 叉燒、燒乳豬、燒鴨、燒鵝都是燒味的一種。也可以選擇做成雙拼或三寶飯。

Char siu, roasted suckling pork, roast duck, roast goose are all kinds of siu mei. Also you can choose the combination of two or three kinds of roast meat.

朋友 B： 那我叫一份燒鴨和燒鵝的雙拼。

I would like to order the combinaton of roast duck and roast goose.

朋友 A： 天氣冷，要不要點老火湯來喝？由於粵地氣候炎熱潮濕，因此大家都愛喝有蔬果、肉類和中藥，可以滋補養身的老火湯。想吃點料也可以點廣東粥。

The weather is cold. Do you want to order the double-stewed soup? Due to the weather is hot and humid in Guangdong area, people all love to eat the double-stewed soup, which has fruits and vegetables, meat and Chinese medicine in it, that is nourishing and nutritious. You can also order Cantonese congee if you want to eat something with an abundant mouthfeel.

朋友 B： 好，我要吃皮蛋瘦肉粥！

Ok, I would like to have minced pork congee with preserved eggs!

飲食小百科 文化大不同
Differences in Cultures

 粥
Congee

廣州：廣東粥 Guangzhou: Cantonese Congee

廣東人會把粥煮爛、使之變得綿滑，廣東粥有時不加配料，稱為「白粥」。也有搭配乾瑤柱絲以增添香味的瑤柱白粥，或是將炸脆的「油炸鬼（油條）」浸入粥內食用。在粥裡加入皮蛋、蔥花和白胡椒粉也是廣東常見的早餐吃法。

Cantonese usually cook the rice to very soft and the soup turns milky, known as Cantonese congee. There are various of them: congee in its simplest form with no ingredients called "white congee," congee with dried scallop to improve its flavor, congee with crispy deep-fried "youtiao," and congee with preserved eggs, chopped shallot, and pepper powder. Those are common breakfast in Guangzhou.

潮州：糜 Chaozhou: Mi

潮洲人將粥稱為「糜」，水量比廣東粥多，吃時佐以乾花生、菜脯或梅菜。潮洲人喜歡將海鮮加到粥裡煮成海鮮粥作為早飯或宵夜。因潮洲地區較中國其他地區相比，保留著更多華夏的文化傳統，而粥早在公元前 2000 年就已經出現，比米飯更早，因此潮州粥亦可視為上古時期華夏人民烹煮稻米

方式的傳承。

Chaozhou people called congee "mi." It contains more water than Cantonese congee, and people eat it with dry peanuts, preserved radish or mei cai. Chaozhou people like to add seafood into congee for breakfast or midnight snack. Chaozhou region, compared to other regions in china, preserves more Chinese culture and tradition. The history of congee is dated even earlier than that of rice. Therefore, Chaozhou congee can be seen as a traditional way of Chinese rice cooking which has been passed down from ancient times.

福建：糜 Fujian: Mi

粥在福建也稱為「糜」，水量比廣東粥少，濃到甚至可以單以筷子食用。福建粥的食材只有白米和清水，著重米香和外觀，與廣東粥相反，不能把米煮爛，也不能過分攪拌以免破壞米粒的形狀。吃時佐以菜脯、肉鬆等。台灣多數人口是由福建移民而來，因此福建粥在台灣亦是相當普遍的早點，吃法與福建類似，除了直接吃粥外還會搭配醬瓜、麵筋、鹹蛋、吻仔魚等。

Congee in Fujian, also known as "mi," has less water than in cantonese congee, and when it is so thick that you can even use chopsticks to eat it. Fujian congee only has rice and water as ingredients, focusing on the smell and appearance of rice, which is opposite to Cantonese congee. The rice can't be boiled until mushy or stir too much, to avoid damaging the shape of the rice. It is serve with preserved radish, pork floss, etc. The population in Taiwan is largely composed of Fujian immigrants. Therefore, the Fujian congee is a quite common breakfast in Taiwan. The way of eating is similar with the way in Fujian. Congee is eaten not only plain but also with pickes, wheat gluten, salted eggs, larval fish, etc.

江蘇、上海及浙江：甜粥 Jiangsu, Shanghai and Zhejiang: Sweet Congee

江蘇、上海及浙江等地會用稻米煮成濃稠的白粥，一般不加高湯等。有時更會加入白糖煮成「糖粥」或「甜粥」。

Jiangsu, Shanghai, and Zhejiang usually boil the rice till thick and creamy, and generally no stock added. Sometimes the congee can be cooked with white sugar and is called "sugar congee" or "sweet congee."

河南 Henan

河南（不包括信陽地區）人所說的粥是指用麵粉加水攪拌均勻成糊狀後，投入沸騰的開水內經過兩至三次沸騰再降溫而煮成的似膠質的稀飯，攪拌不均勻時會有大小不一的麵疙瘩留在稀飯裡。河南稀飯有只以水和麵粉熬煮的，也有加入綠豆、花生等豆類一起熬煮的，或是在已經煮好的稀飯裡打入雞蛋的吃法。

Henan (not including Xinyang region) congee is made with flour and water, and whipped into a smooth paste, then put into boiling water and add cold water before it returns to the boil and repeat 2 to 3 time. This process makes it become a gelatin-like congee with unevenly mixed gnocchi. You can also add mung beans, peanuts and other legumes in the Henan congee, or mix the congee with an egg.

 菜餚的故事 你知道嗎？
Stories About Food

伊麵
Yi Mian

相傳伊麵是起源於鄭州一帶，唐朝鄴城（今河南安陽）有位姓伊的將軍。一次他回家鄉省親，才剛到家皇帝就傳來聖旨要他還朝。伊家來不及置辦酒筵，只能急忙將麵粉用雞蛋和成麵團、桿切成麵條下鍋烹炸，於砂鍋內加入高湯、海參、猴頭菇、熟雞絲、香菇、木耳等材料，並佐以胡椒、辣椒油等端上桌。將軍品嘗之後大為讚賞，此麵從此便在民間流傳開來。

According to folklore, yi mian is originated in Zhengzhou area. During the Tang Dynasty, there was a general surnamed Yi from Ye City (Henan Anyang). Once he went back to visit his family, the emperor decreed him to return to the capital as soon as he arrived. Yi's family did not have time to prepare a banquet for him, so they just mixed the flour with eggs into a dough in a hurry. Then they cut the rolled flat dough into noodles and deep fried the noodles. Then they added broth sea cucumber, Hericium erinaceus, cooked shredded chicken, mushrooms, fungus and other materials in a casserole, and served with pepper and chili oil. After tasting it, the general greatly appreciated this dish, and it spread abroad among people.

另有一說是，清朝乾隆年間，曾任惠州和揚州知府的書法名家伊秉綬在家中宴客，麥姓家廚誤將煮熟的雞蛋麵放入滾燙的油鍋中，情急之下只好撈起來佐以高湯端上桌。由於賓客吃過後皆讚不絕口，於是這道菜就流傳了下來。

Another legend says that in the Qing Dynasty, during the reign of Qianlong, a famous calligraphy, Yi Bing Shou, who had worked in Huizhou and Yangzhou as a frefect. He once held a banquet at home, and the chef surnamed Mai made a mistake by putting egg noodles into the pan full of hot oil. In his anxiety, he served the noodles with broth. As the guests were full of praise after eating, the dish became popular.

實用會話 聊天必備
Useful Phrases

蘭香樓港式餐廳您好。
Hello, this is Lan Hong House Cantonese Restaurant.

您好，我打電話來是想叫外送。
Hi, I call to order food delivery.

好的，請問您要點甚麼？
Alright, what would you like to order?

我要一份廣東炒麵、一份鹹魚炒飯，外加一個叉燒飯便當。
I would like to have Cantonese fried noodles, salted fish fried rice and Char siu rice.

我們要點四份主餐或是滿 4 百元才有外送喔，您還差 40 元，要不要加點小點心或是飲料？
You have to order four main courses or reach 400 dollars for delivery. You are still short by 40 dollars. Would you like to order some snacks or drinks?

那我再來一個招牌冰火菠蘿油好了。
I will get one classic "buttered pineapple bun" then.

不好意思，我們只有冰火菠蘿油不提供外送，因為冷掉就不好吃了。
I'm sorry. "buttered pineapple bun" is not for delivery, because it won't be tasty if it's cold.

這樣啊，那好吧，我再叫一份廣東粥好了，廣東粥應該算主餐吧。
If that so, alright then, I will order Cantonese congee. Cantonese congee should be counted as a main course.

是的，這樣就可以了。請問您貴姓大名，還有您的電話和外送地址是？
Yes, this will be fine. May I have your name, phone number and the deliver address?

我姓李，請幫我送到 XX 路 X 段 XX 號，我的手機是 09XX-XXXXXX。
My surname is Li, please deliver to the address No. XX, Sec. X, Rd. XX, and my cell phone number is 09XX-XXXXXX.

主食

甜點

飲料

點心

好的，現在正值店裡的午餐尖峰時段，約於 40 分鐘後送達可以嗎？
Okay, It's now at the lunch rush hour. Your meal will be delivered in 40 minutes. Is that ok?

沒問題，麻煩你了。
No problem.

好用句型 點餐必會
Sentence Patterns

1. I'd like a restaurant with cheerful atmosphere. 我想去一家有著歡樂氣氛的餐廳。

   atmosphere：氣氛

   👍 **會這句更加分** The atmosphere changed as soon as our teacher walked in the classroom. 當老師一走進教室，班上的氣氛都變了。

2. Where is the main area for restaurants? 請問這附近的餐廳大多集中在那一區？

   main：主要的

   👍 **會這句更加分** What are your main concerns as a politician? 身為一位政治家，你最關心的是甚麼？

3. Is there a Cantonese restaurant around here? 請問這附近是否有粵菜餐廳？

   Cantonese：廣東的、廣州的

   👍 **會這句更加分** Cantonese food is the most popular style outside China. 廣東料理在中國以外也非常受到歡迎。

4. Do you know of any restaurants that's still opening now? 請問你知道現在還有哪些餐廳仍在營業的嗎？

open：開著的

👍 **會這句更加分** Another pharmacy store opened last week. 有另一家藥局開張了。

5. Where is the nearest Hong Kong restaurant? 請問最近的一間香港餐廳在那裡？

nearest：最近的

👍 **會這句更加分** A distant relative is not as good as a near neighbor. 遠親不如近鄰。

6. We'd like a table with a view of fountain. 我們想要可以看的到面對噴水池的位子。

view：景觀、視野

👍 **會這句更加分** The sniper had a clear view of the target. 那位狙擊手可以清楚地看見他的目標。

7. We are a group of ten. 我們總共有 10 個人。

group：團體

👍 **會這句更加分** A group of reporters surrounded the suspect. 一大群記者團團圍住那個嫌犯。

NOTES

主食 Main Course

甜點 Desserts

飲料 Beverages

點心 Snacks

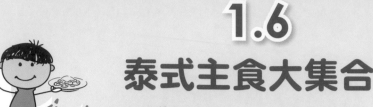

1.6
泰式主食大集合
Thai Main Courses

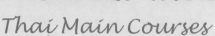

Talking About Food In English

記者 A： 新來的，你怎麼愁眉苦臉的啊？

Rookie, why such a frowning face?

記者 B： 總編說我這篇報導寫的很無聊，要我重寫。前輩，您可不可以給我一點建議？

The chief editor said that the story I wrote is boring. He asked me to rewrite it. Senior, could you give me some advice?

記者 A： 好啊，我看看。「泰國土地肥沃，雨水充足，稻米一年能收三至四次，因此泰國的主食一般便是本土出產的茉莉香米。除了以米飯為主食，還會佐以特殊的紅、綠咖哩、炒菜或其他菜色。」嗯，該怎麼說呢，就是中規中矩的。

Ok, let me see. "Thailand has a fertile land, abundant in rainfall. Its rice can be harvested three to four times a year, so the staple food in Thailand is generally the local jasmine rice. The rice usually served with special red, green curry, stir-fried regetables or others Uhm... how to say, it's satisfactory special.

記者 B： 前輩一開始也有被退稿過嗎？

Have you been refected in the beginning?

66

記者 A： 當然囉。

Of course.

記者 B： 那麼前輩都是怎麼修改的呢？

How did you revise then?

記者 A： 我都是換一個角度想，例如，想想自己會想看甚麼樣的報導？

I always try to think from different points of view. For example, think about what kind of story I want to read.

記者 B： 我知道了！我可以多介紹一些菜色來引起讀者的食慾，例如：「泰國咖哩都是以『顏色』來命名，如黃咖哩、綠咖哩、紅咖哩。綠咖哩的主要成分包括椰奶、茄子、魚露、檸檬和羅勒等食材，可和各種肉類搭配，其中最受歡迎的是牛、豬、雞肉和魚丸。而紅咖哩的主要原料為泰國紅辣椒、香茅、檸檬皮等。」

I got it! I can introduce more dishes to arouse the reader's appetite. For example, "Thai curries are named by 'color,' such as yellow curry, green curry and red curry. The main ingredients of green curry include coconut milk, eggplant, fish sauce, lemon and basil and other ingredients. It can be matched with a variety of meats, among which the most popular are beef, pork, chicken and fish ball. The main materials of red curry are Thai red chili, lemongrass, lemon peel, etc."

記者 A： 就是像這樣！由於華僑定居泰國多年，不少中國的菜色已經被泰國化，你也可以多介紹這類的文化差異。或是一些名稱奇特的菜餚，如泰式打拋豬，是泰國知名的國民美食。得名於它的食材「打拋葉（Holy Basil Leaves）」，是類似九層塔的辛香料，氣味更加濃烈辛嗆。

Just like this! As the Chinese settled in Thailand for many years, a lot of Chinese dishes have been modified, you can also introduce more cultural differences like this. Or you can write about special names of the dish, such as phat kaphrao pork. It's a well-known national Thai dish. Named by its ingredient "Holy Basil Leaves." It's similar to basil spice, but smells stronger and spicier.

記者 B： 我為了採訪有去吃酸辣泰式檸檬魚和咖哩螃蟹（**Fried Curry Crab**），那黃色的咖哩醬汁拌入了滑嫩的滑蛋，融合螃蟹的鮮甜美味，和一般咖哩的味道完全不一樣，好吃到吮指回味，真希望能把這樣的美味傳達給讀者。

For an interview, I once ate Thai style sweet and sour lemon fish and Fried Curry Crab. That yellow curry sauce was mixed with smoothly fried eggs, and fused with the sweet taste of crab. Its taste was completely different from the general curry. It's finger-licking good. I really hope I can transmit that taste to the readers.

記者 A： 你這樣想就對了！

Glad you think like this!

飲食小百科 文化大不同
Differences in Cultures

 ### 各國米食文化
Rice Culture in Different Countries

泰國 Thailand

泰國是全球最大的稻米出口國，亦是當地人的主食之一。農耕節是泰國當地的主要節日，其中以耕田播種儀式最為重要，藉此期盼五穀豐收。最早的稻米種植遺跡在泰北與雲南發現，大約是在公元前 3500 年所種植。

Thailand is the largest exporter of rice in the world. Rice is also one of the staple food for locals. Plow Day (Royal Ploughing Ceremony) is a major local festival in Thailand, and the ceremony of plowing and sowing is the most important part to pray for a plentiful harvest. The earliest rice domestication was found in northern Thailand and Yunnan around 3500 BC.

越南 Vietnam

介於亞熱帶和熱帶的越南，不但全國丘陵以下地形都可以種植稻米，在南越地區還可以一年三穫。在發生越戰以前，越南稻米的輸出量曾高居世界第一。越南人常形容自己的國家為「一根竹扁擔挑著兩個米籮」，就是指越南地形中部狹長，北有紅河三角洲，南有湄公河三角洲，這兩個區域都是稻米的盛產地。越南人常把米製成米線、河粉等食物，至今仍廣受越南人喜愛。

Vietnam is located between subtropical and tropical zones. People can grow rice on the plains and hills all over the country and even have three harvests in south Vietnam every year. Vietnamese often describe their country as "carrying two baskets of rice with a bamboo pole," which

refers to the narrow terrain in central Vietnam, and the Red River Delta in the North and the Mekong Delta in the South, these two areas are fertile of rice. Vietnamese often make rice into mixian (rice noodles), pho, and other kinds of food, still loved by many Vietnamese today.

印度 India

印度產稻的歷史也相當悠久，最早的野生水稻出現在阿薩姆。印度的總人口中約有 65%是以稻米為主食，由於印度的溫和氣候相當適合種植水稻，促使印度成了最大的水稻栽培區，稻米生產量近年甚至超過越南而僅次於中國。

Rice production also has a quite long history in India. The first wild paddy rice appeared in Assam. There are about 65% of total population that have rice as staple food in India. The mild climate suitable for rice cultivation makes India become the largest rice cultivation area in the world. In recent years, the rice production in India even exceeds that in Vietnam and is second only to that in China.

法國 France

阿爾稻米節（Feria du riz）是法國阿爾勒地區慶祝稻米收成的節慶，在每年九月中旬一連三天舉行。慶祝活動包括選出「稻米皇后」、花車巡遊、鬥牛、喝水果酒、吃西班牙海鮮飯等。「稻米皇后」被選出後，會搭乘著大型的平底船於隆河順流而下，接受河畔民眾灑下的稻米。

Arles Rice Festival (Feria du riz) is a festival in Arles, France, to celebrate the rice harvest, held for three days in mid-September each year. The activities include the election of the "Rice Festival Queen," festooned vehicle parades, bullfights, drinking wine, eating Spanish paella, etc. After the "Rice Festival Queen" is being elected, she will take a big punt down to the river Rhone, accepting rice from people by the river.

美國 United States

國際稻米節（International Rice Festival）是位於美國路易西安納州的克勞利市一年一度慶祝稻米的節日，在每年十月的第三個周末舉行。它是路易西安納州歷史最為悠久的農業節日，也是美國最大的農業節日之一。

The International Rice Festival in Crowley, Louisiana, USA, celebrates the rice harvest once a year and is held on the third weekend of October each year. It is the oldest agricultural festival and also one of the largest agriculture festivals in Louisiana.

日本 Japan

水稻的種植方法是在西元前 3 世紀傳入日本的，隨之衍生出各種信仰與禮俗。酒、年糕、點心、醬油、醋等食物也都是以稻米為製作原料之一。

The cultivation methods of paddy rice were spread to Japan in the 3rd century BC, subsequently deriving in a variety of beliefs and rituals. Wine, cakes, snacks, soy sauce, vinegar and many other foods are made with rice as a raw material.

菜餚的故事 你知道嗎？
Stories About Food

咖哩 Curry

相傳咖哩是釋迦牟尼在印度咖哩村的山中修道時賴以果腹的植物香辛料，釋迦牟尼經常帶下山分給村民，不吃豬肉與牛肉的印度人通常以羊肉、雞肉、海鮮魚蝦等為主食，而以釋迦牟尼佛所發明的咖哩調味可以減少食材

的羶腥味，因此經村民改良後大受歡迎，咖哩也傳遍全印度及南亞各國。印度咖哩的特別之處在於，烹調時並不會用所謂的「咖哩塊」或「咖哩粉」，而是邊煮邊加香料進去，煮到最後就成了一鍋咖哩，因此印度咖哩是味道多變的一道菜。而東南亞咖哩與濃郁的印度咖哩截然不同，因為加入了香茅和檸檬皮等材料，風味更為清新。

According to the legend, curry plants were the food for Buddha when he practiced doctrines in a mountain of a village called "curry." Buddha often shared the plants with the villagers. Indians do not eat pork or beef. Their staple food usually are lamb, chicken, and seafood etc., and the curry seasoning invented by Buddha can reduce the smell of mutton. Therefore, after modified by the villagers, it became popular and had spread throughout India and South Asia. Indian curry is unique for not using "curry cubes" or "curry powder" but adding a variety of spices. Hence, Indian curry has so many different flavors. Southeast Asian curry differs from the rich Indian curry by adding lemongrass, lemon peels, and other ingredients, to make the flavor more refreshing.

實用會話 聊天必備
Useful Phrases

先生您好，請問幾位？
Hello, sir, may I ask for how many people?

總共兩位，不過還有一位還沒到，我可以先入座嗎？
Two, but the other one hasn't arrived yet, can I have a table first?

沒問題，先生這邊請。
No problem, sir, this way please.

靠牆的位置啊... 請問可以讓我坐窗邊的位置嗎？
By the wall... Can I have the talde by the window?

不好意思，窗邊的位置是保留位，已經有客人先訂了。
Sorry, tho table by the window has been reserved by other customer.

那好吧。
Well then.

我先為您上兩杯水，請問需要先看菜單嗎？
Let me help you with two glasses of water. Would you like to take a look of the menu first?

等我朋友到再一起看好了。
I will take a look together with my friend when she arrives.

好的，那還有甚麼需要我服務的嗎？
Sure, is there anything I can do for you?

可以幫我把冷氣調低一點嗎？總覺得有點熱。
Would you turn the air conditioner up for me, please? I feel a little bit hot.

我們的冷氣溫度是固定的，我可以先為您的水加一些冰塊，如果還是覺得熱再跟我反應。
The temperature is fixed. I can help you add some ice in your water first. Please let me know if you still feel hot.

好的。我還是先點餐來吃好了，可以給我菜單嗎？
Okay, I think I would like to order first. Can I have the menu?

好的，我馬上去拿您的菜單和冰塊，請稍候。
Sure, I will go get the menu and ice cubes for you. Wait a moment, please.

謝謝。啊，我的朋友來了，菜單和冰水要兩份喔。

Thanks. Ah, my friend is here. Double the menu and iced water, plcase.

好用句型 點餐必會
Sentence Patterns

1. Do you take personal checks? 請問你們收私人支票嗎？

   check：支票

   👍 會這句更加分 The check he wrote to me was bounced.
   他開給我的支票被退票了。

2. I'd like a spaghetti with meat sauce, please.
   我要一份義大利麵搭配肉醬，謝謝。
   sauce：醬料、調味料

   👍 會這句更加分 A good appetite is a good sauce.
   飢不擇食。

3. Please write the amount and sign at the bottom.
   請寫下金額並且簽名在下方。
   bottom：底部

   👍 會這句更加分 Put your shoes on the bottom shelf, please.
   請把你的鞋子放在最下面那一層。

4. I'll put down 5 dollars for the tip.
   我會留 5 塊美金當作小費。
   tip：小費

👍會這句更加分 Don't forget to give the waiter a good tip. He helped a lot. 別忘了給那位服務生豐厚的小費，他幫了大忙。

5. The restaurant's service was awful and the meals were overpriced.

那家餐廳的服務糟透了，餐點也很貴。

awful：可怕的

👍會這句更加分 The garbage can has awful stink.

那個垃圾桶散發出可怕的臭味。

6. A：Something's wrong. This salad tastes weird.

有點不對勁，這道沙拉味道好奇怪。

B：I know. The lettuce looks rotten.

我知道，萵苣看起來已經壞掉了。

weird：古怪的

👍會這句更加分 How weird is it that a man never worries about the future.

一個人從不煩惱未來的事是多麼奇怪！

rotten：腐敗的

👍會這句更加分 The children are poisoned by eating rotten food in school.

孩子們因為在學校吃了腐敗的食物而中毒。

NOTES

主食

甜點

飲料

點心

2號

美食館：甜點
Cuisine Gallery2: Desserts

人們都説「裝甜點的是另一個胃」，的確，不論吃了多少營養豐盛的正餐，看到精緻誘人的甜點仍是會令人食指大動。尤其是當心情不佳或是感到煩悶時，甜點更是能帶給人愉悦的心情，彷彿甜點本身就是一種抗憂鬱劑似地受到大家歡迎。就讓我們來看看甜點到底有著甚麼樣的魔法，能讓大人小孩都為之瘋狂吧！

　　People say "desserts are for the other stomach," indeed. No matter how nutritive your meal is, you still want to have some exquisite desserts. Desserts can bring joys to people, especially when they feel upset or worried, as a kind of antidepressant that is welcomed by everyone. Let's see what kind of magic that can make both adults and children crazy!

2.1
美式甜點大集合
American Desserts

用英文聊美食 聊天必備
Talking About Food In English

客人： 妳好，我在路邊拿到一張傳單，上面寫著這裡是新開幕的甜點專賣店所以過來看看。

Hello, I got a flier, and it says that here is a new dessert specialist, so I came to take a look.

店員： 是呀，我們正在進行開幕酬賓活動，所有美式甜點都有特價喔。

Yeah, we are having a grand opening event, all kinds of American style dessert are on sale.

客人： 請問店裡有哪些是屬於美式甜點呢？

What kinds of American style dessert do you have?

店員： 經典的美式甜點大致可分為派、餅乾和蛋糕這三種，派有波士頓奶油派（Boston cream pie）和胡桃派（Pecan Pie）。餅乾可分為甜、鹹兩種，蛋糕則有魔鬼蛋糕（Devil's Food Cake）、起司蛋糕（Cheesecake）、胡蘿蔔蛋糕（Carrot Cake）等。

The classic American style desserts can be divided in three catagories - pies, cookies and cakes. Famous pies are Boston cream pie and Pecan Pie. Cookies have sweet and salty. And cakes, we have Devil's Food Cake, Cheesecake, Carrot Cake, etc.

客人： 其中有幾種聽起來好特別喔，像是魔鬼蛋糕和胡蘿蔔蛋糕。

Some of them sounds very special, like Devil's Food Cake and Carrot Cake.

店員： 魔鬼蛋糕起源於美國南部，名稱的由來有好幾種說法，主要是因為它的美味讓人嚐了以後會感到罪惡，所以就有人戲稱它為「魔鬼的食物（devil's food cake）」。胡蘿蔔蛋糕則是起源於中世紀，當時糖價昂貴，胡蘿蔔是含糖量最多的蔬菜之一，因此被用於做蛋糕當成甜點。

Devil's Food Cake is originally from southern America. The origin of its name has several interpretations, but the primary reason is that it's so delicious that people feel guilty after tasting it. That is why people called it "devil's food cake." Carrot Cake dates from the mid-century. At that time, sugar was very expensive while carrots are one of the most sugar-rich vegetables, so people used carrots to make cakes as desserts.

客人： 這裡的巧克力布朗尼也算是蛋糕的一種嗎？

Does chocolate brownie count as a kind of cake, too?

店員： 巧克力布朗尼（Chocolate Brownie）又被稱為布朗尼蛋糕、核桃布朗尼蛋糕或者波斯頓布朗尼。加入大量黑巧克力烘培而成，因其高貴的咖啡色澤（brown）而得名（brownie），是一種切塊的小型蛋糕，因此同樣也有特價喔。

Chocolate Brownie, is also called Brownie Cake, Walnut Brownie or Boston Brownie, and baked with a lot of black chocolate, named after its noble brown color. It's a small cake-slice, and it is on sales too.

客人： 那我要巧克力布朗尼。

主食

甜點

飲料

點心

I would like to have Chocolate Brownies then.

店員： 派的口味變化多端，原本是於 17 世紀時，飄洋過海的英國移民將做法帶進新大陸的。因為覆蓋派皮具有讓食物保鮮的作用，所以早期的新移民能將很多東西做成派，尤其是肉類。要買一塊鹹派吃吃看嗎？

Pies have many different flavors. In the 17th century, immigrants from England brought the method of making pies to America. Pie crust is able to keep the ingredients fresh, and the immigrants made a lot of stuffs into pies, especially meats. Would you like to buy a salty pie?

客人： 不了，我比較喜歡吃甜的，尤其是巧克力。

No, I prefer sweet, especially chocolate.

店員： 那推薦您嚐嚐看波士頓奶油派，內餡是鮮奶油，上頭塗上香濃的巧克力糖霜，您一定會喜歡。

Then I recommend you to try our Boston cream pie. It's filled with a cream filling, and frosted with cholocate. You will definitely love it.

飲食小百科 文化大不同
Differences in Cultures

 各國蛋糕的典故
Classical Stories of Cakes from Every Country

奧地利的沙河蛋糕 Austrian Sachertorte

沙河蛋糕起源於 1832 年，一位王子的家廚研發出一種甜美無比的巧克力蛋糕，受到皇室的熱愛。沙河蛋糕獨特的巧克力與杏桃的美味組合卻早已傳遍全世界，被數以萬計的點心主廚不斷繁衍創作，成為代表奧地利的國寶級點心。

Sachertorte originated in 1832. A chef from a prince's house invented a sweet chocolate cake, which was respectively welcomed by royalty. The unique and perfect match of Sachertorte's chocolate icing with apricot is well known all over the world. Thousands of pastry chefs constantly improve it and make it become the most representative Austrian dessert.

德國的史多倫蛋糕 Genman Stollen

在德國，史多倫蛋糕是傳統的水果蛋糕，通常在聖誕節時食用。傳統作法中為4.4kg重，但現今已有較小的尺寸可供選擇。

In German, Stollen is a traditional fruit cake, usually eaten during Christmas. It traditionally weights around 4.4 kg, and the smaller sizes are available nowadays.

法國的木材蛋糕 French Yule log

法國人在耶誕夜時有全家團圓守夜的習慣，時至半夜通常會全家聚在暖爐前一起吃木材蛋糕，一邊喝著咖啡或紅茶驅趕寒意，另一方面也藉機聯絡家人間的感情。

主食 Main Course

甜點 Desserts

飲料 Beverages

點心 Snacks

83

In Christmas Eve, French have the custom stay up late of night vigil with the whole family. They usually stay around the heater, and have Yule log and coffee or black tea to keep warm and, develop the emotional attachment within family.

德國的黑森林蛋糕　German Schwarzwaelder Kirschtorte

相傳古早以前，每當黑森林區的櫻桃豐收時，農婦們除了將剩餘的櫻桃製成果醬外，在做蛋糕時也會大方地將櫻桃塞在蛋糕的夾層內，或是一顆顆裝飾在蛋糕上。而在打製蛋糕的鮮奶油時，更會加入不少櫻桃汁。這種以櫻桃與鮮奶油為主的蛋糕從黑森林傳到外地後，就成了所謂的「黑森林蛋糕」。

It is said in the Black Forest region, when the cherries are harvested , peasant women would used the cherries to make jam. They would also generously fill the cherries into cakes or put cherries on top of them. When they were making the cake, they also added a lot of cherry juice into whipping cream. These cakes are made mainly with cherries and whipping creams, and quickly spread out of the Black Forest region and known as the Black Forest Cake (Schwarzwaelder Kirschtorte).

菜餚的故事　你知道嗎？
Stories About Food

 餅乾的由來
The History of Cookies

距今 160 多年前，一艘航行在法國比斯開灣的英國帆船遇上狂風大浪、不幸觸礁擱淺。船員們急忙放下小舢板逃生，他們來到一個荒無人煙且沒有食物的小島上。等到風停了，他們駛著小舢板回船上搬運食品，可是船

艙裡儲存的麵粉、砂糖、奶油等食物全都被海水泡成糊狀了，他們只好把這些麵糊撈起來裝了幾袋帶回島上，捏成一個個小糰用火烤來吃。沒想到這些混合在一起的麵糊經過發酵，烤出來的成品酥脆可口又美味。船員靠這些烤過的麵糰充饑直到獲救，回到英國後，他們為了紀念在比斯開灣的這場船難，便用同樣的方法烤了小餅來吃，並將之稱為「比斯開（biscuit）」。其他腦筋轉得快的商人比照辦理，製作同樣的小餅出售，這就是現在我們所吃的餅乾。直到現在，仍有許多國家將餅乾稱為「比斯開」。

160 years ago, there was a British ship sailing in the Bay of Biscay, France, when the tempest drove the ship on the rocks. The crew hurried to escape with the lifeboats, but they landed on a desolate and uninhabited island with no food. They waited until the wind stopped, and they rowed the lifeboat back to the ship for food, but all the flour, sugar, butter, etc. were soaked in the brine. They had no choice but to load the dough into few bags and went back to the island. They mashed them into small balls and baked it with fire. They did not expect that it could become crispy, tasty and delicious after baking it. They ate the backed dough until help arrived. After returning back to England, they used the same way to bake the cookie and named it "biscuit," in memory of the wreck. Other smart businessmen started to produce the same cookies for selling. It is the cookie that we eat today. There are still many countries where it is called "biscuit" until now.

實用會話 聊天必備
Useful Phrases

 選購生日蛋糕
Choosing a Birthday Cake

您好，歡迎光臨，請問有什麼我可以為您服務的嗎？

Hello, welcome to the shop. May I help you?

我想買一個生日蛋糕送給朋友，請問有什麼推薦的嗎？

I would like to buy a birthday cake for my friend. Any recommendations?

您可以參考我們展示櫥窗內的蛋糕，每一款旁邊都有標示蛋糕名稱和食材。

You can take a look at the cakes in our window. Each has labeled with its name and ingredients.

嗯，每一種看起來都很好吃耶，真是讓人難以抉擇，請問你們店裡最熱賣的是哪一款？

Uhm... each of them seems very delicious. That's so hard to choose. Which one is the most popular in the store?

 生日蛋糕的話，我們的惡魔蛋糕和草莓奶油蛋糕都很受歡迎。
As for birthday cakes, our Devil's Food Cake and Strawberry Cream Cake are both very popular.

 看起來不錯，不過好大一個喔，我們只有兩個人慶祝，怕會吃不完，有 8 吋以下的嗎？
Looks good, but it's too big. We are only two people to celebrate. I'm afraid we cannot finish all. Is there any cake under 8-inch?

 那您可以參考這裡的切片蛋糕，每塊約一人份，還可以選擇不同的口味。
You can take a look at the sliced cakes here. One piece for one person. And you can choose differene flauors.

 這個好耶，我看看，那就波士頓奶油派和招牌起司蛋糕各一塊。
That's great. Let me see. I'll hace a piece of Boston cream pie and a piece of cheese cake.

 要不要再帶一份巧克力布朗尼或巧克力脆片餅乾呢？
Would you like to have a piece of Chocolate Brownie or Chocolate Biscuit?

我朋友正在減肥，已經很久不碰巧克力了。

My friend is on diet and she has not had chocolate for a long time.

 那麼口味清爽的胡蘿蔔蛋糕如何呢？

How about that light Carrot Cake?

好啊，那來兩份好了，請問這樣一共是多少錢？

Sure, make it two pieces. How much for all?

 一共是 420 元，請稍等，我幫您用禮盒包裝起來。請問生日蠟燭需要的歲數是？

420 dollars. Please wait a moment. I will put all the cakes in a gift box. What is the number you need for the birthday candle?

28，謝謝。

28, thanks.

主食 Main Course

好用句型 點餐必會
Sentence Patterns

1. Q: What would you like for dessert?

   請問您的點心要點什麼呢？

   A: I would like the caramel pudding.

   我想要點焦糖布丁。

   dessert：甜點

   👍 會這句更加分　We went into the cafe for coffee and dessert.

   　　　　　　　　我們到咖啡館喝咖啡和享用甜點。

2. I think I'll skip the coffee/tea. Just bring me my vanilla ice cream.

   請直接幫我上香草冰淇淋，我不需要咖啡/茶了。

   skip：跳過、略過

   👍 會這句更加分　It is important not to skip meals.

   　　　　　　　　三餐都要正常吃，這非常地重要。

3. Waiter: Would you care for any dessert? We have some fancy cakes today.

   　　　　請問要來點甜點嗎？我們今天有一些特別的蛋糕。

   Guest: It sounds worth trying. I might as well try some.

   　　　　聽起來不錯耶。那我想來一些。

   Waiter: Good. I'll be back in a few minutes.

   　　　　好的，馬上為您送上。

   fancy：別緻的

   👍 會這句更加分　That's a very fancy watch.

   　　　　　　　　那是一支非常別緻的手錶。

甜點 Desserts

飲料 Beverages

點心 Snacks

4. Waiter: Would you care for any dessert?

　　　　　請問要來點甜點嗎？

　　Guest A: No, thanks. I'm sure I'll be full.

　　　　　不了，我想我已經飽了。

　　Guest B: They have fantastic chocolate cheesecake here.

　　　　　他們這裡有非常好吃的巧克力起司蛋糕喔！

　　Guest A: They do? Well, maybe we could split some.

　　　　　真的嗎？那或許我們兩個可以分著吃。

　　Waiter: Would you like me to bring two forks?

　　　　　我幫您準備兩支叉子吧！

　　Guest A: Yes, please. Good idea.

　　　　　真是好主意，謝謝。

　fantastic：極好的、極出色的

會這句更加分 What a fantastic movie!

　　　　　多麼棒的一部電影啊！

　split：把…劃分

會這句更加分 The cake has been split up into 8 pieces.

　　　　　這塊蛋糕被切成了八塊。

NOTES

2.2
中式甜點大集合
Chinese Desserts

女兒： 媽媽，我好餓喔，家裡有沒有什麼甜點可以吃？

Mom, I am so hungry, do we have any desserts at home I can eat?

母親： 冰箱裡有冰棒，看妳要不要吃？

There are some popsicles in the fridge, do you want one?

女兒： 冰棒啊…說到吃冰，我還是最喜歡吃剉冰了。一想到那機器磨出來如同雪花般的清涼碎冰，可以選擇加入各種不同的配料，上頭再淋上糖水，料多豐富又美味，夏天來一碗最消暑了。

Popsicle... talking about ice, I like shaved ice. I'm still in favor of it. Thinking of the snowflalce-like ice shaved from that machine, you can also choose a variety of different toppings, and the syrup on top is plentiful and delicious, the best thing to relieve the summer heat.

母親： 媽媽則是最喜歡綿綿冰了，可以單吃也可以另加配料，可惜需要機器才能攪拌出綿密的冰沙口感，跟剉冰一樣，一般家庭沒有機器是很難做出來的。

I like mein mein ice the most. They can be eaten alone and also with toppings. Unfortunately, only the machine can make the foamy smoothie-like mouthfeel, just like shaved ice. It is very difficult to do it without a machine at home.

女兒： 豆花也是很棒的甜點，跟剉冰一樣可以選擇各種不同的配料，冷的熱的都好吃，可惜也是外頭才有賣。

Tofu pudding (douhua) is a great dessert too. As shaved ice, you can choose toppings, and both yummy in cold or hot. It's a pity that they are only sold in the shops.

母親： 女兒啊，既然妳這麼喜歡吃冰品的配料，剛好冰箱裡有一些愛玉跟粉粿，媽媽米煮粉圓，妳幫我煮糖水。

Sweetie... since you enjoy the toppings so much, there are some aiyu jelly and starch jelly in the fridge. I'll cook tapioca pearls and you can help me with the syrup.

女兒： 好啊！太棒了！愛玉加點糖水、檸檬汁或蜂蜜就很好吃了呢。

Sure! Great! Aiyu jelly will be delicious with some syrup, lemon juice or honey.

母親： 對呀，不過愛玉不只好吃而已，早期人們中暑時不是選擇刮痧，就是吃碗不加糖、不加冰的純愛玉，聽說口乾舌燥時吃點愛玉還能降火氣喔。

Yes, but aiyu jelly is not just tasty. In early times, when people had a heat stroke, they chose gua sha or have a bowl of pure aiyu jelly, without syrup nor ice. I heard it can also ease the heat of your body when you are thirsty.

女兒： 不過… 粉粿是什麼？

But... what is starch jelly?

母親： 台灣早期盛產地瓜，當時經濟環境不佳，耐旱的地瓜成了人民的主食之一，也將地瓜的用途發揮地淋漓盡致。只要用地瓜粉加點水，在火爐上邊煮邊攪拌，就成了好吃有嚼勁的「粉粿」。粉粿

在台灣早期是經濟狀況較好的人們才吃得起的甜點，它能消暑、退腸火、防中暑，又可止飢，因此有人會將粉粿當成早餐，也會在下午三、四點時來上一碗，是台灣本土的下午茶甜點。

Earlier in Taiwan, it abounds with sweet potatoes. Due to the poor economic situation, the drought-tolerant sweet potatoes became one of the staple food, and made into various products. By adding some water with sweet potato starch, stir and cook to make the delicious chewy "starch jelly." was a dessert only for the wealthy people in early Taiwan. It helps relieve the summer heat, get rid of the intestinal heat, avoid heatstroke and stop hunger too, so some people take starch jelly as breakfast and have one bowl at 3pm or 4pm. It is a Taiwanese afternoon tea dessert.

女兒： 一樣是加糖水吃嗎？

By adding some syrup as well?

母親： 對呀，等我把粉圓煮好就可以加在糖水裡一起吃囉。

Yeah, it can be eaten with some syrup after I finishes cooking tapioca pearls.

飲食小百科 文化大不同
Differences in Cultures

豆花的多樣化搭配 Tofu Pudding (Dou-hua) Diversification

　　台灣、香港、澳門、馬來西亞、新加坡、廣東、廣西、福建等地通常會在豆花中加入糖水或黑糖水食用。在冬天喝上一碗加了薑汁的熱豆花可以驅寒，還可以加入綠豆、紅豆、各式水果或是湯圓一起食用以增加口感。較為特別的還有將糖水改成使用豆漿的「豆漿豆花」，或是加上巧克力糖漿、巧克力米的「巧克力豆花」、或是搭配芝麻糊的「黑白豆花」以及加入如芒果汁等的「芒果豆花」。除了在湯汁上做變化以外，台灣亦嘗試將其他食材加入豆花製程中，如雞蛋、巧克力等，成了新穎的三色豆花。

　　In Taiwan, Hong Kong, Macau, Malaysia, Singapore, Guangdong, Guangxi, Fujian and etc., the tofu pudding is often eaten with syrup or brown syrup. In winter, eating a bowl of hot tofu pudding with ginger juice can keep out the cold. It can also served with mung beans, red beans, all kinds of fruits or rice balls (tangyuan) to increase the taste of this dessert. Other special recepies include to served with soy milk to make "soy milk tofu pudding", or top with chocolate syrup or chocolate vermicelli to make "chocolate tofu pudding" There are also the sesame flavor "black and white tofu pudding", or "mango tofu pudding" by adding mango juice, etc. Beside making changes in the soup, Taiwanese also add other ingredients in making tofu pudding, such as eggs, chocolate, etc., to make the novel three-color tofu pudding.

愛玉與薛荔 Aiyu Jelly and Climbing Fig

　　愛玉為僅產於台灣之特有亞種，在台灣以外所產的類似愛玉之凍狀食品皆為「薛荔子」所製成。如新加坡的「文頭雪」和武夷山的「薛荔凍」等。「文頭雪」是一塊大果凍上覆蓋一層碎冰，另放上一粒金柑。「雜果文頭

雪」則是加了不同種類的水果塊。薜荔（ㄅㄧˋㄌㄧˋ）是桑科榕屬的攀緣藤本植物植物，雌雄異株，多攀附於樹木或岩石上。性喜溫暖潮濕的氣候，廣泛分佈於亞洲地區，如中國西南部、臺灣、日本、印度等地。由於愛玉與薜荔在台灣原生分布區域重疊，且兩者在分類學上本為同種，雜交後具可育性，因此在野外常可見葉子和果實的特徵介於愛玉與薜荔兩者的個體植株。薜荔可食用的部分為其果實（隱花果），其中成熟種子（瘦果外覆之膠狀物）富含可溶於水的果膠，呈半透明狀或淺黃色，因此也能製成如愛玉凍般凝結的凍狀食品。實際上，在臺灣的市售愛玉子原料成品中也有部分、甚至全部皆為薜荔子的情形。

Aiyu is an endemic subspecie only grown in Taiwan. The other food which is similar to aiyu jelly that produced outside Taiwan is all made with "climbing fig", such as Singapore's "ice jelly" and Mount Wuyi's "climbing fig jelly", etc. "Ice jelly" is a big jelly covered with a layer of ice and put a kumquat on top. "Mixed fruit ice jelly" adds different types of diced fruits. Climbing fig is a species of woody evergreen vine plant of the family Moraceae, dioecious, multi-cling on trees or rocks. It likes the warm and humid climate, widely common in several Asian regions such as southwest China, Taiwan, Japan, India and other places. Due to aiyu and climbing fig are distributed in native area in Taiwan, and both present the same taxonomic species, they can be fertilized after hybridization, and they are often seen in the leaves and characteristic fruits between the individual plants of aiyu and climbing fig in the countryside. Climbing fig edible portion is the fruit (syconium), wherein the ripe seeds (achenes overcoat by jelly) have a rich pectin that is water-soluble, which appear with translucent or light yellow, so it also can be made as a condensation of aiyu jelly. In fact, there are commercial circumstances where some or all aiyu jelly materials are made with climbing fig.

菜餚的故事 你知道嗎？
Stories About Food

愛玉的故事 The Story of Aiyu Jelly

清朝道光年間，有位大陸商人到嘉義做生意，一天因為天氣炎熱，他隨手舀起山區河水解渴，沒想到河上竟浮著一層膠狀的透明物體，吃起來暑熱全消。商人仔細觀察，發現原來是水面上幾顆果實所分泌出來的汁液。商人撿了幾顆帶回家，用水搓揉後果然分泌出果膠而且立刻凝固成凍狀，他發現這些果凍加糖後食用滋味更棒。這位商人有一位名為「愛玉」的女兒，長的楚楚動人、討人歡心，她所帶出門販售的這種飲品也被客人稱為「愛玉凍」。後來一傳十、十傳百，跟著採愛玉、賣愛玉的商人也變多了，甚至一路紅到福建、廣東一帶。

In the Qing Dynasty, there was a mainland businessman who went to Chiayi for business. One day, due to the hot weather, he readily scoop up the water from the mountain river to quench the thirst, but he didn't expect the gelatinous transparent objects floated on the river. After eating those things, the heat had been eased. The businessman observed carefully and found that the gels were out from a few seads. The businessman picked up the seads and went back home. After rubbed with water, they immediately solidified into jelly. He found those jelly tastes even better after combining with syrup. The businessman had a daughter named "Aiyu," who's beautiful and attractive. The drinks she sold were called by customers "Aiyu jelly." After the word was spread, there were more and more shops that sold aiyu jelly, and the drink became popular even in Fujian and Guangdong.

粉圓的歷史 The History of Tapioca Pearls

相傳是清朝年間進貢慈禧的獻壽禮，當時台灣府以木薯粉為主原料做成類似元宵的粉圓甜湯，慈禧太后品嘗後讚不絕口，粉圓從此便成為家喻戶曉

的台灣點心。

It is said that in the Qing Dynasty, Taiwan Prefecture sent tapioca pearls sweet soup which is similar to yuanxiao as tribute to celebrate the Empress Dowager Cixi's birthday. The Empress Dowager Cixi was full of praise after tasting that dessert, and tapioca pearls have become a famous dessert in Taiwan since then.

實用會話 聊天必備
Useful Phrases

 一位台灣人帶外國朋友到冰店品嚐台灣冰品。
A Taiwanese brings a foreign friend to an ice shop to taste Taiwanese frozen dessert.

 從早逛到現在也累了吧？我們休息一會，帶你吃個台灣冰吧！
Are you tired after walking from morning until now? Let's take a rest, I'll bring you to have some Taiwanese frozen desserts!

好啊！我早就聽說台灣的冰和國外的冰淇淋不一樣了，好想見識一下。
Okay! I heard that Taiwanese frozen desserts are soooo special, I want to try it!

這裡有賣豆花跟剉冰，機會難得，兩種都點來吃吃看吧！

Here they sell Tofu pudding and shaved ice. It's a golden chance. Let's try both!

好啊！這一整排琳瑯滿目的食材就是剉冰的配料嗎？全都是我沒見過的東西。

Sure! Is this endless array of toppings for shaved ice? I have never seen all these stuffs before.

在台灣，大部分的豆花和剉冰都可以自由選擇 4 到 5 種配料，讓我來為你介紹一下吧！從基本的紅豆、綠豆、花生到粉圓、芋圓、粉粿、愛玉等。剉冰還可以加當季新鮮水果和各種果醬，就看你想吃甚麼？

In Taiwan, mostly you can choose 4-5 toppings for tofu pudding or shaved ice. Let me introduce them for you! Here are red beans, green beans, peanuts, tapioca pearls, taro balls, starch jelly, aiyu jelly, etc. You can also add a variety of seasonal fresh fruits and jams on the shaved ice. All depends on what you want to eat.

我認得那樣黃澄澄的水果，是鼎鼎大名的芒果對不對？我好想大口大口吃台灣芒果喔！

I know that yellow glistening fruit. It's the famous mango, right? I really want to eat Taiwan's mango!

那就點一碗芒果牛奶冰吧！

Let's order the mango milk shaved ice!

豆花我就沒有概念了，在國外我們甚至連豆腐都很少吃。

I have no idea about Tofu pudding. We seldom eat Tofu in our country.

待會你吃吃看就知道了，口感就像布丁一樣，不同的是可以吃到豆類的風味，其他配料加上黑糖水更是好吃又消暑。

Wait until you try. It tastes like pudding, but the difference is that in this you can taste the flavor of beans. Combining with brown syrup and other toppings, it is so delicious and refreshing.

聽起來的確是夏天裡最棒的選擇，但是到了冬天怎麼辦，賣冰的商家不就都要休息了？

Sounds like the best choice in summer indeed, but how about winter? Are these shops going to close?

台灣的豆花可以做成熱的，其他還有燒仙草和紅豆湯等等，一樣是很受歡迎的冬日點心。
Tofu pudding can be served in hot. Others like hot grass jelly and red bean soup, etc. They are very popular winter desserts as well.

住在台灣真好！冰來了，我等不及要開動了！
It's great to live in Taiwan. Here comes the shaved ice. I can't wait to eat!

好用句型 點餐必會
Sentence Patterns

(訂位相關)

1. We didn't make a reservation. 我們沒有事先訂位。

   reservation：預訂、預訂的席座

   會這句更加分 Do I need to make a reservation? 請問我需要先訂位嗎？

2. Q: Do you take telephone reservation? 請問你們接受電話訂位嗎？

   A: We don't accept reservations on the phone. 我們不接受電話訂位。

   accept：接受

   會這句更加分 Please accept our invitation. 請接受我們的邀請。

3. I'm going to be there 15 minutes late. Would you please hold my table? 我會晚十五分鐘到，可以請你們為我保留一下位子嗎？

   hold：有效、持續、保持

   會這句更加分 Please hold on for a moment. 請稍等一下。

4. May I change this afternoon's reservation to tomorrow at night? 請問我可以

主食 Main Course

甜點 Desserts

飲料 Beverages

點心 Snacks

把今天下午的訂位改到明天晚上嗎？

change：交換、改變

👍 **會這句更加分** Let's eat Chinese food for a change! 我們來吃一下中國菜換換口味吧！

5. I want to cancel my reservation for tonight. 我想要取消今晚的訂位。

cancel：取消

👍 **會這句更加分** The fair was cancelled because of the rain. 那場市集因雨而取消了。

6. Q:How long can you hold the table for me? 請問訂位可以保留多久？

A: We will reserve your table for 10 minutes. 我們會為您保留十分鐘。

reserve：保留

👍 **會這句更加分** Reserve the New Year's money. You may need it someday. 把壓歲錢留起來，有天你會需要的。

7. Customer: A table for 2, please. 請給我們一個兩人座。

Waiter: Sorry, all our tables are full now. 很抱歉，我們目前所有座位都客滿了。

full：滿的

👍 **會這句更加分** Din Tai Fung is always full of foreign customers. 鼎泰豐總是充滿外國觀光客。

NOTES

2.3
日式甜點看這裡
Japanese Desserts

用英文聊美食 聊天必備
Talking About Food In English

記者 A： 我下個月要去日本九州玩，想買一些具有當地特色的甜點回來分送親友，妳對日本比較有研究，能不能給我一點意見？

I want to buy some local desserts for my family and friends when I am off to Kyushu, Japan, next month. You know more about Japan. Can you give me some advice?

記者 B： 說到日式甜點，最具代表性的就是和菓子囉！和菓子是一部分日式點心的統稱，型態有非常多種，古人利用水果及果實加以穀物澱粉做成各式各樣的點心，主要原料包括米、麵粉、紅豆、砂糖、葛粉，並依照不同的口味添加不同的特殊食材。和菓子與抹茶的味道相得益彰，因此和菓子也隨著日本茶道文化的興起而相輔相成至今，形成獨特的甜點文化，不過我建議妳可以在當地品嚐即可，帶回來的話怕會超過賞味期限喔。

Talking about the Japanese desserts, the most representative is Wagashi! Wagashi is kind of Japanese desserts which has many types. Ancient people used fruits with crop starches to make a variety of snacks. The main materials include rice, flour, red beans, sugar, arrowroot flour and extra different special ingredients according to different tastes. Wagashi and Matcha can complement each other's taste. Therefore, with the rise of the Japanese tea ceremony, it has developed a unique dessert culture of Wagashi, but I suggest that you'd better eat Wagashi in Japan, or otherwise I am afraid of that they're all expired when you finish your trip.

記者 A： 這樣啊，那我知道了。和菓子的名稱有其意義嗎？

Is that so? Now I know it. Does Wagashi's name have any meaning?

記者 B： 和菓子的「和」字，取自於大和民族的「和」字；而「菓子」的「果」字，是由水果的「果」字而來，加上草字頭，代表著和菓子是使用草本植物（木的果實）或是水果加工而成的食物。此外，妳這次去九州，剛好可以買到長崎蛋糕。

Wagashi's "Wa" is from the Yamato people's "Yamato," and "gashi" is from the fruit's "fructification," which also represents that the wagashi is made with herbaceous plants (the fructification from wood) or the fruits. Beside, you can buy Castella in Kyushu.

記者 A： 長崎蛋糕？

Castella?

記者 B： 長崎蛋糕（**Honey Cake**）大約在十六世紀時傳入日本，當時的荷蘭商人希望進入日本做生意，特地將荷蘭皇室招待貴賓的蛋糕做為貢品獻給天皇，這種蛋糕立刻博得天皇的讚賞，時至今日儼然已成為當地的特色。

Nagasaki Castella was introduced into Japan around the 16th century. When the Dutch traders wanted to do business in Japan, they sent cakes which only served to honored guests in the Dutch royalty as tribute to the Emperor. This cake immediately won the Emperor's appreciation, and it is a local specialty today.

記者 A： 原來是這樣，聽起來太棒了，我就買那個吧！那還有其他推薦必吃的日式甜點嗎？

So that is how it is. It sounds great, I will buy that then! Is there any other Japanese sweets recommendation?

記者 B： 妳可以吃吃看宇治金時，是日本的傳統刨冰，「宇治」指的是宇治綠茶，而「金時」則是指紅豆。做法是以日式綠茶加砂糖及水煮成糖漿淋在刨冰上，旁邊加上以砂糖熬煮的紅豆和白色的糯米糰子，是一道極富色彩與口感的甜點。在咖啡廳應該不難找。

You may try Uchikinoki, it is a Japanese traditional shaved ice. "Uchi" means the green tea from Uji and "kinoki" refers to the red beans. The method is to cook Japanese green tea with granulated sugar and water into syrup and pour over the shaved ice, served with the red beans paste and white glutinous rice balls. It is a very colorful and tasty dessert. You can easily find it in the coffee shops.

記者 A： 謝謝妳，我到時候一定會找來品嚐看看！

Thank you, I will definitely look for it!

飲食小百科 文化大不同
Differences in Cultures

在明治時代，西洋人帶來了蛋糕及巧克力等西洋點心，日本稱為「洋菓子」，包括糖果、餅乾、冰淇淋等，並開始對各種西日合併菓子下功夫。如在明治7年（1874年），銀座的木村屋推出「紅豆麵包」。

In the Meiji era, Westerners brought cakes, chocolate and other Western snacks, including candies, cookies, ice cream, etc. to Japan, which called "okashi" in Japan. They started to modified the western desserts with the Japanese elements. For instance, in Meiji 7th year (1874), Kimuraya started to sell "red bean bread" in Ginza

在台灣也有出產羊羹及大福等「和菓子」，據說是由日本的和菓子師傅傳承下來的技術為基礎，在台灣根深蒂固地發展而來，在台灣也有好幾家已經創業將近 100 年的老字號和菓子店。不過在風味方面，有些是台灣自行開發的，例如羊羹，有茉莉花茶及咖啡、蘋果、鳳梨等在日本很難看得到的口味。

In Taiwan, there are also shops make "Wagashi" such as Yōkan and Daifuku. It is said that based on the skills which inherited from the Japanese wagashi chefs and deeply developed in Taiwan, and those wagashi shops are nearly century-old. But in flavors, there are some variations in Taiwan. For example, flavors of jasmine tea, coffee, apple, pineapple, and etc. for Yōkans, which are rare in Japan.

和菓子的製作費工，命名也相當講究，通常是以連歌、俳句、歷史典故或自然風景為靈感。其外觀的多樣性也是世界上首屈一指，點心師傅會把和

菓子作成栩栩如生的花鳥魚蟲，或者配合季節營造出當季的氣氛，讓和菓子有如巧奪天工的藝術品一樣捨不得吃下。帶有藝術性的和菓子在日本人看來是日式矜持的完美呈現。特別精巧、具有藝術效果的和菓子也可以稱為工藝菓子，特色是以食材來表現花鳥風月的世界觀，這正是日本人精緻文化的體現。

The production method of Wagashi is very labor-intensive and it is also very particular in naming, usually inspired by renga, haikus, historical stories or natural landscapes. The diversity of its appearance is outstanding in the world. Dessert chefs normally shape the Wagashi into different kinds of animals vividly, or create the atmosphere as the reflection of season. They make Wagashi looks like a piece of exquisite artwork, and people would feel pity to eat it. For Japanese, the artistic wagashi is the perfect presentation of the Japanese reserved character. Particularly delicate in artistic effects, Wagashi features by using ingredients to express a world view towards nature, which is a manifestation of the Japanese refined culture.

賞心悅目的和菓子常作為年節送禮之用，也是日常招待客人必備的點心，在日本各地都有獨特風味的和菓子作為名產，日本人出差、觀光總會買個幾盒和菓子回來，由此可見和菓子在日本人生活佔有相當大的重要性。

Eyeable wagashi are often given as the New Year gifts, and also the necessary desserts for guests. In Japan, each place has a unique flavor of wagashi as a local special. When Japanese go for business or trips, they always bring back several boxes of Wagashi. Therefore, Wagashi occupies an important part in Japanese life.

菜餚的故事 你知道嗎？
Stories About Food

　　長崎蛋糕最早起源於古國 Castella。十七世紀，葡萄牙的傳教士和商人遠渡重洋來到長崎，他們帶來的東西，例如玻璃、煙草、麵包等等對當地人來說都是新奇的玩意兒，為了建立彼此的友誼，這些外地人想了一些辦法來討好當地人，傳教士對貴族分送葡萄酒、對平民分送甜點，希望藉此傳播基督教。商人更是大量製造糕點在街中分送民眾。當時，一種用砂糖、雞蛋、麵粉作的糕點大受歡迎，日本人問：「這是甚麼？」葡萄牙人回答：「這是從 Castella 王國傳來的甜點」結果，日本人就誤將「Castella」(日文以片假名記為「カステラ」)當作甜點的名字流傳下來。西元 1965 年，日本「長崎本舖」在台灣成立公司，由日本首席師傅遵行古法調製原料、引進專用烤爐慢火烘培，專業生產長崎蛋糕，從此「長崎蛋糕」也就成了蜂蜜蛋糕的代名詞。

Castella originated from an ancient country named Castella. In 17th century, Portuguese missionaries and traders came from far away to Nagasaki. The products they brought, such as glass, tobacco, bread and so on, were novelty stuff to locals. These outsiders thought of some ways to curry favor with locals in order to establish mutual friendship. Missionaries distributed wine to aristocracy and dessert to civilians, hoping to spread Christianity. Businessmen even distributed a lot of confectionery for people in the streets. At that time, there was one popular kind of pastry made from granulated sugar, egg, and flour. Japanese asked, "What is it?" Portuguese replied: "This is the dessert coming from the Kingdom of Castella." In turn, Japanese had mistakenly "Castella" (in Japanese katakana known as "カステラ") as the dessert's name and handed down. In 1965 AD, the Japanese "Nagasaki shop" established in Taiwan. Japanese masters modulated materials, imported the special simmered

baking ovens and professionally produced Castella. Since then, "Castella" has become a synonymous of honey cake.

實用會話 聊天必備
Useful Phrases

女兒啊，從日本回來的表姐帶了幾盒和菓子過來，快點來吃。

Daughter, your cousin came back from Japan with a few boxes of wagashi. Come and have some.

好。表姐，好久不見了。
Ok! Cousin, didn't see you for a long time.

才幾年不見，妳已經長成像草莓大福一樣甜美的小美人了。

Only a few years gone, you have grown up like a sweet strawberry Daifuku, sweet and pretty.

哪有啦！這就是和菓子嗎？有好多種類喔，而且每一個都好精緻。

Not really! Is this Wagashi? There are so many kinds, and each of them is so elaborated.

剛才我也跟妳表姐談到，每一個都像藝術品一樣，真捨不得吃呢！

I just talked with your cousin about that. Each of them is like a piece of artwork. What a pity if we eat them.

我剛到日本的時候也覺得很稀奇，和菓子被形容為「日本飲食文化中的花」，因為和菓子就像繪畫和陶瓷等手工藝品一樣，是靠師傅的美感和手藝來表達內心的感性，更與季節和節日息息相關，是日本人引以為傲的文化。

When I first arrived in Japan, I also feel that quite a fancy. Wagashi has been described as "the flower of Japanese food culture," because Wagashi is as same as paintings, ceramics and other handicrafts, all depended on the aesthetic perception and handicraft of the master to express inner sensibility, even related to the seasons and holidays, is a kind of culture they are so proud of.

旁邊這一盒大福也算是和菓子嗎？

Can this big box of Daifuku be considered as Wagashi as well?

和菓子種類很多，仙貝、包餡饅頭、羊羹和糯米糰子都算是，我們趁鮮來享用吧。

There are many kinds of Wagashi. Popped rice crackers, stuffed buns, Yōkan and glutinous rice balls are all included. Let's enjoy when they are still fresh.

好用句型 點餐必會
Sentence Patterns

1. Do you have a menu in Japanese or English?

   請問你們有日文或英文的菜單嗎？

   Japanese：日本人、日語

   👍 會這句更加分　The girl speaks Japanese very well.

   那個女孩說得一口流利的日語。

2. What's the today's special?

   請問今天有甚麼特別料理嗎？

   special：特別的

   👍 會這句更加分　The new cell phone was nothing special.

   那款新手機沒甚麼特別之處。

3. Could you recommend something else?

   可以請你推薦一些其他的嗎？

   else：其他、另外

   👍 會這句更加分　What else can I do for you, sir?

   還有其他我可以幫忙的地方，先生？

4. Do you have any local teas?

  請問你們有任何當地盛產的茶嗎？

  local：當地的

  👍 **會這句更加分** We reach Tokyo at 10:00 local time.

  我們於當地時間 10 點抵達東京。

5. Q: May I take your plate?

  我可以收走您的盤子嗎？

  A: Yes, please.／Not yet.

  好的，麻煩你。／不，謝謝。

  plate：盤子

  👍 **會這句更加分** She left a tip under her plate.

  她把小費留在她的盤子底下。

6. My order hasn't come yet.

  我點的餐點還沒來。

  yet：還沒

  👍 **會這句更加分** The boy hasn't finished his homework yet.

  那個男孩還沒有完成他的回家作業。

7. I ordered it thirty minutes ago.

  我在三十分鐘前就點餐了。

  ago：在…以前

  👍 **會這句更加分** I went to Japan with my family a year ago. It was a wonderful trip.

  我一年前曾和家人去日本，那是一趟非常棒的旅行。

2.4
義式甜點看這裡
Italian Desserts

用英文聊美食 聊天必備
Talking About Food In English

A 女： 妳還記得我們上次去台中旅遊認識的義大利男生嗎？妳看，他回我 e-mail 了耶！

Do you still remember the Italian guy we met in the last trip to Taichung? He replied to my e-mail. Look!

B 女： 妳還真的主動跟他聯絡啊！是想發展異國戀情嗎？

Did you really take the initiative in contacting him? Are you looking for a exotic romance?

A 女： 也不是啦，只是交個朋友增廣見聞啊，而且他好像對甜點很有研究呢！

Not really, just making friends to enrich my knowledge, and he seems to know a lot about desserts!

B 女： 他信裡寫些甚麼？

What did he write in the letter?

A 女： 一開始是「很高興認識妳」還有「當時天氣那麼熱，謝謝妳告訴我哪裡有賣冰淇淋」，再來就是介紹自己國家的甜點特色，還有和台灣吃到的甜點的不同之處，滔滔不絕寫的好像論文喔！

At the beginning, he wrote something like "very nice to meet you" and "thanks for telling me where to buy ice cream on the burning hot day." After that, he started to introduce the special desserts from his country and compare them with Taiwan's. He wrote a mile a minute, like writing a paper.

B 女： 我看看...「製作冰淇淋最有名氣的國家是義大利和美國…」，雖然有點不服氣，但也無法反駁甚麼。剩下的都是像這樣的內容嗎？

Let me see... "the most famous producers of ice cream are Italians and Americans..." Although a little unacceptable, have no point to deny. Is the rest of the content like this?

A 女： 其實他只是在介紹自己國家的甜點而已，並沒有要批評台灣的意思喔！像他就跟我說了很多小知識，妳知道提拉米蘇（Tiramisù）在義大利原文是「帶我走」的意思嗎？據說在二戰時期，有一位義大利士兵要出征，可是家裡幾乎什麼也沒有了，愛他的妻子為了給他準備乾糧，用家裡所有能吃的餅乾、麵包製成了一個糕點，就叫提拉米蘇。每當這位士兵在戰場上吃到提拉米蘇就會想起他的家，想起家中心愛的人。

Actually, he just introduced the desserts from his country, not for criticism, as he gave me many tips, do you know Tiramisù in Italian means "take me away?" It is said that during the World War II, there was an Italian soldier who was going to battle, but there was nearly nothing left at home, but for preparing his rations, his wife made a dessert by using all the cookies, bread and anything eatable, named Tiramisù. Every time when this soldier had Tiramisù, it reminded him that his home and lovely wife.

B 女： 不愧是義大利人，真是浪漫。

So romantic. No wonder he is an Italian.

A 女： 現在正當紅的法國代表甜點馬卡龍（Macaroon）其實最早是出

現在義大利的修道院，當時有位名為 Carmelie 的修女製作了這種以杏仁粉為主的甜點來替代葷食，又被稱為修女的馬卡龍，直到 1533 年才被帶到法國。

Nowadays, Macaroon is the representative French dessert, but actually it first appeared in an Italian monastery. There was a nun named Carmelie who made this dessert based on almond flour to replace the meat seasoning, also called nun's macaroon. It was not introduced in France until 1533.

B 女：　第一次回信就跟妳說這麼多，是不是有點怪啊？

Isn't it a little bit weird for the extremely long first reply?

A 女：　不會啊，讀著讀著會很想吃甜點呢！他還寫到泡芙也是源自義大利的小點心，在 16 世紀傳入法國。而巧克力也是…。

Not really. I'd love to have some snacks after reading it! He also wrote that puff is from Italy and it was introduced in France in the 16th century. Chocolate as well...

B 女：　夠了，我不想聽了，我們直接去吃甜點吧！

That's enough. I don't want to hear that anymore. Let's go get some desserts!

飲食小百科 文化大不同
Differences in Cultures

巧克力 Chocolate

　　16 世紀初期的西班牙探險家在墨西哥發現當地的阿茲特克國王飲用一種可可豆加水和香料製成的飲料，探險家品嚐後將可可帶回西班牙，並在西非一個小島上種植可可樹。西班牙人將可可豆磨成粉、加入水和糖，如此加熱後所製成的飲料便是「熱巧克力」。不久其製作方法被義大利人學會，並且很快地傳遍整個歐洲。目前全世界大約三分之二的可可是由西非生產的，其中有 43%是來自象牙海岸。在英國，大多數巧克力生產者都是購買巧克力，然後自己融化，注模並用自己的設計包裝。

　　In the early 16th century, Spanish explorers found that the King of Aztecs was drinking one kind of beverage made with cocoa, water and spices in Mexico. After tasting it, the explorers brought cocoa back to Spain and planted it on a small island in West Africa. Spanish ground cocoa into powder and put water and sugar in, so it became "hot chocolate" after heating. Soon the method was learned by Italian and spread into Europe quickly. Currently, there is about two-third of world cocoa production produced in West Africa, and 43% in Ivory Coast. In England, most of chocolate producers purchase chocolate to melt, mold and package to their own designs.

馬卡龍 Macaron

　　馬卡龍（法語：Macaron），又稱作法式小圓餅，是一種用蛋白、杏仁粉、白砂糖和糖霜所做的甜點，是法國西部維埃納省最具地方特色的美食，在法國東北地區偶爾可見。「Macaron」在台灣是以英語發音，較接近於「馬卡龍」，但這已脫離了法語發音方式，實際上的法語發音較接近「馬卡

紅」。

Macaroon (French: Macaron), also named Luxemburgerli, is made with meringue, almond powder, white sugar and icing sugar. It's the best local dessert in the West French province of Vienne and occaisnally can be seen in the North East region as well. The pronunciation of the word "Macaron" in Taiwan is based on the English pronunciation of the word. Its pronunciation is similar to "Makalong," different from the French pronunciation of the word, which is actually similar to "Makahong."

菜餚的故事 你知道嗎？
Stories About Food

冰淇淋 Ice Cream

在南宋時，中國已掌握用硝石放入冰水作為致冷劑，以奶為原料，邊攪拌邊冷凝製作「冰酪」的方法。元朝開國皇帝忽必烈很喜歡冰酪，將它列為宮廷消暑食品，經御膳房多次改進，風味更佳。這位皇帝曾降旨下令冰酪的製作方法不得外傳，於是成了皇宮的專利品。據說義大利旅行家馬可波羅來到中國時，忽必烈待以國賓之禮，盛宴款待，賜與冰酪。後來馬可‧波羅欲回國時，忽必烈特別教授他冰酪的製法。馬可波羅回大利後將冰酪的食譜獻給王室。國王視為珍寶，對外秘而不宣，直到 1553 年，從義大利出嫁到法國的凱瑟琳德美第奇皇后才將冰淇淋的製作工藝帶到法國，並藉由這個技術得到了作為冰淇淋製作者的一份終身退休金。

In the Southern Song Dynasty, Chinese people had already mastered the method of making "milk ice" which is the ancestor of ice cream; they dissolved saltpeter in the water as the refrigerant, and stirred a pot of milk in it. Kublai Khan, the first emperor of the Yuan Dynasty who liked milk ice very much and listed it as a royal dessert for relieving the summer heat.

After continuous improvements, the imperial kitchen made the taste of milk ice even better. Kublai Khan had decreed to keep the secret of how to make milk ice, and it became the exclusive dessert only served in the imperial palace. It's said that when Italian explorer Marco Polo traveled to China, Kublai Khan treated him as an honored guest, and feasted him with milk ice. When Marco Polo returned to Italy, the emperor even bestowed the milk ice recipe on him. Marco Polo dedicated the recipe to the royal family after his return to Italy. These milk ices soon became popular in the upper class. In 1553, the Queen Catherine de Medici brought the Italian sherbet recipe to French and earned herself a lifelong pension.

霜淇淋是冰淇淋的一種，但比一般的冰淇淋來得軟，並也因其柔軟的質地而得名。霜淇淋綿密、滑順的口感最近在台灣掀起了一股新風潮，並引起了兩家主要的便利超商連鎖店之間的「冷戰」。然而，販售軟質冰淇淋的這個主意卻是來自於一個「爆胎」。在1934年時，有一個冰淇淋小販的冰淇淋車爆胎了，他將車子推到一個停車場，並販售有些融化的冰淇淋給路過的人。出乎他意料的是他賣光了他所有的冰淇淋，還給了他研發霜淇淋配方及販賣軟質冷凍甜點的想法。有趣的是在1940年後期，年輕的鐵娘子瑪格麗特・柴契爾在一家食物製造商裡擔任化學家的職務。在那一段時間中，這一家食物製造商正與美國的一家經銷商共同研發霜淇淋的製作方法。一般相信這位前任的英國首相瑪格麗特・柴契爾曾經參與發明Mr. Whippy這一種霜淇淋的團隊。

Soft serve is a type of ice cream which is softer than the regular ice cream, and named after its soft texture. Its creamy and smooth taste has created a new fashion in Taiwan recently, and brought on a "cold war" between two major convenience store chains. However, the idea of serving soft ice cream was actually from a "flat tire." In 1934, an ice cream vender suffered a flat tire in his ice cream car, and he pulled the car to the parking

lot, and sold the melting ice cream to passers-by. It was an unexpected turn to him that he sold out his entire supply of ice cream, and gave him ideas of developing the soft serve ice cream formula and selling soft frozen dessert. Interestingly, during the late 1940s, the future Iron Lady Margret Thatcher worked in a food manufacturer as a chemist. At that time, the food manufacturer was developing a soft serve recipe with an American distributor. It is commonly believed that the former UK Prime Minister Margaret Thatcher was a part of the team that invented the soft serve ice cream named Mr. Whippy.

實用會話 聊天必備
Useful Phrases

天氣好熱，我好想吃冰消消暑喔！
The weather is so hot. I want to have an ice cream to cool down!

走啊！前面就有便利商店，我們去買冰棒來吃。
Let's go! There is a convenience store in the front. Let's go get a popsicle.

可是我不想吃那種含有色素的市售冰棒，附近有沒有哪裡可以吃到真材實料的冰淇淋啊！
But I don't want to the popsicle which contains artificial coloring. Is there any place where we can have a real ice cream?

我知道附近的百貨公司地下街有一家專門賣冰淇淋的店，標榜使用新鮮水果製成的冰淇淋，還吃的到水果的果肉。

I know there is a ice cream shop in the basement of the department store which guarantees that their ice creams are made from fresh fruits and you can even taste the fruit flesh.

對！我就是想吃那種綿密又富有食材風味的冰淇淋。

Yeah! Creamy and tasty, that's the king of ice cream I want to have.

不過光是一球好像就不便宜喔！你應該只是熱瘋了想吃點涼的，不一定要花大錢吧！？

It's not that inexpensive for every scoop. I think you're just trying to get something cold to relieve the annoying heat. You don't really want to spend big money, do you?

說的也是，而且走到百貨公司還有一大段路，我們還是先到前面的便利商店吹吹冷氣再說。

That's true. Besides, it is still far away from the department store. Let's go to the convenience store in the front and enjoy the cold air first.

121

最近的便利商店也開始賣起霜淇淋了，我一直想去吃吃看是不是真有大家説的那麼好吃。

Convenience stores have started to sell soft serve lately. I always want to try and see if it's really like everybody says.

好吧，那百貨公司的冰淇淋就等下次再犒賞自己了。

Alright, the department store's ice cream will be scheduled until next time for rewarding myself.

好用句型 點餐必會
Sentence Patterns

1. Could you wrap this up for me? 可以幫我打包嗎？

   wrap：包起來

   👍會這句更加分 Please wrap it up carefully for me.
   請幫我將這個小心地包起來。

2. We like to pay separately. 我們想要分開結帳。

   separately：分別地

   👍會這句更加分 Let 's go finish the work separately.
   我們分頭去完成這份工作吧。

3. I think there is a mistake in the bill. 我認為帳單上有一些錯誤。

   mistake：錯誤

   👍會這句更加分 Never make the same mistake twice. 切勿重蹈覆轍。

4. Can I pay with this credit card？ 請問我可以用這張信用卡付帳嗎？

credit：信用

👍 會這句更加分 Sorry, I left my credit card at home.
對不起，我把信用卡忘在家裡了。

5. May I have the receipt, please? 請給我收據，謝謝。

receipt：收據

👍 會這句更加分 Ask the cashier to give you a receipt when you pay the check. 結帳的時候記得向收銀員要一張收據。

6. Could you wipe off the table for us, please? 可以幫我們清理桌面嗎，謝謝。

wipe：擦拭

👍 會這句更加分 The young mother wiped her baby's hands on a paper towel. 那位年輕媽媽用紙巾擦拭嬰兒的雙手。

7. Can I have some fruit instead of the dessert？ 可不可以不要甜點改成水果？

instead：代替

👍 會這句更加分 She gave her son some useful advice instead of money.
她給她的兒子一些有用的建議而不是金錢。

2.5
港式甜點大集合
Hong Kong Desserts

同事 A： 我先下班囉！明天見。

I am getting off work. See you tomorrow.

同事 B： 妳今天這麼準時下班啊！平常妳都還會留下來跟大家聊聊天再走的。

You get off work on time today. Usually you will stay after work and have some chat with everyone.

同事 A： 我今天要去排隊買點心，不趕快走就買不到了。

I am in a hurry for lining up to buy snacks today, otherwise I might not get them.

同事 B： 什麼點心這麼有魅力啊？

What kind of snacks are so fascinated?

同事 A： 就是車站附近那家新開的港式餐廳所賣的冰火菠蘿油啦！上次吃過一次之後就念念不忘，每次下班經過都已經賣光了。

It's a Hong Kong restaurant that sells "pineapple bun" which is newly opened near the station! It became an obsession after last time I had it. Every day when I get off from work, they have been already sold out.

同事 B： 冰火菠蘿油，那是什麼？

"Bing huo bo luo you," what's that?

同事 A： 妳不知道嗎？菠蘿油是從菠蘿麵包發展而來的食品，切開剛出爐的菠蘿麵包，夾上一塊厚切的奶油，這樣奶油就會被菠蘿麵包的溫度溶化，吃起來奶油香味超濃厚，吃過都會上癮。

Don't you know? "Pineapple bun" is a variant of pineapple bun, cut the bun which is just baked, stuff a thick butter inside, so the butter will be melted by the temperature of pineapple bun, which have a super strong flavor of butter and will be addictive after taste.

同事 B： 聽起來好誘人喔！可以幫我買嗎？

It sounds so attractive. Can you buy one for me?

同事 A： 可是冰火菠蘿油冷掉就吃不出奶油融化的風味了，妳要不要現在就下班收一收跟我一起去？

But you won't be able to taste the melting butter once it gets cold. Do you want to pack your things up and go together with me?

同事 B： 可是我還有團購的事情要處理耶…

But I still have group buying to deal with...

同事 A： 妳是説上次我帶蛋塔來跟同事們分享，結果大家覺得好吃想要一起團購的那件事嗎？

Do you mean the egg custards I shared with colleagues last time, which turns out everyone wants to group buy after tasting them?

同事 B： 對呀，就是那次。後來大家發現那家港式甜點店還有賣芒果布丁和奶皇包，所以就委託我一起開團購，今天要統計大家要買的數量和金額。

Yes, that's it, and then they found out that restaurant also sells mango pudding and custard bun, they asked me to organized a group buying. I have to confirm the purchasing quantity and amount.

同事 A： 那真是辛苦妳了… 這也算是因我而起，我待會就外帶港式餐廳的西米露，明天上班再帶來給妳吃吧！

Thank you for all the troubles you've taken… My bad, I will buy you some sago puddings from that Hong Kong restaurant, and bring them to you tomorrow.

同事 B： 好啊！西米露可以冰，明天再吃也沒問題。

Ok, sago pudding can be kept inside a refrigerator. It won't be any problem eating it tomorrow.

同事 A： 那家港式餐廳的西米露有哈密瓜，橘子等創新口味，還可以依自己的口味添加水果粒，我每一種都買看看吧。

They have cantaloupe, orange and other innovative flavors of sago pudding in that Hong Kong restaurant, and you can choose differeut fruit topping as well, I will buy one of each.

同事 B： 謝謝妳！那妳有要一起團購嗎？

Thank you! Do you want to join the group buying?

同事 A： 我也跟進買一些馬拉糕好了，那我先走囉！拜拜！

I will buy some Cantonese sponge cakes then. I am leaving now. See you.

飲食小百科 文化大不同
Differences in Cultures

 蛋塔
Egg Custard

早在中世紀，英國人已知利用奶類、糖、蛋及不同香料製作類似蛋塔的食品。在 1399 年英格蘭國王亨利四世的一次宴會中便有食用蛋塔的記載。

As early as the Middle Ages, British had known how to use milk, sugar, eggs and different spices to make the food which similar to egg custards. According to records, egg custards were served in a banquet that given by the King Henry IV of England in 1399.

蛋塔深受香港人喜愛，但其實在香港的歷史尚短。根據考證，在 1920 年的廣州，當時各大百貨公司競爭激烈，為了吸引顧客，百貨公司的廚師每週都會設計一款「星期美點」來招攬生意，蛋塔正是此時出現於廣州。

Egg custard is very popular in Hong Kong, but in fact the history of egg custard in Hong Kong is still short. According to research, in 1920 in Guangzhou, when there was a intense competition between main department stores. In order to attract customers, chefs of the department stores would design a "weekly delicacy" each week to generate the business. Egg custards first appeared in Guangzhou at the time.

香港引進蛋塔的年代尚未有準確的紀錄，有一說是自 1940 年起，香港的餅店內便已出現蛋塔，並於 1950 年至 1980 年間打入多數茶餐廳的市場。起初茶餐廳的蛋塔都比較大，一個蛋塔便可以成為一份下午茶。

There is no accurate records of the time when egg custards were

introduced in Hong Kong. It is said that egg custards already appeared in a Hong Kong bakery in the 1940s, and it also got into the market of most of the tea restaurants between 1950-1980. Initially, the egg custard in the tea restaurants was relatively larger, an egg custard can well served the wholafternoon tea.

長期以來，蛋塔一直是台灣各家麵包店的必備產品，但不是非常熱門。直到澳門安德魯餅店的葡式蛋塔在台灣掀起一股熱潮，在安德魯餅店大受歡迎，業者也紛紛群起仿效。這波葡式蛋塔熱日漸衰退後，目前只剩下肯德基仍在販售葡式蛋塔。

Over the years, egg custard has been a basic product of bakeries in Taiwan, but it is not very popular. Until the Portuguese egg tart of Lord Stow's Bakery, Macau stirred the interest in Taiwan. Lord Stow's Bakery was so popular, and other food manufacturers had patterned on it. After this interest in Portuguese egg tart declined, KFC is the only manafacturer that currently sells Portuguese egg tarts.

菠蘿麵包源於香港，亦稱菠蘿包，是一種沒有內餡的普遍甜味麵包。因烘烤過後表面呈現金黃色的凹凸脆皮狀貌似鳳梨（菠蘿）因而得名，菠蘿麵包實際上並沒有鳳梨的成分。菠蘿麵包的產生，其中一種説法是因為早年香港人認為包子的風味不足，因此在包子上加上砂糖等甜味餡料而成。在台灣販賣的菠蘿麵包是源自於日本的蜜瓜包，雖然在外型上和港式菠蘿麵包相似，但是製作方式和味道並不一樣。

Pineapple bun, also known as pineapple bread, is originated in Hong Kong, and it's a kind of sweet bun without stuffing. Golden, crispy checkers appear on the surface after baking, and named after the pineapple-like sugary crust top. However, pineapple buns don't actually have any pineapples as ingredient. There's one saying that in early times, Hong Kong people thought the steamed bun tastes bland, so they added sugar and something sweet on top of it to become the pineapple bun. In Taiwan, pineapple bread is derived from the Japanese melon bun. Although they are similar in appearances, the tastes and production methods are not the same.

芒果布丁是在香港流行的甜品之一，雖然算是西式甜品的一種，但廣泛普及於香港的中式酒樓，並流行到日本、台灣等地。在西方國家，芒果布丁更是被視為發源自香港的一種東方甜品。

Mango pudding is one of the most popular desserts in Hong Kong. Although regarded as a Western dessert, it's popular in Chinese restaurants in Hong Kong and spread to Japan, Taiwan and etc. In Western countries, mango pudding is regarded as one kind of oriental dessert from Hong Kong.

菜餚的故事 你知道嗎？
Stories About Food

 樹婚
Tree Marriage

在泰國南部宋卡府的一座小村莊有個奇特的風俗，那就是在每年 6 月至 8 月的某個特定日子，只要年滿 21 歲的男子都要與大樹舉行婚禮，就算是離家工作的人也必須在那個日子趕回來「結婚」，否則就得終身打光棍。和大樹結婚必須和舉辦真正的婚禮一樣隆重，因此結婚時送給「樹新娘」的聘禮也相當豐盛，包括馬拉糕、炸麵圈、糖、點心、雞、豬頭、水果等。當結婚儀式開始時，會由 30 名當地少女頭頂著聘禮，在長鼓樂隊的帶領下列

隊從新郎家向新娘樹出發。抵達後，穿著禮服的新郎必須在選定的新娘樹下點蠟燭誦經，接著象徵新娘的老太太會出來受禮，接著大家分食聘禮，結婚典禮就算完成。要和樹結婚的起源已不可考，但當地男子依然遵守這樣的風俗習慣，因為他們相信有了樹新娘的保佑，未來的生活才能過得平順幸福。

There is a peculiar custom in a small village named Changwat Songkhla, in southern Thailand. From June to August each year, in a certain date, every man who is 21 years old must have a wedding with a tree. Even if the person is away from work, he has to come back "to get married" on that day, otherwise he would become a lifelong bachelor. Tree marriages must be held as the grand wedding. Therefore, the gift to the "Tree Bride" must be sumptuous, including Cantonese sponge cakes, deep fried doughnuts, candy, snacks, chickens, pig heads and fruits. When the wedding ceremony begins, thirty local girls led by the long drum band would carry the dowry on the head and head to the groom's house and the tree bride. Upon arrival, the groom has to wear a dress, and must be chanting with candles at the selected tree. An elderly female would come out tot receive the gift at the tree bride's behave, and everyone would share the dowry before the wedding ceremony is completed. The origin of this marriage are not clear, but the local men still comply with such customs, because they believe that the bride is blessed by the tree, so the future life will be full of happiness.

實用會話 聊天必備
Useful Phrases

您好，請問有甚麼可以為您服務的嗎？
Hello, may I help you?

你好，我打來是想訂位。
Hi, I would like to make a reservation.

好的，請問您要訂位的日期和時間是？
Ok, would you please Inform the date and time?

這個禮拜六的晚餐時段，2 個人。
This Saturday's dinner time, a table for 2 people.

好的，目前還有空位，請問您的大名和電話。
Ok, we still have vacancies now, may I have your
name and phone number?

我姓王，手機是 09XX-XXXXXX。對了，請問你
們有服裝上的規定嗎？
My surname is Wang, my cell phone number is
09XX-XXXXXX. By the way, do you have any
dress code?

主食 Main Course

甜點 Desserts

飲料 Beverages

點心 Snacks

餐廳規定需著正式服裝。
The dress code in the restaurant is that you must wear formal clothes.

正式服裝是指⋯男生要穿西裝打領帶、女士要穿禮服和高跟鞋嗎？
Formal clothes mean... men have to wear suits and ties, ladies have to wear dresses and heels?

現在已經沒有那麼嚴格了，只要男士不穿露趾涼鞋、拖鞋，女士穿裙裝或非牛仔褲的褲裝就可以了。
It's not so strict now, it's fine for men as long as they don't wear sandals or sloppers; for ladies, just wear dress or pants, not jeans.

女生連牛仔褲也不能穿啊⋯不過你們畢竟是講求氣氛和強調、在情侶間很熱門的求婚必勝餐廳，如此要求也不過份。
No jeans allowed for ladies⋯? After all, as a popular "sure victory in proposing marriage" restaurant which emphasize on the atmosphere so much, it's not really an excessive request.

是的，大部分客人不用説都會精心打扮，其實只要照平常約會的穿著就沒有問題了。

Yes, most of the guests are well dressed. In fact, there won't be any problem with usual dating dress.

好用句型 點餐必會
Sentence Patterns

1. **Do you have any dress code?** 請問貴餐廳是否有任何服裝上的規定？

   code：規則、準則

   👍 **會這句更加分** You must live up to the code of the company. 你必須遵守公司的規定。

2. **Would the ladies wear formal dresses?** 請問女士是否需要穿著正式的服裝？

   formal：正式的

   👍 **會這句更加分** His formal clothes made him got a good job. 他正式的穿著助他得到一份好工作。

3. **May I have just a little of it?** 可以給我一點這個嗎？

   little：少量的

   👍 **會這句更加分** I left the bus and walked for a little. 我下巴士走了一小段路。

4. **What flavor do you want for your ice-cream?** 你想要點什麼口味的冰淇淋？

   flavor：滋味、風味

   👍 **會這句更加分** These tomatoes have a vinegar flavor. 這些番茄帶有醋的滋味。

5. **Are you still serving your breakfast menu?** 你們現在還有供應早餐嗎？

   breakfast：早餐

133

👍 會這句更加分　We make a good breakfast before go to school. 我們在上學前吃了一頓好早餐。

6. How many ingredients/cheeses does it include? 請問這裡面加了幾樣配料/起司？

ingredients：原料、食材

👍 會這句更加分　What are the ingredients of this pie? 這個派是用哪些原料做成的？

7. Excuse me, what does brown mustard taste like? 不好意思，請問吃起來是甚麼味道？

taste：嘗起來

👍 會這句更加分　Beers taste better if they are chilled. 啤酒冰過以後更好喝。

NOTES

2.6
泰式甜點大集合
Thai Desserts

Talking About Food In English

料理教室老師：今天我們要來教三種經典的泰式甜點，都是炎炎夏日中好吃又好看的消暑聖品。

Today we are going to teach three classic Thai desserts. All are tasty and very refreshing in the middle of summer.

料理教室學生：太棒了！端出少見的泰式甜點上桌，老公和小孩一定都很開心。

That's great! My husband and children must be very happy to see the rare Thai desserts placed on table.

料理教室老師：而且做法也很簡單喔！首先是芒果糯米飯（Glutinous Rice with Mango），我先簡單講解一下做法再來實際操作。傳統的做法是把洗淨的糯米用清水浸 4-6 小時，把水瀝乾後，用乾淨的薄紗布包好，放在蒸籠隔水蒸 45 分鐘。蒸好後把糯米放至大碗內，趁熱加入椰奶糖汁，放置半小時以上即可。要吃的時候再依個人喜好淋上一些椰奶糖漿，或灑上椰絲、芝麻等。

And the method is also very simple! The first one is Glutinous Rice with Mango. Let me briefly explain how to make it. The traditional approach is to use the clean glutinous rice soak in clean water for 4-6 hours. After draining off and warpped up with clean cheesecloth, place it in a special double steamer and steam for 45 minutes. After steaming, put the glutinous rice in a large bowl, add coconut milk syrup while it is still hot, cover it up and place it more than half an hour. You can top it with some coconut milk syrup, sprinkled coconut, sesame, etc. when you want to eat it.

料理教室學生：加了椰奶的糯米配上芒果，吃起來不知道怎麼樣？

What is the taste of the glutinous rice with coconut milk and mango?

料理教室老師：待會實際操作妳們就知道了，淋在上面的鹹椰奶漿可以中和芒果和糯米的甜，吃起來甜而不膩。接下來這道香蕉蛋餅（Roti）和芒果糯米飯一樣，都是在泰國極受歡迎的路邊小吃。外皮就像我們在台灣常吃的蛋餅一樣，但又比蛋餅更有嚼勁，只不過吃起來是甜的。做法是先用奶油將餅皮煎至焦香，鋪上香蕉切片，煎好後在蛋餅上淋一層煉乳、糖漿或巧克力，覺得不夠甜的人還可以再灑上一點砂糖。

You guys will know it when you make it. The topping salty coconut milk can balance the sweetness of mango and glutinous rice. It tastes sweet but not too much. Then, this Roti is as same as mango glutinous rice, both are very popular snacks in Thailand. The pancake is just as same as the Chinese omelet that we often eat in Taiwan, but more chewy, and the taste is sweet. Use the butter to fry pancake until semi-cooked, then cover with banana slices, and pour a layer of condensed milk, syrup or chocolate on Roti. People who don't think it's sweet enough can also sprinkle a bit granulated sugar.

料理教室學生：好特別喔！等不及要趕快來動手做了。

So special! Can't wait to start making it.

料理教室老師：最後一道「摩摩喳喳」（Bubur Cha Cha）是泰國最有名的冰品，極具南洋風味。做法很簡單，在煮熟的西米上放上繽紛的熱帶水果、紅豆及椰漿即可。

The last dish is the most famous frozen dessert in Thailand, "Bubur Cha Cha", which is very of Southeast Asian style. The method is very simple, only by putting the colorful tropical fruits, red beans and coconut milk syrup on the cooked sago.

料理教室學生：一定要加椰漿嗎？如果改用糖水可以嗎？

Is it necessary to add coconut milk? Can we use syrup instead?

料理教室老師：如果沒有椰漿就不是摩摩喳喳了，椰香可以增進食欲，小朋友應該也會很喜歡。好，接下來我們就開始動手做看看吧！

It would not be Bubur Cha Cha without coconut milk. Coconut can increase appetites. Children may also like it. Now let's start to do it!

飲食小百科 文化大不同
Differences in Cultures

各國特色水果
Features Fruits in Different Countries

日本：哈蜜瓜&草莓&西瓜 Japan: Cantaloupe & Strawberry & Watermelon

哈蜜瓜在日本給人的感覺是一種非常昂貴的水果，常用於饋贈親友或帶去探望病人。在精心管理的溫室中栽培出的哈密瓜一個可賣到 1 萬日圓以上。

Cantaloupe gives the impression of a very expensive fruit in Japan, used commonly as gift for relatives or to visit patients. Cantaloupes grow in a greenhouse cultivation with careful management, and can be sold by more than 10,000 yen each.

日本種植草莓的產量及銷量目前稱得上世界第一。日本的草莓色澤、外觀堪稱一絕。值得推薦的品種為「女峰」和「豐之華」，兩者都酸甜適中、香醇可口。

Strawberry production and sales volume in Japan are currently regarded as the best in the world. The color and appearance of Japanese strawberry are well-known as wonderful. The varieties of "Nyohou" and "Fung" are the most recommended, both tastes are well-balanced between sweet and sour, and delicious.

西瓜是日本夏季最具有代表性的水果。日本的西瓜品種很多，外觀有圓形、橢欖球形、白紋及無白紋的，果肉也有紅、黃、橙等種類。

Watermelon is the most representative of Japanese fruits in summer.

There are many varieties of watermelon in Japan, round or oval, white stripes and non white stripes. The flesh can also be red, yellow, orange, etc.

法國：無花果 France: Fig

無花果於公元 10 世紀傳入法國、英國，17 世紀傳到美國加州，唐代傳入中國，西藏是主要產區。無花果在《聖經》中被稱為「神聖之果」、「生命果」、「太陽果」，可新鮮食用，同時也是一種中藥材。

Figs were spread to France and England in the 10th century, to California in the 17th century, and to China in the Tang Dynasty. Tibet is the main producing area. Figs are referred to as "sacred fruit," "fruit of life," and "sun fruit" in the Bible. They can be eaten fresh, and are also a traditional Chinese medicine.

美國：蔓越莓&酪梨 United States: Cranberry & Avocado

蔓越莓目前在北美地區被大量種植，因為蔓越莓本身的酸味較強，收成後的果實會加糖再做成果汁、果醬等。蔓越莓醬便是美國感恩節主菜火雞的傳統配料。

Cranberry is grown in large quantities in North America, because cranberry itself has a strong sour taste. People use cranberries and sugar to make juice and jam. In the American Thanksgiving tradition, the cranberry sauce is served with the roasted turkey.

酪梨原產於中美洲和墨西哥，是一種水果，但在美國通常會加入各種料理中食用，如壽司、沙拉、墨西哥捲餅或是夾進三明治內當配料。

Avocado is one kind of fruits from Central America and Mexico, but in

the United States it can be made into a variety of dishes, such as sushi, salads, Mexican burritos or sandwiches.

英國：西洋梨 United Kingdom: Eupropeam Pear

西洋梨原產於英國，仕歐洲、北美洲及澳洲等地被廣泛栽培食用。西洋梨的熱量低、富含豐富的膳食纖維，果實成熟後柔軟多汁，帶有清甜香氣，風味極佳。

European pear originated in the United Kingdom. It has been extensively cultivated in Europe, North America and Australia. The pear has low calories, and is rich in dietary fiber, soft and juicy during ripening, with sweet aroma and excellent flavor.

紐西蘭：奇異果 New Zealand: Kiwi

奇異果又稱為獼猴桃，原產於中國。1904 年伊莎貝爾女士把中國的獼猴桃種子帶回紐西蘭之後，輾轉送到當地知名的園藝專家亞歷山大手中，培植出紐西蘭第一株奇異果樹。奇異果含多種維生素，並可製成果醬或釀酒。

Kiwi, also known as kiwi fruit, originated in China. In 1904, after Ms. Isabel brought back kiwi seeds from China to New Zealand, through many hands, these seeds reached the local well-known gardening expert Alexander. He cultivated the first kiwi tree in New Zealand. Kiwi has lots of vitamins, and also can be made into jam or wine.

菜餚的故事 你知道嗎？
Stories About Food

 芒果
Mango

　　芒果原產於印度，是印度人眼中不可或缺的美容聖品。芒果又被視為「愛情之果」。印度民間流傳著許多在芒果樹下締結良緣的愛情故事，在當地的傳說中，芒果會為戀人帶來幸福。

　　Mango originated in India. It's a tropical fruit of the family of Anacardiaceae. Indian folklore has many lovely stories of marriage under mango trees, so the mango is also known as "the fruit of love" in India. During the mango flowering period, pairs of Indian lovers will go under mango trees for romancing, because in the local legend, mango will bring happiness to lovers.

　　台南玉井會被稱為台灣的芒果之鄉，其實都要歸功於一位叫鄭罕池的農民。在民國50年代，農復會至美國佛羅里達州進行考察，帶回了數十種新的芒果品種，在台灣各地進行試種。經過多年的嘗試後，終於發現最適合愛文芒果生長的地方，玉井便是其中一個。正因為他不畏困難，堅持鑽研種植愛文芒果的技術，才讓許多農民開始跟進大量種植芒果，並不斷進行技術與品種的改良，這樣的成就也使他被尊稱為「愛文芒果之父」。

　　Yujing District, Tainan City, is known as mango district in Taiwan. All achievements are due to a local farmer named Zheng Han Chi. In 1961, the Joint Commission on Rural Reconstruction went to Florida for investigation, and brought back around forty new varieties of mangos and tried to grow them throughout Taiwan. Zheng was not afraid of difficulties, and he insisted in developing cultivation techniques for Irwin mango. After years of trying, he finally found the most suitable place to grow Irwin mango, Yujing district. Since then, farmers began to plant a large number of mangos and improved in technologies and varieties. Thus, he was called "the father of Irwin mango."

實用會話 聊天必備
Useful Phrases

您好，現在為您上一下飯後甜點。
Hello! Here is the dessert for you.

謝謝…咦，等等，為什麼芒果旁邊會有米飯？妳不是說這是一道甜點嗎？
Thanks... hey, wait, mango with rice? I think you were saying that it's a dessert.

先生，請容我說明一下，這在泰國的確是一道知名的甜點，叫做「芒果糯米」。
Sir, please allow me to explain. This is a famous dessert in Thailand indeed, named "Glutinous Rice with Mango."

糯米！？糯米不是難以消化嗎？你們餐廳在飯後上這種甜點是什麼意思？

Glutinous rice!? Isn't glutinous rice difficult to digest? What do you mean by serving this kind of dessert?

這個… 糯米的確有消化上的疑慮，不過只要適量食用的話是沒有問題的，因此我們餐廳的芒果糯米分量也有拿捏，目前還沒有客人吃過後反應有消化不良的狀況。

Well... glutinous rice indeed is a kind of heavy food for stomach, but there won't be any problem by eating an appropriate portion. Therefore, we serve a small portion of mango glutinous rice in our restaurants. We don't have any guests suffered from indigestion after eating this dessert so far.

可是…芒果配糯米會好吃嗎？

But... does glutinous rice with mango taste good?

我個人希望先生您可以先嚐一口看看再決定，不過我還是會請廚房為您準備另一種飯後甜點，希望先生您能用的開心。

I personally hope that you can try it first and then decide, but I will still ask the kitchen to prepare another dessert for you and hope that you can enjoy it, sir.

> 嗯… 吃起來是比我想像中還要好吃啦！不過既然可以吃到另一種甜點，那我就不客氣了。
> Uhm... it tastes better than I thought, but since I can have another kind of dessert, I will go ahead and try it then.

好用句型 點餐必會
Sentence Patterns

1. What is the most popular dessert? 請問最受歡迎的甜點是甚麼？

   popular：受歡迎的

   👍會這句更加分 He is now a popular singer. 他現在是很受歡迎的歌手。

2. A: Let's split the bill. 帳單我們來平分吧！

   B: No, I'll pick up the tab. 不，我來付就好。

   tab：帳款、費用

   👍會這句更加分 Thanks for paying the tab at the bar last night for me. 謝謝你昨晚在酒吧為我付了帳。

   pick up：拾起（指拿起帳單的動作）

   👍會這句更加分 I picked up your suitcase by mistake. 我錯拿了你的皮箱。

3. Do you have a table available tonight? 請問你們今晚還有空位嗎？

   available：可利用的

   👍會這句更加分 The hotel has a twin room available for us. 那間飯店還有一間雙人房可以給我們。

4. Could you please tell me the restaurants where only local people go? 你能告訴我有哪些餐廳是只有本地人會去的嗎？

   only：只

145

👍 **會這句更加分** My home is only a bus stop from the train station.
我家離火車站只有一班公車的距離。

5. Do you charge extra fee for more than 5 people?
請問超過 5 個人會額外收費嗎？
charge：收費

👍 **會這句更加分** How much do they charge for delivering?
他們索取多少運送費用？

6. Your server is coming up very soon. Please wait for a moment.
你們的服務生馬上就來，請稍等一下。
server：侍者

👍 **會這句更加分** The server was very rude to me the whole time.
整個用餐時間那位侍者都對我非常無禮。

7. I have a reservation under my name, John Smith.
我有用我的名字訂位，John Smith。
under：下面的

👍 **會這句更加分** Children under 12 years of age are not charged for movie.
十二歲以下的孩童看電影不收費。

NOTES

3號

美食館：飲料
Cuisine Gallery3: Beverages

飲料是經過人們加工後可供飲用的液體，主要成分為水及其他添加物。飲料的種類繁多，可依包裝方式分為罐裝飲料、瓶裝飲料、鋁箔包飲料，亦可依溫度分為冷飲、熱飲，也可依是否含有酒精分為酒類、無酒精飲料，及含糖和無糖飲料。飲料雖無法當作正餐，卻也是各國飲食文化中不可或缺的一環。不僅可解渴、調劑身心，更可達到人際交流的作用。這一章就讓我們來看看各國的飲料吧。

Beverages are the processed drinks for people to enjoy. Main ingredients are water and other additives. There are many kinds of drinks that can be classified by packs, such as cans, bottles, retort pouches, or by temperature, such as hot and cold drinks. It also can be divided into alcoholic or non-alcoholic sugared or sugar-free drinks. Even though beverages can't be a meal, they are important to every culture as well. Beverages are not just for quench, but also to provide physical and mental relaxation. Let's take a look at beverages in different countries.

3.1
美式飲料大集合
American Beverages

Talking About Food In English

飯店員工 A：前輩，剛剛有一位美國客人交代說下午回來時要在房內看到「熱的」、「現做的」美式飲料，怎麼辦？我甚至不知道哪些飲料是屬於美式的。

Senior, there was an American customer asking for a cup of "hot" and "fresh" American style drink in his room when he comes back in the afternoon. What should I do? I don't even know which kind of beverages are American style.

飯店員工 B：先冷靜下來，那你是怎麼回應的呢？

Calm down. What did you reply?

飯店員工 A：我照著飯店的標準程序答應客人會照辦，待客人離開櫃台後就來問前輩您了。

I followed the standard of the hotel and promised him that I will make it. When he left, I came here to ask you.

飯店員工 B：嗯，處理得很好。就我所知，經典的美式飲料有美式咖啡（Americano）、可樂（Cola）、薑汁汽水（ginger ale）和檸檬汁（Lemonade），客人有沒有說要哪一種？

Uhm... well done. As I know, classic American style beverages are Americano, Coke, ginger ale and lemonade Did the customer mention any of them?

飯店員工 A：沒有耶。

No.

飯店員工 B：讓我想想，檸檬汁源於十七世紀的法國，原本是檸檬原汁加入開水、不加糖或是加入蘇打水，傳到美國後才開始瘋狂地改造並發揚光大，因此種類也很多，但就我所知沒有熱的。至於可樂這種碳酸飲料更不可能熱著喝了。

Let me think. Lemonade was originally from France in the 17th century. It used to be sugar-free lemon juice, with water or soda water. When it spread to America, it started to change and be promoted. In America, there are many kinds of lemonade. However, it's not a hot drink, and it can't be Coke either.

飯店員工 A：我知道了，那就只剩美式咖啡了，因為薑汁汽水一定也不是熱著喝的。

I get it. It must be Americano then, because people don't drink hot ginger ale.

飯店員工 B：那可不一定喔，在十九世紀時，英國的酒館會在吧台準備研磨成粉狀的薑讓客人灑在啤酒上，這就是薑汁汽水的前身。一般的薑汁汽水的確是喝冰的，但是現在也有業者推出熱的薑汁汽水，所以客人想要的熱飲或許正是指薑汁汽水。

I'm not sure about that. In the 19th century, British bars prepared ginger powder for customers to put on top of beers, and this is where ginger ale comes from. Normally, ginger ale is a cold drink, but some merchants launch hot ginger ale as well. Maybe that customer wants ginger ale.

飯店員工 A：薑汁汽水我們有辦法現做嗎？

Can we make ginger ale?

飯店員工 B：這點我倒沒想到，你反應很快嘛！薑汁汽水一般無法現做，那一定是美式咖啡沒錯。美式咖啡（義大利語：Caffè Americano）一般是由義式濃縮咖啡加入熱水製作而成，或者是用義式咖啡機萃取完 espresso 後，繼續讓機器供水直到斟滿一杯完整的咖啡。的確滿足客人想喝熱的且現做的條件。

I didn't think about it. You are quick-witted! In general, we don't have homemade ginger ale, so it must be Americano then. Americano (Italian: Caffè Americano) is usually made with espresso and hot water, or with hot water in a coffee machine extracting from espresso until the cup is full. That can really satisfy the customer's request: hot and fresh.

飯店員工 A：那我這就去交代吧台，在客人回房前準備好。

I'm going to the bar right the way and I will prepare it before the customer comes back.

飲食小百科 文化大不同
Differences in Cultures

部份歐洲人並不喜歡香味受到破壞的美式咖啡，因此法國人會將美式咖啡戲稱為「jus de chaussette」，意思是「襪子汁」。

Some Europeans don't like Americano, because its taste is different from regular drip coffee. Some French people even refer to Americano as "jus de chaussette," which means "socks juice."

在美國、澳大利亞和紐西蘭，有些時候會將勾兌時先放入熱水、後放入濃縮咖啡的做法稱為 Long Black。某些時候，一些簡單的滴漏式咖啡機也會被稱為美式咖啡機。

In America, Australia and New Zealand, sometimes when they are blending coffee, they will put hot water before espresso. This method is also named Long Black. In some cases, regular coffee machines are also named American coffee machines.

薑雖然最早是從印度和中國傳到西方的，但西方人對於薑的喜愛卻完全不下於東方人。自從西元九世紀開始，西方人就已經開始用薑來調味，可以說是最早期的香料。薑受到歐洲人歡迎的程度甚至和胡椒粉、鹽巴並駕齊驅。據傳薑在中古世紀甚至被拿來治療黑死病，至於功效則已不可考。薑在古老的梵語中被稱為「stringa-vera」，意思是「像牛角般的身體」，用以形容薑的獨特形狀。中國人拿薑入藥的歷史已非常悠久，遠在孔子的著作當中就有提及。不只在中國，就連寫於七世紀中葉的古蘭經裡面也有關於薑的記載。

Although the earliest ginger spread to Europe from India and China, Westerners enjoy ginger no less than Asians. Since the 9th century AD,

Westerners started to use ginger for flavor, being the earliest spice. Ginger was equally popular with pepper and salt among Europeans. Allegedly, ginger can be used to cure black disease, but its efficacy lost in the mist of past. In old Sanskrit, ginger is called "stringa-vera," which means "a body like a horn," alluding to ginger's special shape. For a long time, Chinese people have been using ginger for medicine, far from the works of Confucius. Apart from China, there were also related writings in the Quran, which was written in the mid-7th century.

在東方料理中無論是雞鴨魚肉、蒙古烤肉醬、日式沙拉醬,或是粵菜裡出名的薑蔥油雞、薑蔥龍蝦、甚至現在在高雄一帶還能吃到拿來沾番茄的醬油裡面都有薑。在日本,吃生魚片時少不了醃漬的嫩薑;若沒有加進磨碎曬乾的薑粉也稱不上是真正的印度咖哩。

In Asian cuisine, no matter if it's meat, Mongolian barbecue sauce, Japanese salad dressing, Cantonese ginger chicken, or ginger lobster, you can always find ginger in them. In Kaohsiung, you can even find ginger in the dipping soy sauce for tomatoes. In Japan, you also see a lot of pickled ginger while having sushi. If you do not add dried, smashed ginger powder, it can't be a real Indian curry.

相對於東方人通常用薑來作料理;西方人則喜好用薑來作甜品,尤其是蛋糕、餅乾等,如薑餅人。薑還被用來放在布丁、果醬等醃漬物裡面,薑茶也是很普遍的飲品。

Compare with Asians, who usually use ginger for cooking, Westerners like to use ginger in desserts, especially in cakes or cookies, such as ginger cookies. Ginger is also used to make puddings, jellies and other desserts. Ginger tea is also a common drink.

菜餚的故事 你知道嗎？
Stories About Food

可樂的故事 The story of Coke

1886 年，美國有位名叫約翰潘伯頓的藥劑師，一天他將碳酸水、糖及其它原料混合在一起，意外的調配出原始的可樂。潘伯頓將它放在藥局販售，某天下午，一個酒鬼跌跌撞撞地來到了彭伯頓的藥局想買治療發燒頭痛的藥水。營業員本來應該到水龍頭那兒去兌水，但他懶得走動，便就近拿起蘇打水往可口可樂裡摻。結果那位酒鬼喝了一杯又一杯，不停地說：「好喝！」酒鬼事後到處宣傳這種飲料的神奇功效，就此展開了「可樂」這個美國飲料的傳奇。

In America, 1886, there was a pharmacist named John Pemberton. Coke was formulated by John Pemberton unexpectedly, by mixing carbonated water, sugar, and other raw materials together. Pemberton put it in the drug store for sale. One afternoon, there was a drunkard bumped into Pemberton's drug store for liquid medicine to cure his fever and headache. The clerk supposed to get the water from the tap, but he was too lazy to get it. Instead, he took the closest soda water and put it into coke. The drunkard drank one after another and kept saying "tasty!" After this, the drunkard started to advertise Coke's magical effects, and the legend of American drink "Coke" began.

檸檬可預防壞血病 Lemon Can Avoid Scurvy

18 世紀時，英國船員之間曾因缺乏維生素 C 引起壞血病，先後死亡約 1 萬人。經過實驗研究才發現檸檬中的維生素 C 能夠治療壞血病，此後，英國相關部門規定船上的船員必須每天攝取足夠的檸檬汁才能啟航。

In the 18th century, about ten thousands sailors died from scurvy,

美式飲料

which is caused by lack of vitamin C. After experiment, researchers realized that lemon had vitamin C to cure scurvy. Ever since then, British related departments regulated by law that the sailors have to drink enough lemonade before they get on the boat.

實用會話 聊天必備
Useful Phrases

您好，請問可以點餐了嗎？
Hi, may I have your order please?

好的，我要一份沙朗牛排和一份兒童特餐。
Ok, I would like to have a sirloin steak and a kid's meal.

一份沙朗牛排和一份兒童特餐，好的，請問需要點些飲料嗎？
A sirloin steak and a kid's meal, sure. Would you like to drink something?

請問你們有哪些無酒精的飲料可以給孩子喝的呢？
Which kind of soft drinks do you have for kids?

我們有可樂、檸檬汁和薑汁汽水。
We have coke, lemonade and ginger ale.

可樂含有咖啡因，我怕孩子晚上睡不著會吵鬧，
薑汁汽水的話，不知道孩子會愛喝嗎？
Coke has caffeine. I'm afraid that the kid won't
sleep at night. Do kids like ginger ale?

我們的薑汁汽水酸酸甜甜的，有許多客人和小孩
都喜歡喝喔。
Our ginger ale is sweet and sour. Many
customers and children like it.

喝起來不會有薑的味道嗎？
Won't it taste like ginger?

只有一點點喔，還可以做成熱的，保有汽水氣泡
的同時又可以驅寒。
Only a little bit, and we can also make it hot to
keep the soda bubbles and get rid of cold.

那就點一杯來試喝看看吧！為了保險起見，另一
杯飲料還是點檸檬汁好了。
A cup of ginger ale then, and a lemonade, for
safety.

主食 Main Course

甜點 Desserts

飲料 Beverages

點心 Snacks

 好的,一杯檸檬汁和薑汁汽水,請問薑汁汽水要做熱的還是冰的呢?
Alright, a lemonade and a ginger ale. How would you like your ginger ale, hot or cold?

先喝喝看冰的好了,謝謝你。
We will try the cold one first. Thank you.

好用句型 點餐必會
Sentence Patterns

1. Waiter: What would you like to drink after your meal?

   請問您餐後要喝甚麼飲料呢?

   meal:一餐、餐

   👍 會這句更加分 Please enjoy your meal. 請享用你的餐點。

2. I'd like a small Coke, but don't add too much ice please.

   請給我一杯小可樂,但冰塊不要太多。

   add:添加

   👍 會這句更加分 She added salt into the soup. 她在湯裡加了鹽巴。

3. Q: Excuse me. May I have a refill of coffee? / Can I refill my coffee?

   請問一下,咖啡可以續杯嗎?

   A: The first refill is free. 可以免費續杯一次

   有些地方的飲品不確定是否可以續杯,此時便可事先詢問店員。

   refill:再裝滿

   👍 會這句更加分 Let me refill your cup. 讓我再幫你倒一杯。

5. Waiter: Would you like coffee or tea? 請問您要喝咖啡或是茶？

　　Guest: Please bring me a cup of Americano. 請給我一杯美式咖啡。

　　bring：帶來、拿來

👍 **會這句更加分** I'll bring you a souvenir from Japan.

　　　　　　　　我會從日本帶紀念品回來給你。

6. Could you please bring me some more water? 請問可以幫我加水嗎？

　　could：能，可以，本來可以

👍 **會這句更加分** Could I smoke here? 我可以在這裡抽煙嗎？

7. Waiter: Good afternoon, sir. Here is our menu. Would you like something to drink before you order?

　　　　　先生午安，這是我們的菜單，請問在點餐前需要喝點甚麼呢？

　　Guest: Yes. Sparkling water, please. 好的，礦泉氣泡水，謝謝。

　　　　　（點餐中）

　　Waiter: Very good, sir. I will get your order into the kitchen and be right back with your sparkling water.

　　　　　沒問題，先生。我這就將您的菜單送進廚房，並為您送上氣泡水。

　　Sparkling：起泡沫的

👍 **會這句更加分** She was drinking the Sparkling water. 她在喝氣泡酒。

　　mineral：礦物的、礦泉水

👍 **會這句更加分** Why mineral waters taste different from water?

　　　　　　　　什麼礦泉水喝起來和水不一樣？

3.2
中式飲料大集合
Chinese Beverages

用英文聊美食 聊天必備
Talking About Food In English

孫子 A： 爺爺，好香喔，你在喝甚麼呀？

Grandpa, what are you drinking? Smells so good!

爺爺 B： 乖孫，這是杏仁茶。

Good boy, this is almond tea.

孫子 A： 有一種好獨特的香味喔。

It has a unique fragrance.

爺爺 B： 對呀，這是鮮杏仁的獨特香氣。杏仁茶是由古代宮廷傳入民間的一種風味小吃。

Yeah, this is the unique aroma of fresh almonds. Almond tea is a snack from the ancient palace that circulated into the civil society.

孫子 A： 這麼厲害？那爺爺多喝點！

Cool! Grandpa, you should drink more then!

爺爺 B： 呵呵，你們年輕人現在都流行喝什麼…珍珠奶茶對不對？其實很多中式飲料都對身體很好、也很好喝喔。

Hehe, What's the popular drink for young people now... pearl milk tea, right? In fact, there are many healthy and tasty Chinese drinks.

孫子 A： 比方説呢？

For example?

爺爺 B： 像是豆漿跟米漿啊。

Soybean milk and rice milk.

孫子 A： 爺爺，這個我知道，豆漿是以黃豆或黑豆為原料製作的；米漿則是由米和花生為主要材料製成的，在中式早餐店都喝的到。

Grandpa, I know that. Soybean milk is made with soy beans or black soy beans, rice milk is made with rice and peanuts. You can find them in Chinese breakfast shops.

爺爺 B： 嗯，還有你奶奶最愛喝的酸梅湯。酸梅湯是中國傳統的消暑飲品，在夏天不僅可開胃還可補充水分。酸梅湯最初是清宮御膳房為皇帝製作的消暑飲料，比歐洲傳入的汽水還早一百五十年喔。

Uhm... there is also your grandma's favorite drink, plum juice. Plum juice is a traditional Chinese refreshing drink. It is not only appetizing, but also moisture replenshing. In the beginning, plum juice was the refreshing drink of Qing emperors made by the imperial kitchen. It is 150 years earlier than the European soda.

孫子 A： 現在台灣的珍珠奶茶也流行到東亞、歐洲、美國甚至中東國家等地方了，中式的飲料真是厲害！

Taiwan's pearl milk tea is also popular in East Asia, Europe, United States and even places like Middle East now. Chinese beverages are really amazing!

爺爺 B： 厲害的還有麵茶。

They is also the formidable seasoned millet mush.

孫子 A： 甚麼是麵茶？

What is seasoned millet mush?

爺爺 B： 麵茶是用小米麵粉熬成的糊，本身沒有味道，在販售時會淋上用麻醬、焦麻仁和花椒鹽混合製成的調味料，有時為了增添口感還會撒上一些薑粉。伴隨佐料一起喝，香氣四溢，是六〇年代台灣相當風行的鄉土小吃，不過隨著時代改變，麵茶已逐漸走進歷史囉。

Seasoned millet mush is made with the paste of millet flour. It has no taste itself. It is topped with the mixture of sesame, fructus cannabis and Sichuan pepper-salt. Sometimes, in order to increase the taste, it will sprinkle some ginger powder. It was scented to drink together with sauces. It was a quiet popular snack in Taiwan in the sixties, but with the time, seasoned millet mush gradually went into history.

孫子 A： 好可惜，我來上網查查還有哪裡喝的到？

What a pity. Let me check on the Internet to see where I can still find it.

飲食小百科 文化大不同
Differences in Cultures

南杏與北杏 Apricot Kernels and Bitter Almonds

杏仁有「南杏」與「北杏」之分，在香港統稱「南北杏」，藥膳同源。在中藥材店有按重量出售的粒裝南北杏，可自行磨成粉，或是部份中藥材店備有電動磨粉機可代客磨粉。北杏含有微量毒素，用於中藥或煲中式湯水時，中藥材店會按比例出售，大部份是南杏加上少量北杏。

There is a difference between apricot kernels and bitter almonds. Collectively named "almonds" in Hong Kong, they serve for the same purpose both in medicine of food. In Chinese herbal medicine chops, almonds are sold by weight. People can ground it into flour themselves, or some of the Chinese herbal shops have the mortar to help grounding it into flour. Bitter almonds contain traces of toxins. Chinese herbal medicine shops will sell proportionately when it is used in Chinese medicine or soup pot, with a larger amount of apricot kernels and a smaller amount of bitter almonds.

豆漿的食用變化 The Change of Soybean Milk

豆漿有多種食用方式，不加任何調料的稱為「白漿」或「清漿」；加糖的為「甜漿」；加醋、加鹽、醬油、醬菜等調料的為「鹹漿」。豆漿是中式的營養早餐，通常搭配油條一起吃。越是新鮮、富含豆味的豆漿越被視為豆漿中的極品。

There are many ways of edible soybean milk- without any seasoning, called "white jiang" or "clear jiang"; with sugar, "sweet jiang "; with vinegar, salt, soy sauce, pickles and other spices, named "salt jiang". Soybean milk is a nutritious Chinese drink, usually eaten together with fried bread sticks

(youtiao). The richer the soybean milk is, the better.

　　星巴克等咖啡店會使用豆漿替代牛奶來沖調咖啡，以供不喝牛奶的顧客選擇，因為豆漿不含乳糖，對乳糖不耐症患者不會產生影響。

Starbucks and other coffee shops use soybean milk to substitute milk to make coffee for customers who do not drink milk, because soybean milk does not have lactose, so there's no problem for lactose intolerant individuals to soubeam milk drinking.

　　在日本，豆漿亦被用來當作火鍋的湯底，是高級日本料理的吃法。

In Japan, soybean milk is also used as the base of hot pot soup. It is a classic way to eat Japanese food.

「波霸」風潮席捲全世界 "BOBA" Wave Weeping the World

　　在臺灣以外亦常見波霸 BOBA 或 Bubble 的稱呼，起源於 1980 年代末期移居北美洲的台裔新移民。他們以「波霸奶茶」的名稱為號召，加州各地因此如雨後春筍般出現 BOBA Tea House、BOBA Planet、BOBA World 等茶坊。如今非台裔的美洲居民依然滿口 BOBA 或 Bubble。他們會用英語向櫃枱的服務生說：Give me latte, and add some BOBA in, please.（給我一杯紅茶拿鐵／奶茶，加點「波霸」。）如今「波霸」已成為一種粉圓的代名詞。

Outside Taiwan, it is also common to see the title of "BOBA" or "Bubble," originated in the late 1980s. The new immigrants from Taiwan named it "Boba milk tea," so shops like "BOBA Tea House," "BOBA Planet," "BOBA World" and other tea places are sprung up throughout California. Now, American will still say "BOBA or "Bubble." They will use English and say to the waiter in counter: "Give me latte, and add some BOBA in, please." Today, "BOBA" is synonymous of tapioca pearls.

菜餚的故事 你知道嗎？
Stories About Food

豆漿的起源 The Origin of Soybean Milk

一般相信，1900 多年前西漢孝子淮南王劉安於母親患病期間，每日將泡好的黃豆磨成豆漿給母親飲用，劉母之病逐漸好轉，豆漿也隨之傳入民間。另一個傳說出於《金華地方風俗志》和《中國風俗故事集》，戰國時代燕國大將樂毅因父母年老嚼不動黃豆，於是就把黃豆磨成豆漿。

People usually believe that 1900 years ago there was a filial son Liu An, who was King of Huainan under the Western Han Dynasty, who soaked the soy bean and grounded for his mother who is in illness. When she gradually got better, soybean milk was introduced to civil society. Another folklore from "Jinhua local customs" and "Chinese customs stories" say that there was an general in the Warring States period named Leyi whose parents couldn't chew soy beans, so he grounded them into soybean milk.

珍珠奶茶的爭議 Controversy of Tapioca Pearl Milk Tea

春水堂創辦者劉漢介宣稱自己是珍珠奶茶發明者，於 1983 年開始實驗製作珍珠奶茶，由店內女職員林秀慧調製成功。另一說是，臺南市翰林茶館的涂宗和先生宣稱他於 1987 年，以在鴨母寮市場看到的白色粉圓為靈感所發明。為了爭論誰是發明珍珠奶茶，春水堂和翰林茶館曾互相告上台灣法院，但也因為這兩家店皆未申請專利權或商標權，才使得珍珠奶茶如今能成為臺灣最具代表性的國民飲料。

Chun Shui Tang's founder, Hanjie Liu, declared himself the inventor of tapioca pearl milk tea. He began experimental production of tapioca pearl milk tea in 1983, and modulated it successfully by a female staff named Xiuhui Lin in the store. Others say that Mr. Zonghe Tu, from Hanlin Tea House, in Tainan City, declared that he invented it by inspiration of white tapioca pearls at Ya Mu Liao market in 1987. To determine who was the inventor of tapioca pearl milk tea, Chun Shui Tang and Hanlin Tea House sued each other in the court in Taiwan. However, both of them did not apply for the patent or trademark. Nowadays, tapioca pearl milk tea is the most representative drink of Taiwan.

實用會話 聊天必備
Useful Phrases

 一位台灣人帶著外國朋友到手搖飲料店點餐
A Taiwanese brings a foreign friend to order in a handmade drinks store

 您好，請問要點甚麼？
Hello, what would you like to order?

我想要一杯烏龍綠茶。你呢？
I would like to have a cup of oolong green tea, and you?

好多選擇喔，我研究一下好了。
There are so many choices here. Let me study a little bit.

請問烏龍綠茶的甜度和冰塊正常嗎？
How would you like your oolong green tea, ice and sweetness?

半糖去冰好了，謝謝。你決定好要點什麼了嗎？
I would like half sweetness and without ice.
Thanks. Are you ready to order?

我想喝喝看台灣正統的珍珠奶茶。
I want to drink the traditional Taiwanese tapioca pearl milk.

兩位再加一杯珍珠奶茶嗎？請問甜度和冰塊呢？
Another cup of tapioca pearl milk for you, right?
How would you like your ice and sweetness?

原來連甜度和冰塊都可以選擇啊！那我先喝喝看正常的好了。
Even sweetness and ice can be chosen! I would like to try the original first.

主食 Main Course

甜點 Desserts

飲料 Beverages

點心 Snacks

167

好的，兩位請稍等。
Ok, wait a moment, please.

咦，怎麼沒有問我們要帶走還是內用呢？
Uhm... why he didn't ask us if we are going to drink it here or take it away?

因為在台灣，大部分的手搖飲料都是買了後帶著走的。
Because in Taiwan most of handmade drinks are for to go.

難怪路上這麼多人都人手一杯飲料，在台灣的生活真的好方便啊！
No wonder so many people are having a drink in hand on the road, it's really convenient to live in Taiwan!

好用句型 點餐必會
Sentence Patterns

1. Could you please circle the location of the restaurant on this map?

   你能幫我在地圖上圈出餐廳的位置嗎？

   circle：圈出

   👍 **會這句更加分** Please circle the correct answers. 請圈出正確的答案。

   location：位置、場所

   👍 **會這句更加分** We have to find a new location for our picnic.

   我們必須找一個新的野餐地點。

2. Can I walk there? 請問走路去可以到嗎？

3. It's too noisy here. Could you move me to another table?

   這裡實在太吵了，可以請你幫我換到另外一桌嗎？

   noisy：吵雜的

   👍 **會這句更加分** The classroom were as noisy as always.

   教室裡跟平常一樣吵。

4. Can I take some pictures in the restaurant? 請問你們介意我在餐廳裡拍照嗎？

   May I have a photo with you? 請問我可以跟您合照嗎？

   mind：介意

   👍 **會這句更加分** Do you mind if I smoke here? 你介意我在這裡抽菸嗎？

   photo：照片

   👍 **會這句更加分** My sister is next to me in the photo.

   照片裡，在我旁邊的是我妹妹。

5. This milk is spoiled. 這牛奶酸掉了。

   spoil：變壞、腐敗

   👍 **會這句更加分** Don't eat spoiled food or you will get sick.

   不要吃腐敗的食物，不然你會生病的。

169

6. Where can I get some napkins and straws?

　　請問我可以在哪裡拿到紙巾和吸管？

　　napkin：紙巾

👍 會這句更加分　Please hand me a napkin. Thanks.

　　　　　　　　請遞給我一條餐巾，謝謝。

　　straw：吸管

👍 會這句更加分　No one will use a straw to drink beer.

　　　　　　　　沒有人會用吸管喝啤酒。

7. Please clear away our table. 請幫我們清理一下桌子。

8. Please help yourself with the drinks. 飲料請自取。

NOTES

主食
Main Course

甜點
Desserts

飲料
Beverages

點心
Snacks

3.3
日式飲料大集合
Japanese Beverages

用英文聊美食 聊天必備
Talking About Food In English

貿易公司主管：公司考慮代理日本飲品進口販售，今天特地舉辦產品説明報告，希望大家能仔細聆聽並協助調查市場需求。

The company has considered to import Japanese drinks as an agent, so we are going to held a special product description report today. Hope everyone listens carefully and assists in the investigation of market demands.

貿易公司員工：是的。

Yes.

貿易公司主管：這次公司著眼在三款日本經典飲品上，首先介紹的是抹茶。抹茶起源於中國隋朝，在唐、宋達到頂峰，特別是宋朝的寺院抹茶茶藝，又稱為「點茶」，至今已有一千多年的歷史。自明朝以來此技幾乎絕跡，所以中國開始流行用茶葉泡湯棄渣的喝法。在九世紀末，抹茶隨日本隨遣唐使進入日本，點茶被日本人民所接受並推崇，發展成為今天的日本茶道。

The company is going to focus on three kinds of Japanese classic drinks this time. First, we are going to introduce Matcha. Matcha originated in Sui Dynasty in China, and reached the pinnacle during the Tang and Song Dynasties. Especially in the Song Dynasty, the art of Matcha in the temple, also known as "tencha," have reached a thousand years of history today. This technique was almost extinct since the Ming Dynasty, so in China, it became popular to make tea by steeping tea leaves in water and straining off leaves. In the late 9th century, Japanese kentoshi brought Matcha back to Japan, and "tencha" was accepted and respected by Japanese people and developed into today's Japanese tea ceremony.

貿易公司員工：抹茶的原料是綠茶，是碾磨成粉狀的、蒸青的綠茶。在日本經過多年的改良，綠茶已經很少有苦澀的味道了，因此在台灣的接受度應該很高。

Matcha is made from steamed green tea powder. After years of improvements in Japan, there is less bitter taste left, so it should be highly accepted in Taiwan.

貿易公司主管：再來是清酒，清酒是以米、米麴和水發酵而成的傳統酒類，在日本又稱為日本酒（にほんしゅ）或是直稱為酒（さけ），佛教僧侶則將其稱為「般若湯」，酒精濃度平均在15%左右。最適合飲用清酒的溫度介於攝氏五度到六十度間，是世界上飲用溫度範圍最大的酒類。清酒亦可應用在料理上，如用來除去魚類的腥臭味。

The next one is sake. Sake is fermented by rice, aspergillus oryzae and water, becoming the traditional alcoholic drink in Japan. It is also known as Japanese sake（にほんしゅ）or alcoholic drink (さけ) instead. Buddhist monks called it "Wisdom Soup (hannyato)," its alcohol by volume is about 15%. Most suitable temperature for drinking sake is between five to sixty degrees Celsius, which is the alcoholic beverage of the largest serving temperature range

in the world. Sake is also used for cooking, to remove the stench from fish.

貿易公司員工：根據我的調查，因為洋酒大舉進入日本，使的清酒近來在日本的銷量日漸低落，反倒是隨著日式料理流行至西方國家後，歐美地區也逐漸出現飲用日本酒的風潮，我想台灣亦有相同的市場。

According to my research, due to the large amount of alcoholic drinks imported from Western countries in Japan, the sales of sake gradually declined, but after Japanese cuisine started to spread it to Western countries and get popular, sake becomes a usual drink in Europe and America. I think it will also have the same market in Taiwan.

貿易公司主管：最後是乳酸菌飲料可爾必思（カルピス），為日本飲料製造商可爾必思株式會社（**Calpis Co., Ltd.**）的主要產品，經初步調查已經有其他公司代理了，因此今後針對前兩項飲品進行研究即可。

The last one is the main product of Japanese beverage maker Calpis Co. Ltd., the fermented lactic drink Calpis（カルピス）. After preliminary research, there's one company which already got the dealership, so in the future we only need to do research on the first two drinks.

貿易公司員工：是的。

Yes.

飲食小百科 文化大不同
Differences in Cultures

日本茶道 The Tea Ceremony in Japan

　　日本鎌倉時代的臨濟宗留學僧南浦紹明在宋朝時來到中國，將徑山茶宴帶回日本，成為日本茶道的起源。中國徑山茶宴進入日本之後，日本很快就發展出自己的風格與流派。最著名的是千宗旦的三個兒子所創設的三個流派：表千家流的不審庵、裏千家流的今日庵以及武者小路千家流的官休庵，合稱三千家。日本茶道是一種儀式化的、為客人奉茶之事，原稱為「茶湯」（茶湯、茶の湯）。日本茶道和其他東亞茶儀式一樣，都是一種以品茶為主而發展出來的特殊文化，但內容和形式則有別。茶道歷史可以追溯到 13 世紀，最初是僧侶用茶來集中自己的思想，後來才成為分享茶食的儀式。

　　In the Kamakura period, there was a monk called Nampo Shao-ming who studied abroad in China during the Song Dynasty and brought back the Jingshan tea party to Japan. This was the origin of the Japanese tea ceremony. After Chinese Jingshan tea party spread to Japan, Japanese quickly developed its own styles and genres. The three most famous tea schools were created by sons of Sen Sotan: Omotesenke's Fushin'an, Urasenke's Konnichian, MushanoKojisenke's Kankyuan, which together are known as "three Sen houses/families (the san-senke)." The Japanese tea ceremony is a ritual and serving tea to guests, former known as "tea ceremony" (tea' soup, 茶の湯). The tea ceremony in Japan is like in other East Asian countries. All developed a special culture based on the taste of tea, but with different forms and content. Tea ceremony can be traced back to the 13th century. It was initially for monks to be concentrated on their thoughts with the tea and it gradually became a ritual for sharing tea desserts.

現在的日本茶道分為抹茶道與煎茶道兩種。由主人準備茶與點心（和菓子）招待客人，而主人與客人都按照固定的規矩與步驟行事。除了飲食之外，茶道的精神還延伸到茶室內外的佈置、品鑑茶室的書畫佈置、庭園的園藝及飲茶的陶器，都是茶道的重點。

Nowadays, the Japanese tea ceremony is divided in two kinds - Matcha and Sencha. The tea and desserts (Wagashi) will be prepared by the host to entertain the guests. Host and guests have to act in accordance with fixed rules and procedures. Besides the diet, the spirit of the tea ceremony also consists of arranging tea house's interior and exterior decorations, apperciating the room's paintings, gardening and pottery for tea. These are all main points of the tea ceremony.

台灣茶藝 The Tea Ceremony in Taiwan

不論是清治時代或是日治時代，台灣人早期喝茶並無特別講究的文化。1970～1980 年代台灣經濟起飛，人們對於生活與飲食有了更高的要求，茶藝館便順勢興起。茶藝館一方面受工夫茶影響，一方面在內部擺設與美感上則受融入禪宗文化的日本茶道影響，演變成為台灣獨特的人文景觀，甚至傳到其他華人地區。茶藝一詞正式定名於 1970 年代後期，由台灣茶藝愛好者命名。此名字的採用是經過討論，以區分於源自日本的茶道。

Either in Qing Dynasty or Japanese colonial era, Taiwanese did not have a special tea culture. From 1970 to 1980, Taiwanese economy took off, people had higher living and diet standards, and tea houses seized the opportunity to rise. Tea houses received on the one hand the influence of Gongfu tea and on the other hand the elegant interior furnishings integrated with Zen of the Japanese tea ceremony. It evolved into a unique cultural in Taiean, and even spread to other Chinese regions. The art of tea formally grown in the late 1970s, being named by a Taiwanese art tea's enthusiast. This name was adopted after a discussion to make a distinction from the Japanese tea ceremony.

菜餚的故事 你知道嗎？
Stories About Food

 可爾必思
Calpis

　　可爾必思企業的創業者為僧侶出身的三島海雲。1902 年，年僅 25 歲的三島海雲造訪中國內蒙古，嚐到馬奶酒。他以這種當地飲料為基礎，於 1919 年開發出「可爾必思」。創業初期以「初戀的味道」為文宣，生產全世界第一瓶乳酸菌飲料。基於「公司發售的第一種飲料要與公司同名」的商業技巧，此飲品和公司名稱是由「鈣(Calcium）」加上梵語「salpis」（漢字翻譯為「熟酥」，第二種味道之意）組合而來。由於 Calpis 的發音，在英語中近似 Cow piss（牛的尿），為了避免讓顧客有不良的聯想，因此在英語國家中改用 CalPico 的名稱銷售。

　　The entrepreneur of Calpis company was a former monk, Mishima Kaiun. In 1920, Mishima Kaiun visited Inner Mongolia, China, when he was 25, and tasted Kumiss. Based on this local drink, he founded "Calpis" in 1919. When he started the business by using "taste of the first love" as slogan, he produced the first bottle of fermented lactic drink in the world. Based on the business skills of "the first beverage on sale must have the same name as the company", this drink and the company names were the combination from "Ca (Calcium)" plus the Sanskrit "Salpis" (its kanji characters means "the second flauor"). Due to Calpis pronunciation in English is close to "Cow piss" (cow's urine), in order to avoid customers had adverse associative connection, in English-speaking countries the

company's business is under the name "CalPico."

實用會話 聊天必備
Useful Phrases

爺爺，好香喔！您又在泡茶了嗎？
Grandpa, it smells so good. Are you making tea again?

乖孫，這是你奶奶在泡抹茶所發出來的香氣。
Good boy. This is the aroma from your grandma's Matcha.

抹茶？顏色好綠喔！奶奶，等泡好了我可以喝喝看嗎？
Matcha? Its color is so green. May I try after you finish brewing, grandma?

當然可以囉！來，雙手捧著茶碗慢慢喝。
Of course. Come here. Hold the bowl with two hands and drink slowly.

喝起來有點澀澀苦苦的！
It is a little bit puckery and bitter!

所以喝抹茶要搭配著和菓子吃呀！來，吃一口。
So drinking Matcha has to be enjoyed with Wagashi. Come on. Have a bite.

嗯，好甜，跟抹茶搭配起米剛剛好。奶奶好聰明喔！
Uhm, very sweet, just matches with Matcha perfectly. Grandma is so smart!

不是奶奶聰明，是奶奶受過日本時代的教育，有按觸過一點茶道，真正的茶道可是很講究的喔。
Not because grandma is smart, but grandma has been educated in the Japanese era, so I have learned a bit of the ceremony. It's very particular about the real tea ceremony.

爺爺現在正在喝的日本清酒更講究，可惜你還小，不然就能訓練你跟我對飲小酌一番了。
It's more particular about the sake that I'm drinking. You are still too young to drink it; otherwise we could drink it together.

哪有做爺爺的鼓勵小孩子喝酒的啊？乖孫不要聽爺爺亂說，如果喜歡的話奶奶可以常泡給你喝。
What kind of grandpa would encourage children to drink? Good boy, don't listen to your grandpa's nonsense. If you like the drink, grandma can make it for you.

 我想，我已經開始喜歡上抹茶了，因為可以光明正大吃到好吃的點心！
I think I started to like Matcha, because I can eat delicious snacks.

好用句型 點餐必會
Sentence Patterns

1. We have 3 sizes for coffee, Small, Medium and Large. Which size would you like? 我們有三種分量的咖啡，小杯、中杯和大杯。請問您要哪一種？
   medium：中等的
   會這句更加分 The model is of medium stature. 那位模特兒只有中等身材。

2. Sorry, we don't have iced coffee in our menu. How about a regular coffee instead?對不起，我們的菜單中沒有冰咖啡，來一杯招牌咖啡如何呢？
   regular：一般的、標準的
   會這句更加分 Do you want regular or king size for your bed?
   請問您要標準床還是大床？

3. Take a number and wait at your table, thanks.
   請領取號碼牌並至您的座位上稍後，謝謝。

4. Just leave the tray there. We'll take care of it.
   將托盤放著就可以了，我們會處理。
   tray：托盤
   會這句更加分 The waitress carried some cocktail with a tray.
   那位女服務生用托盤端著一些雞尾酒。

5. Please bring back the tray to that section. 請將托盤拿至專屬放置區。
   section：區域、部分

👍 會這句更加分 A small section of rock juts out into the harbor.
有一小部分的岩石突出至港口內。

6. We have hot and iced coffee. Which do you prefer?
我們備有冰咖啡和熱咖啡,請問您想要哪一種?
prefer:喜歡…而不喜歡、寧可…而不

👍 會這句更加分 I prefer rock music to classical music.
比起古典樂,我更喜歡搖滾樂。

7. I'm sorry, but I'm afraid you've given me the wrong order.
不好意思,恐怕你搞錯我的餐點了。
afraid:擔心、害怕

👍 會這句更加分 I'm afraid you have to go to the party by yourself.
恐怕你必須自己一個人去參加那場派對了。

wrong:錯的

👍 會這句更加分 The official always answered the wrong things.
那個官員的回答總是牛頭不對馬嘴。

181

3.4
義式飲料吧
Italian Beverages

Talking About Food In English

朋友 A： 謝謝你來參加我的開幕儀式，乾杯。

Thanks for coming to my opening ceremony, cheers.

朋友 B： 恭喜你開了自己的義大利餐廳，乾杯！哇，這紅酒真好喝！

Congratulations to you that you're running your own Italian restaurant, cheers! Wow, this red wine is very tasty!

朋友 A： 義大利是世界上最古老的葡萄酒產區。早在公元前二世紀便開始出產葡萄酒，兩千年後，義大利成為世界上最重要的生產國之一，葡萄酒在義大利非常受歡迎，消費量位居世界前列，每年平均消費量也多出美國 8 倍之多。因其地理位置之利，義大利幾乎所有地區都耕作葡萄，並擁有超過 100 萬座葡萄園。

Italy is the oldest wine producer in the world. Starting to produce wine in the 2nd century BC, after 2000 years, Italy became one of the most important producing countries. Wine is very popular in Italy, where per capita consumption each year is 8 times higher than in America, and the consumption is at the forefront of the world. Due to its geographical location, most of the districts produce grapes, and there are over one million of vineyards.

朋友 B：　不愧是喜愛義國文化到開了餐廳的達人！那麼紅酒和白酒的區別呢？

No wonder you are an expert in Italian culture and running this restaurant! So what is the difference between red wine and white wine?

朋友 A：　和紅酒不同的是，白酒在釀造時使用的是去皮的葡萄。當他們從壓碎的葡萄中擠壓萃取出用以釀酒的葡萄汁之後，就立刻將葡萄皮取出，不讓葡萄皮中所含的色素滲入葡萄汁中。據研究表明，攝取適量紅酒對健康有益，部分原因是因為葡萄皮中含有兒茶素、多酚、逆轉酮等物質，能降低癌症的發病風險。

Unlike the red wine, white wine is made from grapes without skins. Once they extract the grape juice by pressing crushed grapes for wine, they remove the grape skins immediately to avoid pigment from grape's skin into the wine. Studies show that as long as you drink an appropriate quantity of red wine, it's good for the health. Part of reason is because there are catechin and polyphenols, resveratrol and etc. full contained in grape's skin that can lower the risk from cancer.

朋友 B：　那我一定要常來這裡多喝幾杯！

I must come here more often to drink a couple more then!

朋友 A：　沒問題！你的餐後咖啡想喝濃縮咖啡、卡布奇諾還是拿鐵？

No problem! Which kind of coffee do you want to have after your meal, espresso, cappuccino or latte?

朋友 B：　我一直不懂它們的分別耶！

I never understood the diffrences between them!

朋友 A：　義式濃縮咖啡是藉由高壓沖過磨細的咖啡粉來沖出咖啡。量通

常是以「份(shot)」來計算，常作為其他咖啡飲料的基礎而不會過度稀釋咖啡成份。卡布奇諾是在濃縮咖啡上倒入以蒸汽發泡的牛奶，與拿鐵咖啡的差別在於多了奶泡，調法是濃縮咖啡、鮮奶與奶泡各 1：1：1，還可以在奶泡上灑上肉桂粉、可可粉或是橙橘檸檬類的果皮絲裝飾或增加風味。拿鐵則是三分之一的濃縮咖啡加三分之二的鮮奶，與卡布奇諾相比有更濃的鮮奶成分。

Espresso is one of the coffees made by the ground coffee via high pressure. It's usually count by "shot" and it is also used as a base of other coffee drinks. Cappuccino is made by steam milk with foam on top, and it's different from latte is the milk foam. It consists of espresso, milk and milk foam in the propotion of 1:1:1. You can also decorate or add some flavor by either cinnamon, cocoa powder or lemon orange peel. Latte is made by 1/3 of espresso and 2/3 of milk, having more milk than cappuccino.

朋友 B： 給我一杯拿鐵吧，謝謝！

I'd like to have a cup of latte, thanks!

飲食小百科 文化大不同
Differences in Cultures

葡萄酒 Wine

在幾千年前釀酒葡萄使用以釀製葡萄酒，直到希臘殖民時代，義大利的釀酒業才開始蓬勃發展。公元前二世紀羅馬人被迦太基人擊敗後，義大利的葡萄酒釀造開始進一步蓬勃發展。大面積的奴隸種植園在沿海地區興起，並蔓延至廣大區域。在公元 92 年，羅馬皇帝圖密善下令摧毀大量的葡萄園，以騰出土地生產糧食。在這段期間，在義大利以外的地區種植葡萄是被法律禁止的。義大利藉此出口葡萄酒到各省以換取更多的奴隸，而高盧（現在的法國）對此種貿易的需求極為強烈，主要由於當地居民相當風靡義大利葡萄酒。隨著葡萄栽培法的限制在各省逐漸放寬，大片的葡萄園開始在歐洲其它國家蓬勃發展，特別是高盧和西班牙。同時這也促成了新葡萄品種的發展，促使義大利最終成為各省葡萄酒的進口中心。

Wine grapes have been made into wines for several thousand years, and Italy's wine industry began to flourish after Greece colonial period. In the 2nd century BC, after Romans were defeated by Carthaginians, Italy's wine industry production began to further flourish. There were large plantations by slaves in the coastal and spread to other places. In 92nd AD, the Roman Emperor Domitian ordered to destroy most of the vineyards to produce food. Meanwhile, it was against the law if you grow grapes outside of Italy. Therefore, Italy took this opportunity to sell wines for more slaves, and the demand of wine in Gaul (France) was extremely high. With the looser grape restriction law in every province, many vineyards began to flourish in other European countries, especially in France and Spain. This also facilitated the development of new varieties of grapes, and in the end Italy became the wine import center of every province.

拿鐵咖啡 Caffè Latte

　　拿鐵（latte）在義大利語意思是鮮奶，若你身處義大利，記得不要只對咖啡店店員說你要一杯 Latte，不然你只會得到店員狐疑的眼神以及一杯鮮奶。在英語的世界裡，Latte 則早已是 Coffee Latte 的簡稱，泛指由熱鮮奶所沖泡的咖啡。而法語單字 lait 與義大利語單字 latte 同義，都是指牛奶。Caffè Latte 就是所謂加了牛奶的咖啡，通常直接音譯為「拿鐵咖啡」、「拿鐵」或「那提」。至於法文的 Cafe au Lait 就是咖啡加牛奶，一般稱為「咖啡歐蕾」。

　　Latte in Italian means milk. If you are in Italy, remember not to tell the waiter in the coffee shop for a cup of latte, otherwise you will get a cup of milk, and the suspicious look from the waiter. In English-speaking world, latte is the short form of coffee latte, which means generally the coffee pour in hot milk. In French "lait" and Italian "latte" are synonyms, both mean milk. And "Caffè Latte" means coffee with milk and is usually transliterated as "coffee latte" or "latte." In French, "Cafe au Lait" is coffee with some milk, named generally as "Latte."

　　創設於 1525 年以後的方濟會的修士都穿著褐色道袍，頭戴一頂尖帽子，傳到義大利時，當地人為這種服飾取名為 Cappuccino，因為修士的服飾顏色看起來就像非洲的一種僧帽猴（Capuchin），而卡布奇諾咖啡的顏色就像修士深褐色的外衣，卡布奇諾咖啡因此得名。

　　The monks and nuns of Franciscans, which was established in 1525, all wore brown hooded robes and pointed hats. When they arrived in Italy, people named their dress "Cappuccino," because the color of the hooded robes worn by monks and nuns were like a kind of African monkey called Capuchin and the color of cappuccino was just like the color of the robe. That is where the name of the drink, cappuccino, came from.

菜餚的故事 你知道嗎？
Stories About Food

　　據說在一千多年前，一位牧羊人發現羊吃了一種植物後，變得非常興奮活潑，進而發現了咖啡。也有説法是由於一場野火燒燬了一片咖啡林，燒烤咖啡的香味引起周圍居民注意。人們最初咀嚼這種植物果實來提神，後來烘烤磨碎摻入麵粉做成麵包，做為勇士的軍糧以提高作戰的勇氣。直到 11 世紀左右，人們才開始用水煮咖啡做為飲料。13 世紀時，衣索比亞軍隊入侵葉門，將咖啡帶到了阿拉伯世界。因為伊斯蘭教義禁止教徒飲酒，有些宗教人士認為這種刺激性的飲料違反教義，一度禁止並關閉咖啡店，但埃及蘇丹認為咖啡不違反教義因而解禁，咖啡飲料迅速在阿拉伯地區流行開來。「Coffee」一詞就是源於阿拉伯語「Qahwa」，意思是「植物飲料」，後來傳到土耳其，成為歐洲語言中咖啡一詞的語源。

　　Allegedly 1000 years ago, a shepherd found that a goat got excited after eating certain kind of plant, and then discovered coffee. It is also said that the residents who lived around the forest smelt the aroma after a wild-fire burnt down all the wood, thus discovered coffee. In the beginning, people chewed coffee beans to fresh up, and mixed it into flour to bake breads to excite the warriors. People started to make coffee with water until the 11th century. In the 13th century, Ethiopia invaded Yemen and brought coffee into the Arab world. Due to Islam's doctrine, alcoholic drinks are forbidden, and some Muslims think that coffee is against the doctrine, so they prohibited and closed coffee shops. However, the Sudan of did not agree with it, and the prohibition of coffee was lifted. Coffee started to become popular in the Arab world. "Coffee" is a word from the Arabic "Qahwa," which means plant drink. The etymology of coffee in Europe derives from the Turkish.

實用會話 聊天必備
Useful Phrases

 您好，請問需要甚麼呢？
Hi, may I help you?

我要一杯卡布奇諾和一杯拿鐵咖啡。
I want a cup of cappuccino and latte.

 請問都是熱的嗎？
Would you like both hot?

對。
Yes.

 要中杯還是大杯呢？
Regular or large?

都要大杯。
Both large.

 請問卡布奇諾要撒肉桂粉還是可可粉呢？
How about cinnamon or cocoa powder on top of cappuccino?

都不要，請幫我加糖。

Neither of them. Please add some sugar for me.

好的。那麼拿鐵咖啡要加糖嗎？

Alright. How about latte with sugar?

直接給我糖包和奶球就好。

Just a packet of sugar and a coffee-creamer for me.

糖包和奶球各一份可以嗎？

Is it enough one of each?

糖包兩包。請問一共多少錢？

Two packets of sugar. How much for all?

一共是 240 元。

Total is 240 dollars.

我要刷卡。

I want to pay by credit card.

現在我們有推出刷卡的優惠活動，消費兩杯大咖啡送一杯小咖啡。

Now, we have an offer to buy two large coffees will get a small coffee for free by credit card payment.

有哪些種類的咖啡可以選呢？

Which kind of coffee can I choose?

只要是小杯的飲料都可以選擇。

Any small size of coffee is available.

那我選焦糖瑪奇朵好了，冰的。

I would like to choose iced caramel macchiato.

好的。您要外帶還是內用？

Okay. Would you like to drink here or take away?

全部外帶，裝在一起就可以了。

All take away. It is fine to put them all together in a bag.

好的，這是您的信用卡和咖啡，謝謝您的光臨。

Alright. Here is your credit card and coffees. Thank you for coming.

好用句型 點餐必會
Sentence Patterns

1. May we have a wine list, please? 請問可以給我們酒單嗎？

   list：清單

   👍 **會這句更加分** Make a list of the groceries you need. I will get it for you later. 把你所需要的雜貨用品列成一張清單，我晚一點會幫你買。

2. Can you recommend a nice wine at a reasonable price?

   可以請你們推薦價格合理又不錯的酒嗎？

   price：價格

   👍 **會這句更加分** The car is good except for its price.
   那輛車很棒只是價格太貴。

3. Do you have some inexpensive whiskey? 請問你們有低價位的威士忌嗎？

   inexpensive：廉價的

   👍 **會這句更加分** Sweet potato is an inexpensive food in Taiwan.
   地瓜在台灣是一種廉價的食物。

4. What kind of drinks do you have for an aperitif? 請問你們有甚麼餐前酒呢？

   aperitif：餐前酒

   👍 **會這句更加分** Can we skip the aperitif and order straight away?
   我們可以跳過餐前酒直接點餐嗎？

5. Waiter: Would you like some wine before your meal?

   請問上菜前要喝點酒嗎？

   Guest: Please give us two glasses of red wine. 請給我們兩杯紅酒。

   wine：酒

   👍 **會這句更加分** After drinking some wine, she feels sleepy and dizzy.
   喝了一些酒之後，她覺得有點想睡且頭暈。

主食 Main Course
甜點 Desserts
飲料 Beverages
點心 Snacks

6. May I order a glass of wine？ 請問我可以點杯酒嗎？

　　glass：玻璃杯、一杯

　👍會這句更加分　Would you go and get me a glass of orange juice?
　　　　　　　　你可以去幫我倒杯柳橙汁來嗎？

7. Could you show me something to certify your age？

　　能否請您出示能證明年紀的文件？

　　certify：證明

　👍會這句更加分　I can certify that this is her signature.
　　　　　　　　我可以證明那是她的簽名。

NOTES

3.5
港式飲料大集合
Hong Kong Beverages

Talking About Food In English

祖母： 乖孫啊，謝謝妳今天帶奶奶來吃飲茶。

Good boy, thank you for bringing grandma to have dim sum lunch today.

孫女： 不客氣，孝順您是應該的啊。我們剛剛已經點了好多籠茶點，現在來點飲料吧！奶奶您想喝甚麼？

You're welcome. We are supposed to be filial to you. We just order a lot of dim sum. Let's order the drinks now. What would you like to drink, grandma?

祖母： 有甚麼好推薦的呢？

Any recommendations?

孫女： 有鴛鴦奶茶、絲襪奶茶和凍檸茶。

There are Mandarin style milk tea, Hong Kong style milk tea and lemon tea.

祖母： 這三種聽起來都好奇特啊！又是絲襪又是鴛鴦的，到底是什麼奇怪的飲料啊？

These drinks sound special. Mandarin style? Hong Kong style? What are those?

孫女： 奶奶您別緊張。鴛鴦奶茶在東南亞又稱為咖啡茶，是由 7 成港式奶茶和 3 成咖啡混和而成的飲品，能同時享受咖啡的香氣和奶茶的濃郁。喝的時候可以自行添加砂糖或煉乳。

Don't get too nervous, grandma. Mandarin style milk tea (Yuanyang - Mandarinducks coffee tea), also known as Mandarin coffee with tea in Southeast Asia, is a beverage mixed by 70% of Hong Kong style milk tea (silk-stocking milk tea) and 30% of coffee, enjoying simultaneously the aroma of coffee and the rich from tea. Granulated sugar or condensed milk can be added by yourself while drinking.

祖母： 原來裡面沒有加鴛鴦啊！

So there is no Mandarin duck inside!

孫女： 呵呵，當然沒有。鴛鴦奶茶也被視為香港文化的象徵，用來比喻香港華洋文化交融的現象。

Hehe, of course not. Mandarin style milk tea is also seen as a symbol of Hong Kong culture, and it is used to describe the phenomenon of Hong Kong cosmopolitan culture.

祖母： 原來如此。

I see.

孫女： 絲襪奶茶也是極具香港特色的一種奶茶，是香港人下午茶和早餐常見的飲品。基本上，在香港茶餐廳所供應的奶茶都是用「絲襪奶茶」的方式泡製的。

Hong Kong style milk tea is one kind of milk tea characteristic of Hong Kong. It's a common drink for Hong Kong people as afternoon tea or breakfast. Basically, the tea restaurants that supply milk tea in Hong Kong are also made by the same way as "Hong Kong style milk tea."

祖母： 為什麼要叫絲襪奶茶呢？

Why is it called Hong Kong style milk tea?

孫女： 所謂「絲襪奶茶」，是把煮好的紅茶用棉線網先行過濾，除了濾掉紅茶渣以外，也使紅茶口感更為香滑，再加入淡奶和糖調味。由於棉線網經奶茶浸泡後顏色與女性穿的絲襪非常接近，因此被戲稱為「絲襪奶茶」。

Hong Kong style milk tea refers to use a sackcloth bag to filter the cooked black tea in advance, expect to filter the residues from the black tea, and also to make the black tea taste more creamy. Then it would be seasoned by adding the evaporated milk and sugar. Due to the color of the sackcloth bag after soaked into the black tea is very similar to the stockings women wear, it is referred to as "Hong Kong style milk tea" (Stocking milk tea).

祖母： 原來跟絲襪一點關係都沒有，那奶奶就放心了。

So it's nothing to do with silk-stockings. I am more comfortable with it now.

孫女： 凍檸茶分為熱飲和冷飲兩種，是以檸檬調味的紅茶飲品。

Lemon tea is divided into two kinds of drinks, hot and cold, which are black tea drinks flavored with lemon.

祖母： 那就是一般的檸檬茶囉？

So it's normal lemon tea?

孫女： 港式檸檬茶一定會搭配三四塊厚約 3 到 5 毫米的切片檸檬在杯中，加入紅茶葉沖泡的港式紅茶。客人可以用隨附的茶匙或吸管將檸檬搗碎以自行調節酸性。

Hong Kong style lemon tea, they usually put 3 or 4 pieces of 3-5 mm thick slices of lemon in the cup, and add the Hong Kong style black tea which brewed with black tea leaves. Customers can adjust the acidity by using a teaspoon or straw to mash lemon.

祖母： 原來是這樣啊，可以自行調節酸度的檸檬茶不錯耶，那奶奶就喝這個吧。

I see. Sounds pretty good that I can adjust the acidity by myself. I will drink this then.

飲食小百科 文化大不同
Differences in Cultures

下午茶 Afternoon Tea

英式下午茶一般在下午三點半到四點半進行，然而喝茶並不是主要的環節，品嘗各種點心反而成了最重要的部分。正統的下午茶點心一般是以「三層架」的形式擺盤，第一層放置各種口味的三明治，第二層是英國的傳統點心司康（scone），第三層則是小蛋糕和水果塔，順序是由下往上吃。

British afternoon tea is generally held around 3:50 pm - 4:30 pm. However, the most important thing about afternoon tea is not about tea, but enjoying a variety of snacks. In general, the traditional afternoon snacks are present in a "three tiered dessert stand." The first layer is for all the different kinds of sandwiches, the second layer is a traditional British dessert scone and the third layer is for the small cakes and fruit tarts. The order of tasting is from the bottom to the top.

自英國開始殖民統治香港，也一併把「下午茶」的概念帶進香港。和一

般華人習慣在早上喝茶不同，西方人偏好在下午三點左右，也就是午飯到下班之間的這段時間享受茶和西點。而西方人喝茶習慣加牛奶和糖，使茶入口後更香更滑，因此這也成了製作香港奶茶的基本原則。由於錫蘭出產的紅茶味道既好價格又便宜，所以錫蘭紅茶在香港十分流行。香港餐廳會把下午二點半到五點半稱為「下午茶時間」。大部分快餐店、西餐廳和茶餐廳都會在此時段提供分量較午餐少的餐點，價格也比午餐便宜。

When the British began their colonial rule in Hong Kong, they also spread the concept of "afternoon tea" to Hong Kong. Chinese usually drink tea in the morning, which is quite different from Westerners who prefer it in mid-afternoon around 3 pm, the period between lunch and the evening. Westerners accustomed to drink tea with milk and sugar for making the tea more fragrant and slippery to drink, so it has become the basic principles of the milk tea produced in Hong Kong. Due to the black tea produced from Ceylon is both savor and affordable, Ceylon black tea is very popular in Hong Kong. The "tea time" in Hong Kong is between 2:30 pm and 5:30 pm. In this period, most of the fast food shops, Western restaurants and tea restaurants provide a tea-time set, which is lighter and more affordable than lunch.

隨著英國在 19 世紀末的強盛，下午茶文化從英國本土帶入歐洲和其他殖民地，成為一種世界性的文化標誌之一。幾乎在每一家西式餐廳都會供應下午茶餐點。英國下午茶又被香港人稱為 High tea，而在紐西蘭，他們的 Tea time 習慣在早上而非下午，所以又稱為 Morning tea time。

With the prosperity of Britain in the 19th century, the culture of afternoon tea spread to Europe and other colonies of the United Kingdom, becoming a worldwide cultural icon. The afternoon tea are mostly served in every Western restaurant. The British afternoon tea is also called "high tea" by people of Hong Kong, but in New Zealand, they used to have the "Tea time" in the morning instead of afternoon, so it is also named "Morning tea time."

飲茶 Yum cha

　　飲茶，又稱為品茗，是一種源自中國廣州的粵式飲食，而後流傳至世界各地，成為廣東文化的一大特色。在香港，飲茶一開始是叫做「上茶樓」或「上酒樓」，後來就叫做「去飲茶」，慢慢又簡化為「飲茶」，此後就成為上茶樓喝茶吃點心的代名詞。飲茶的茶樓在歐美被稱為「Dim Sum House」（點心屋）。紐澳則將飲茶的場所同樣稱呼為「飲茶」，在日常對話中亦會說「Let's go to Yum Cha」（我們去飲茶吧）。

Yum cha, also known as tea drinking, it's a Cantonese food from Guangzhou, China, that spread to the rest of the world, becoming the major feature of Guangdong culture. In Hong Kong, yum cha was called "go to the Tea house" or "go to the Cantonese restaurant" in the beginning, then "go Yum cha" and after slowly and simplified as "Yum cha", which become synonymous of "Dim Sum House" in Europe. New Zealand and Australia still call it "Yum cha" in the Yum cha restaurant, in the daily conversation they say "Let's go to Yum Cha."

菜餚的故事 你知道嗎？
Stories About Food

ⅰ⅟ㅇ 維多利亞下午茶
Victorian Afternoon Tea

　　在英國維多利亞時代（西元1840年），貝德芙公爵夫人安娜瑪麗亞（Anna Maria）女士每到下午時刻就覺得提不起勁、百般無聊。此時距離穿著正式的晚餐還有一段時間，可是她又覺得肚子有點餓，於是就要女僕在

她的起居室準備幾片烤麵包、奶油和茶先讓她滿足口腹之慾。公爵夫人很滿意這樣的茶點內容與過程，開始邀請知心好友加入她的下午茶會，伴隨著茶和精緻的點心，共享輕鬆愜意的午後時光。沒想到這樣的活動漸漸在當時的貴族社交圈內流傳開來，形成一種優雅自在的下午茶文化，後來更一躍成為正統的「英國紅茶文化」，這就是所謂的「維多利亞下午茶」的由來。

In Victorian England (1840 AD), Anna Maria, the Duchess of Bedford, felt dispirited and bored every afternoon. There was still a span of time to the dinner, which she had to wear formal dresses with complicated etiquette, but she also felt a bit hungry, so she asked the maid to prepare few slices of bread, butter and tea to satisfy her appetite. She felt that this was a really quite perfect afternoon snack. Later on, The Duchess began to invite close friends to join her afternoon tea in the living room, along with tea and delicate desserts to share the relaxing moment in the afternoon. She didn't expect such activity gradually spread to the aristocratic social circles at the time, making aristocratic ladies scrambled for it. it became an elegant and relax afternoon tea culture, even became the traditional "British black tea culture" after, which is the story of "Victorian afternoon tea."

實用會話 聊天必備
Useful Phrases

小姐，不好意思，我年紀大了，菜單上的字太小看不清楚，可以請妳告訴我圖片上這個綠色的飲料是什麼嗎？

Excuse me, miss. I'm getting old. The words on the menu are too small. I can't see them very clearly. Can you please tell me what is the green drink on this picture?

這是新鮮現榨的小麥草汁。
This is fresh wheatgrass juice.

是冷的還是熱的啊？
Is it cold or hot?

是冷的喔！小麥草汁沒有在做熱的。
It's cold. There is no hot wheatgrass juice.

我身體虛，不能喝冷的，有沒有熱的飲料呢？
I am feeble. I can't drink cold. Is there any hot drinks?

我們有熱咖啡和熱的絲襪奶茶。
We have hot coffee and Silk Stocking milk tea.

絲襪奶茶！？是用絲襪下去泡的嗎？不要，我不敢喝。
Silk Stocking milk tea!? Is this brewed with silk stockings? No, I don't dare to drink it.

絲襪奶茶是形容喝起來的口感絲滑柔細，不是用絲襪泡的，您別擔心。
Silk Stocking milk tea is a drink which tastes silky and smoothly, not brewed with silk stockings. Don't worry.

主食 Main Course

甜點 Desserts

飲料 Beverages

點心 Snacks

奶茶這種東西我喝了會拉肚子，還是不要好了，有沒有單純茶類的飲料？
Better not. If I drink milk tea, it will cause me diarrhea. Are there any pure tea drinks?

我們的凍檸茶很有名，可惜是冰的，如果幫您去冰可以嗎？
Our lemon tea is famous, but it's cold. Will it be fine for you to take off the ice?

有加檸檬？我怕我的敏感性牙齒會酸痛。
Is there lemon in it? I'm afraid that my sensitive teeth will hurt.

那，就只剩下熱紅茶了。
Well, the only thing left is hot black tea.

那就熱紅茶吧，謝謝妳啊！
Hot black tea then. Thank you!

好用句型 點餐必會
Sentence Patterns

1. Please give me a little extra/less caramel syrup, please. 請給我多／少一點焦糖糖漿，謝謝。

   syrup：糖漿

   👍 **會這句更加分** I would like my pancakes with maple syrup.
   我的鬆餅要加楓糖漿。

2. I want more/less milk in my milk tea, please.
   我的奶茶要加多／少一點牛奶，謝謝。

   less：較少的

   👍 **會這句更加分** The roads should be less crowded when it's raining.
   雨天的時候路上應該比較不會那麼擁擠了。

3. I heard that the drinks here are good. 我聽說這裡的飲料很好喝。

   drinks：非酒精飲料

   👍 **會這句更加分** Do you know these drinks are not for free?
   你知道這些飲料不是免費的嗎？

4. Is it hot or cold? 請問那是冷的還是熱的？

   cold：冷的

   👍 **會這句更加分** The cold weather won't last forever, don't worry.
   這冷天氣不會持續到永遠，別擔心。

5. Which one sells better? 請問哪一個賣得比較好？

   selling：銷售

   👍 **會這句更加分** This company does more selling than production.
   這家公司從事的銷售多過生產。

主食 Main Course

甜點 Desserts

飲料 Beverages

點心 Snacks

6. Do you have any fat-free ice cream? 請問你們有任何不含脂肪的冰淇淋嗎？

   fat-free：不含脂肪的

   👍 **會這句更加分** Fat-free milk is not the guarantee for health.

   低脂牛奶並不保證健康。

7. Do you have drinks with fruits? 請問你們有含水果的飲料嗎？

   fruits：水果

   👍 **會這句更加分** These fruits will not keep over this week.

   這些水果無法存放過這週。

NOTES

3.6
泰式飲料大集合
Thai Beverages

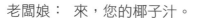

用英文聊美食 聊天必備
Talking About Food In English

老闆娘： 來，您的椰子汁。

Here is your coconut juice.

客人： 喔... 謝謝妳，可是我沒有點飲料啊！

Oh... thank you, but I didn't order any drink.

老闆娘： 您是第一次來消費吧？我們的椰子汁是免費招待的。

You come here the first time, right? Our coconut juice is on the house.

客人： 這麼好啊，您真大方。

That's great. You are so generous.

老闆娘： 這沒什麼啦！椰子是泰式料理的精隨，吃泰式料理當然也少不了椰子汁囉。

It's nothing. Coconut is the essence of Thai cuisine, and of course you can't eat Thai food without coconut juice.

客人： 聽老闆娘這麼一說我才想到，自己對泰式飲料完全沒有概念耶。

I realized that I have no idea of Thai diet by listening to you.

老闆娘： 除了椰子汁以外，泰式奶茶也是純正的泰式飲料。泰式奶茶的茶葉接近印度紅茶，特色是沖泡出來的茶湯是橘紅色的，茶湯先沖泡完成才會倒進加了牛奶、煉乳、冰塊的杯子裡。我泡一杯請你喝吧！

Apart from the coconut juice, the Thai milk tea is also an authentic Thai drink. The Thai milk tea is similar to the Indian black tea. Its special brewed color is orange, after the completion of brewed, poured tea in a cup which has milk, condensed milk, ice inside. Let me give you a cup of brewed tea!

客人： 不行啦！已經讓您免費招待一杯椰子汁了，這杯我自己付帳。

No, I already have a cup of free coconut juice. I will pay for this cup.

老闆娘： 唉呀～ 不要客氣啦！如果你覺得好喝的話，就多多幫我宣傳囉。

Oh, don't worry! If you think It tastes good, then help me to promote it.

客人： 那就恭敬不如從命了。

Obedience is better than politeness.

老闆娘： 來，泰式奶茶沖好了，你喝喝看。

Here, here is your Thai milk tea. Try it.

客人： 甜度適中，冰冰涼涼的，好好喝喔！

Moderate sweetness with ice. Very tasty.

老闆娘： 你還可以推薦長輩或女性朋友喝泰式香茅茶 Lemongrass Tea （namtakrai），印度醫學專家認為，香茅可以解毒及幫助消化。此外，相傳香茅也具有殺菌和治療神經痛和肌肉痛的效果，最重要是可以利尿、消腫及滋潤皮膚。

You can also recommend elderly or female friends to have lemongrass tea (namtakrai). Indian medical experts believe that the lewongrass can help digestion and detoxification. Besides that, according to the folklore, lemongrass has also bactericidal effects and contributes to treat neuralgia and muscle pain. The most important is a diuretic, swelling and moisturize the skin.

客人： 這麼厲害？感覺不只女性，大人小孩都可以喝耶！

Is it really that good? It seems like it's not only for women, but also for children and adults.

老闆娘： 對呀，由於香茅茶被證實具有淨化腸道的效果，所以常被當作餐後茶飲用。在泰國餐廳裡都會備加了班蘭葉的香茅茶。來，我再泡一杯請你。

Yeah, because lemongrass tea has been proved that it can purify the intestines, so it is often used as the tea after meal. In Thailand, restaurants always have lemongrass tea with pandan leaves. Here, let me give you another drink.

客人： 感謝，喝完這杯真的不要再請我了，不然就要虧本了。

Thanks, but please don't give me any free drinks again, or you are going to lose money.

飲食小百科 文化大不同
Differences in Cultures

 ### 各種果汁及其益處
A Variety of Juices and Their Benefits

番茄汁 Tomato Juice

番茄汁內所含的番茄紅素具有防止乳癌的效果，特別是像番茄醬、番茄汁或是番茄湯等經過加工的番茄食品，當中的番茄紅素特別容易為人體吸收，降低罹患乳癌的效果比直接生吃番茄還要好。另外番茄汁還可以減低罹患癌症、心血管等疾病的機率。

Tomato juice contains lycopene, which has the effect of preventing breast cancer. Lycopene can be intaken from tomato sauce, tomato juice, tomato soup, or other tomato processed food which is more easily to be absorbed by human body than to eat tomatoes directly. Tomato juice can also reduce the risk of cancer, cardiovascular disease and other diseases.

蘋果汁 Apple Juice

蘋果汁富含多酚類物質。除了大多數水果都富含的維生素 C 之外，蘋果汁也含有硼等有益於骨骼健康的礦物質。

Apple juice is rich in polyphenols. Most fruits are rich in vitamin C, and apple juice also contains beneficial minerals, such as boron, for bones health.

葡萄柚汁 Grapefruit Juice

葡萄柚汁略帶酸味，富含維生素 C 對健康有益，但不可與藥物併用。

Grapefruit juice is a little sour, rich in vitamin C and good for health.

However, it cannot be taken together with medicines.

鳳梨汁 Pineapple Juice

鳳梨汁的營養價值與新鮮鳳梨果肉差異不大，由於鳳梨果肉含有能分解蛋白質的酵素，故經常飲用鳳梨汁能夠幫助消化與吸收。鳳梨中亦含有各種豐富的維生素，尤其是維生素 C，可以降低罹患腎臟疾病、高血壓與支氣管炎等疾病之風險。

The nutritional value of fresh pineapple juice and pineapple pulp does not have many differences, since pineapple contains enzymes that break down proteins. Drinking pineapple juice can help digestion and absorption. Pineapple also contains a rich variety of vitamins, especially vitamin C, that may reduce the risk of kidney disease, hypertension and bronchitis disease.

葡萄汁 Grape Juice

葡萄汁和葡萄酒一樣，含有抗氧化劑如類黃酮，已被證明可幫助肌膚抗老化且有益於身體健康。

Grape juice is like wine. Both of them contain antioxidants, such as flavonoids, and also have shown the benefits to help skin anti-aging and health.

椰子汁 Coconut Juice

椰子汁的成分與人的體液類似，容易被人體吸收，因此腹瀉時喝椰子汁也有幫助。

Coconut juice composition is similar to human body fluids, and it's easy for human body to absorb. Drinking coconut juice is also helpful when diarrhea.

草莓汁 Strawberry Juice

草莓汁能幫助通便，且草莓富含對免疫系統有益的維生素 C，亦能治療失眠。

Strawberry juice can help purge, and strawberries are rich in vitamin C, beneficial to the immune system and can also treat insomnia.

木瓜汁 Papaya Juice

木瓜中的木瓜蛋白酶可將脂肪分解為脂肪酸，且含有一種酵素能消化蛋白質，有利於人體對食物進行消化和吸收，因此木瓜汁能健脾助消化。

Papaya's papain can break lipid down into fatty acids, and contains an enzyme that can digest proteins, help the body to digest and absorb food. Papaya can help digestion.

奇異果汁 Kiwi Juice

奇異果富含維生素 C，含量為柳橙的 2 倍，更有 β 胡蘿蔔素、維生素 E 及多酚等營養成分，是一種營養價值非常高的水果，因此奇異果汁也對健康有益。

Kiwi is rich in vitamin C, about double the amount of oranges. It is also rich in nutrients β-carotene, vitamin E and polyphenols, having very high nutritional value of fruits. Kiwi juice is good for your health.

西瓜汁 Watermelon Juice

西瓜汁含有豐富的維生素 A 及維生素 C、鉀及鎂，可以消暑解渴，亦有能對抗癌症和防止太陽灼傷皮膚的功效。

Watermelon juice is rich in vitamin A and vitamin C, potassium and magnesium. It can be refreshing, and it can also fight cancer and prevent sun burns.

菜餚的故事 你知道嗎？
Stories About Food

在古代傳說有一位叫「木耶」的方士，他駕船到海上尋找仙山，不幸遇上大風浪，眼看著船就要被巨浪所吞噬時，有一條黑龍載起他飛到一座孤島，一頭撞在礁石上就再也沒有醒過來。此時天外突然飛來一位仙女，將手中玉瓶裡的水淋在黑龍的頭上，只見黑龍瞬間化為一棵大樹，大大的葉子上結滿了奇怪的果實。原來那位仙女正是南海觀音的化身，她不忍見到島上瘟疫橫行，如今正巧遇上精通醫術的方士，希望他能到島上治病救人。方士找到村莊後帶著村民來到仙樹下，喝下神水的百姓果然不久後就病癒。木耶方士得到百姓的愛戴，便留在孤島教導百姓醫術和耕田的知識。後人為了紀念木耶，便把「木」「耶」二字合併為「椰」字，並將仙樹取名為「椰樹」。

In ancient times, there was a legend of an alchemist called Wood Ye. He sailed out to the sea looking for the Mountain of Immortals. Unfortunately, he met a big storm. When he saw the waves going to engulfed the ship, a black dragon flew him up to an island. He didn't wake up since the crash. At this time, there comes a fairy. She poured the water from the jade jar to the Black Dragon's head, the Black Dragon then turned into a tree which has some strange fruits covered with big leaves. The fairy was an incarnation of Nanhai Guanyin Buddha. It could not bear to see the rampant island plague. It wants the alchemist to cure the sickness of the people. The alchemist found the villages and brought villagers over to the fairy tree. People recovered after drinking the magic water. Alchemist Wood

Ye was beloved by the people, and he stayed in the island to teach the people the knowledge of medicine and farming. To commemorate Wood Ye, people put together "wood" and "ye" into the word "coconut," also named the magic tree as "coconut tree."

實用會話 聊天必備
Useful Phrases

我想買兩顆椰子。
I would like to buy two coconuts.

好的，要剖開嗎？
Ok, do you want we to open them for you?

不用，我想帶回家冰過再喝。
No, I want to bring them home to drink after iced.

妳家裡有剖開椰子的工具嗎？
Do you have the tool to open coconuts at home?

沒有耶… 用一般的菜刀可以嗎？
Nope... can I use a kitchen knife?

椰子的外殼很厚，要用大刀，像是柴刀順著纖維一刀一刀砍下來，我怕小姐妳帶回家不好處理。
Coconut shell is thick. You have to use a broad knife, like a machete knife, knifed down along with the fiber. I'm afraid that you can't deal with it if you bring them back home, miss.

可是我想要帶回家再慢慢喝，現在剖開的話我就拿不回去了。
But I want to bring them back home to drink slowly, I can't bring them back home if you open them now.

我可以先幫妳處理外殼，等妳回家再挖個小洞來喝。
I can help you to deal with the shell first, once you get back home, you can make a small hole to drink.

這倒是不錯的方法。
This is a quite good idea.

兩顆椰子我都幫妳去殼了，來，妳看，去殼後的椰子上面有三個小孔，有兩個長的一樣，剩下一個長的不一樣。妳回家後拿小刀挖一下不一樣的那個小孔，就可以插吸管進去喝椰子汁了。

I have dehusked the two coconuts for you, here, take a look. Above the dehusked coconut , there are three apertures; two of them look the same, and the other doesn't. You can use a knife to dig the hole which is different when you get back home, then you can insert a straw into it to drink the coconut juice.

謝謝！
Thanks!

如果妳有辦法在家裡把椰子敲開的話，別忘了椰子肉也可以吃喔。

If you have a way to knock coconuts open at home. Don't forget that coconut meat can be eaten too.

好用句型 點餐必會
Sentence Patterns

1. I'll have two cakes and a decaf. 我要兩塊蛋糕和一杯去掉咖啡因的茶。

   decaf：去掉咖啡因的茶

   👍 會這句更加分 He is sipping his decaf latte over there.
   他正在那裏喝著他的低咖啡因拿鐵。

2. A：Is it your first time here? 這是你第一次來嗎？

   B：No. I've been here a couple of times. 不，我來過好幾次了。

   couple：（口語）幾個，三兩個

   👍 會這句更加分 They spent a couple of days in Paris during their honey moon. 他們蜜月的時候在巴黎待了幾天。

3. Can I have a box for to go? 可以用盒子裝讓我帶走嗎？

   box：箱子、盒子

   👍 會這句更加分 The wooden box was a present that my father made for me.
   這個木盒子是我爸爸做給我的禮物。

4. What time is the last order? 請問最後一次點餐是甚麼時候？

   last：

   👍 會這句更加分 Do you always leave the best bits till last as well?
   你也會把最好的東西留到最後嗎？

5. A：Can I go outside and smoke a cigarette? 我可以到外面抽根菸嗎？

   B：Sure. There's an ashtray near the door. Please feel free to use it.
   當然可以，門附近有菸灰缸，請隨意使用。

   cigarette：香菸

   👍 會這句更加分 He has gone through three packs of cigarettes in just one
   day. 他在一天內就抽完了三包香菸。

ashtray：菸灰缸

👍 會這句更加分 Please drop your cigarette ashes into the ashtray over there. 請將你的煙灰彈進那裏的菸灰缸裡。

6. I'd like to order some drinks. Do you have any suggestion? 我想點一些飲料，請問你有甚麼建議嗎？

suggestion：建議

👍 會這句更加分 My brother give me many helpful suggestions when I have none. 當我沒有主意的時候我的哥哥都會給我很多有用的建議。

4 號

美食館：點心
Cuisine Gallery4: Snacks

剛吃過正餐卻還是有點嘴饞，想吃點東西又怕影響下一餐的食量，此時小點心便是正餐之間最佳的選擇啦！種類豐富的小點心有甜有鹹，有可以迅速帶著走補充熱量的外食小點心、也有精緻到值得花時間坐下來好好品嚐的下午茶小點心。小點心不但上的了廳堂當飯桌佳餚，也很適合請客送禮，這一章就讓我們來一窺小點心的奧妙吧！

Snack is the best choice between meals, if you still feel like to eat something but don't want to quash the appetite for the next meal. There is a variety of sweet and salty snacks. There are snacks to replenish calories, and also delicate snacks that worth spending the time and having an afternoon tea. Snacks are not only suitable to be excellent cuisines on the dinner table, but also to be good gifts. Let's see the subtleness of snacks in this chapter!

4.1
美式點心大集合
American Snacks

用英文聊美食 聊天必備

Talking About Food In English

大學生 B： 每到下午就好想吃一些小點心喔！

I want to have some snacks badly every time in the afternoon!

交換學生 A： 對呀，在美國這個時候大家通常都會去熱狗攤買熱狗來吃。法蘭克福香腸配上多種配料，如番茄醬、美乃滋、芥末、生菜絲等，一想到就流口水了。

Yeah, in America, people usually get some hot dogs at this time. Frankfurters with ketchup, mayonnaise, mustard, lettuce, etc. Once I think of it, I start to drooling.

大學生 B： 熱狗的確很好吃，不過我很好奇，美國的小點心除了熱狗和薯條（French Fries）以外還有甚麼呢？

Hot dogs are tasty indeed, but I'm curious about what else are the snacks from America apart from hot dogs and French fries?

交換學生 A： 甜甜圈也是很方便的小點心，最普遍的兩種形狀是中空的環狀，以及麵團中間可包入鮮奶油、卡士達醬等甜餡料的封閉型甜甜圈。在美國有許多人以甜甜圈作為早餐的主食，甚至還為此設立了「甜甜圈日」呢！

Doughnut is also a convenient snack. There are two

common shapes- ring doughnut, and round daught ball doughnut which stuffed with cream or custard. In America, many people take doughnuts as staple of breakfast, and even set up the "Doughnut Day."

大學生 B： 亞洲人對美國點心的印象的確就是熱狗、甜甜圈和薯條，不知道除此之外還有其他種類嗎？

For Asians, impression of American snacks are hot dogs, doughnuts and French fries indeed, but is there anything else?

交換學生 A： 還有英式鬆餅（Muffin）跟杯子蛋糕啊！Muffin 有英式與美式之分，英式 Muffin 的歷史略為悠久，可追溯自十、十一世紀的威爾斯。英式 Muffin 水分含量高，口感比美式 Muffin 更加鬆軟，吃法多侷限在原味 Muffin，以淋上蜂蜜、果醬或加上乳酪的方式稍加變化。美式 Muffin 的口味更為多元，會在麵糊裡添加不同配料以作出不同的口味，像是巧克力、核桃、香蕉等。

There are muffins and cupcakes. There are British and American style muffins. British style muffins have a long history, tracing back to the 10th, and 11th century in Wales. British style muffins are more moisture and tasty than American style. You may also enjoy different style of muffins by having honey, jelly or cheese. American style muffins have more flavors by using different ingredients to put inside the dough, such as chocolate, walnuts, bananas, etc.

大學生 B： 那麼杯子蛋糕呢？

How about cupcakes?

交換學生 A： 近幾年在美國本土流行在 Muffin 上擠上鮮奶油、巧克力、

放上軟糖做點綴，讓美式 Muffin 的造型更加多采多姿，這就是所謂的杯子蛋糕（Cupcake），也有人稱為小仙子蛋糕（fairy cake）。現在美國各大城開始出現許多杯子蛋糕專賣店，這些造型可愛、可自由組合的杯子蛋糕可是非常流行呢！

Recently in America, it has become popular to put cream or chocolate on top of the muffins in order to decorate them. That is what people call cupcakes, or fairy cakes. Many big cities have special stores for cupcakes, and these cupcakes are very popular in America today.

大學生 B： 可惜我們現在能吃到的只有學生餐廳的薯條，走，我們去吃一些薯條解饞吧！

What a pity that we can only eat French fries from students' restaurant. Let's go grab some French fries then!

飲食小百科 文化大不同
Differences in Cultures

 ### 甜甜圈的歷史
The History of Doughnuts

在 19 世紀中葉，甜甜圈被稱為荷蘭油蛋糕（olykoeks），因此有一種理論認為，甜甜圈是被荷蘭定居者引入北美的，他們也同時促使其他美國甜點，包括餅乾和鮮奶油餡餅開始流行起來。然而，也有證據表明，這種糕點是由舊時在美國西南部的原住民發明的。到 19 世紀中葉，甜甜圈的樣式和味道就和今天看到的基本相近了，並開始被視為一種徹頭徹尾的美國食品。

In the mid-19th century, doughnuts, also named "oil cake" (Dutch: olykoeks), were introduced by Dutch settlers to North America. They also made other desserts, including cookies and cream pies, which all became popular in America. However, there is also a prove that this kind of dessert was invented in old times by a southwest American aboriginal. In the mid-19th century, the style and taste of doughnuts were similar to today's, and people began to regard doughnuts as American food.

美國人漢森格雷戈里聲稱，他早在 1847 年乘坐一艘做石灰生意的船舶出國時就已經發明了環形的甜甜圈，那時他只有 16 歲。格雷戈里厭惡普通油炸餅那種油膩的、被扭曲成各種形狀的感覺和總是炸不熟的中心部分。他説自己那時用船上的胡椒罐在甜甜圈麵糰的中心打洞，後來又把這種技術教給他的母親。

Gregory Henson of the U.S. claimed that he invented the ring-shaped doughnuts in 1847, when he was on a trading ship, when he was only 16 years old. Gregory was dissatisfied with the greasy twisted rope-shaped doughnuts. He claimed that he punched a hole in the center of dough with a pepper can on the ship and later taught the method to his mother.

在蘿拉英格爾斯懷爾德的書《農民男孩》中，Almanzo 的母親做了麻花形和環形兩種甜甜圈，環形的那種被稱為「新發明」。書裡提到，油炸時，麻花形的會自己翻轉；而環形的需要自己動手去翻動。

In Laura Ingalls Wilder's book *Farmer Boy*, Almanzo's mother made two kinds of doughnuts, ring and twisted, the ring shape was "newly invented." It is mention in the book that it will flip itself when deep frying the kind of twisted shape and the other ring shape have to flip by yourself.

據人類學家保羅·R·穆林斯説，甜甜圈首次被提及是在 1803 年的一本英文版美國食譜附錄中。

According to the anthropologist Paul R. Mullins, the first cookbook to mention doughnuts was a 1803 English edition of an appendix of American recipes.

Muffin 名稱溯源 The Origin of Muffins

muffin 這個名詞在英文最早出現的拼法是出現於 1703 年的 moofin，可能來自於古德文的 muffen（為 muffe 的複數，意指小蛋糕）；或是來自法文的 mouflet（意指麵包的柔軟）。muffin 在 19 世紀英國人已經工業化生產，成為下午茶的主食。Muffin 有兩種型式，一種是以酵母發酵的扁平麵包，在美國稱為 English Muffin。一種是用發粉膨發的快速麵包。

The name muffin is first found in 1730 spelled "moofin," possibly derived from the ancient German "muffen" (the plural of muffe means small cake), or possibly from the French "mouflet" (which means soft as a bread). In the 19th century, the United Kingdom had already industrialized its production, and muffins became the staple of afternoon tea. There were two types of muffins - one was yeast fermentation's compressed bread, also named "English Muffin" in America. The other was the quick bread by using baking powder as leavening agents.

菜餚的故事 你知道嗎？
Stories About Food

 熱狗不是狗
Hot Dog Is Not a Dog

熱狗約於 19 世紀傳入美國，當時叫做 Frankfuters，最暢銷的熱狗品牌是 Dachshund Sausages。據説當時有位漫畫家在運動場看見小販叫賣熱狗，於是畫下情境，回到公司想寫上説明時卻記不起 Dachshund 的發音，

而因為 Dachshund 亦可解釋為德國臘腸犬，故他索性寫上 Hot Dog，從此成了這個食品的代號。有人認為直到 1904 年舉行的路易西安那購物博覽會才首次出現熱狗這種食品，然而類似熱狗的另一食品－臘腸在當時的歐洲市面上已頗為普遍，而德國早在紀元前 64 年就有了。

Hot dogs have been in America since 19th century and they were also named "Frankfurters." The best sale brand was "Dachshund Sausages." Allegedly, there was a cartoonist who saw a vendor selling hot dogs in a sports ground, so he drew the cartoon, but he couldn't recall the name "Dachshund," when he was back to his office. So he wrote down Hot Dog instead, because Dachshund can also be referred to as dachshund. Later people also started to use the name "hot dog." Some people believe that hot dogs first appeared at the Louisiana Purchase Exposition. However, other products similar to hot dogs were very common in the market, and Germany had hot dogs long time before, in 64 BC.

到了 1860 年代，第一個熱狗麵包才在紐約市布魯克林區中首次推出。另一說是，這個以麵包夾著香腸來吃的食物，是源自德國香腸世家，當時只為了方便進食燙手的香腸而夾上麵包，傳統食法更是不加任何醬料或配料，以吃出香腸的原味。

The first hot dog bun was only shown in Brooklyn in the 1860s. Others said that this hot dog bun was originated from the German sausage family, and used only for the convenience while eating the hot sausage. In the traditional way, no sauce or extra toppings are added to keep the original flavor of the sausage.

實用會話 聊天必備
Useful Phrases

 一對好姊妹約在一家充滿貴族氣息的下午茶餐廳
A pair of good sisters making an appointment for afternoon tea in an aristocratic restaurant

好久不見了，這家店好找嗎？
Hi, long time no see. Is this restaurant easy to find?

真的好久沒跟妳出來喝下午茶了，這家店很有名啊，我一直想來卻沒機會。
It's really been a while to have an afternoon tea with you. This restaurant is very famous. I've always wanted to come, but have no chance.

那我真是挑對地方了！聽說這裡的英式下午茶非常正統喔！
I chose the right place then! I heard that the British afternoon tea here is very traditional!

喔？那我們就趕快點一份來品嚐吧！能請服務生幫我們介紹一下嗎？
Oh? Let's order one then! Can we ask the waiter to introduce it for us?

主食 Main Courses
甜點 Desserts
飲料 Beverages
點心 Snacks

我們的三層英式下午茶由下而上依序是佐以燻鮭魚、小黃瓜、火腿和美乃滋的三明治；第二層則是英式奶油鬆餅，搭配果醬或奶油食用，最上層則是季節水果塔和蛋糕、餅乾。

Our three layers of British afternoon tea, from the bottom to the top, the first layer is smoked salmon, cucumber, ham and mayonnaise sandwich, the second layer is British muffin with jelly or cream, and the top layer are seasonal fruit tart, cake and cookies.

份量好多喔，可以兩個人分著吃嗎？
Such a huge plate. Can we two share it?

可以的，會分別為您送上兩壺茶，請問兩位要紅茶還是奶茶呢？
Sure. We will serve you two pots of tea. What would you like your tea, black tea or milk tea?

我要紅茶。
I would like to have black tea.

那我要奶茶。
Then I'll have milk tea.

227

好的，待會送上三層點心盤時，建議您由下層依序往上層食用，這樣的口味才會由鹹而甜，讓味蕾品嚐到食物的原味。

Ok. I'd suggest you to eat from the bottom to the top, so the flavor will be salty to sweet and also you can taste the original flavor of the food.

英國人喝下午茶好慎重喔，感覺自己也變得淑女起來了。

British are very cautious about having afternoon tea. I feel myself a lady.

對呀，就連使用的茶具器皿等都很講究呢！今天就讓我們像歐洲貴婦一樣優雅地談天吧！

Yeah, even fastidious about fea sets! Let's chat like European ladies!

好用句型 點餐必會
Sentence Patterns

1. Can I have a hot dog, please？ 我可以點一份熱狗嗎，謝謝。

2. Q: Which would you like for bread？White or whole wheat？
   您想要什麼口味的麵包？白吐司或全麥麵包？

   A: Whole wheat, please. 請給我全麥麵包，謝謝。

   wheat：小麥

   會這句更加分 Flour is made from wheat. 麵粉是用小麥做的。

3. What are the hours for afternoon tea? 請問喝下午茶的時間是甚麼時候？

hour：小時、時刻

👍會這句更加分 It took me 6 hours to finish the work.

那份工作花了我六個小時才完成。

4. What kind of cake goes well with Assam tea? 阿薩姆茶搭配甚麼蛋糕好呢？

kind：種類、性質

👍會這句更加分 This kind of problems are easy to solve.

這種問題是很容易就可以解決的。

5. Do you have any snacks or desserts? 請問有甚麼小菜或點心嗎？

snack：小吃、點心

👍會這句更加分 I always ate a snack between meals.

我總是在兩餐之間吃點小點心。

6. What is the minimum per person? 請問每個人的最低消費是多少？

minimum：最小值、最低限度的

👍會這句更加分 This is the minimum rate for a single room.

這是一間單人房的最低價錢了。

per：每

👍會這句更加分 How many kilometers can a human run per hour?

一個人一小時可以跑幾公里？

常見的茶
Popular Tea
☑ Milk tea 奶茶
☑ Earl Grey tea 伯爵茶
☑ Darjeeling tea 大吉嶺茶
☑ Russian Caravan 俄國茶
☑ English breakfast tea 英式早餐茶
☑ Nilgiri tea 尼爾吉里茶

主食 Main Course

甜點 Desserts

飲料 Beverages

點心 Snacks

4.2
中式點心大集合
Chinese Snacks

 用英文聊美食 聊天必備
Talking About Food In English

班長 A： 各位同學，現在我們來討論一下這次園遊會班上要賣的項目。主題是「中式點心」請大家踴躍提議。

Hey guys. Let's discuss about the items we are going to sell in the garden party. The theme is "Chinese snacks," so please give me some proposals as many as we can.

學生 B 賣鹹酥雞好不好！鹹酥雞最好吃了！

How about fried salty chicken! Fried salty chicken is the best!

學生 C： 你是自己想吃吧！？鹹酥雞準備起來好像很麻煩耶！

That's what you want to eat, right!? There are a lot of troubles preparing Fried salty chicken.

學生 B： 不會啊，只要把雞肉切成小塊，先用醬料醃漬入味再裹上油炸粉油炸，我們還可以一併販賣炸甜不辣、豬血糕、雞皮、馬鈴薯條、番薯條、四季豆、芋粿、青椒、銀絲卷、豆乾、雞心、雞屁股、薯餅等，只要把食材先準備好就行了。

Not really. You just need to cut the chicken in small pieces, first marinated in sauce, then wrapped them with flour before you fry them. We can also sell tempura, rice cake, chicken skin, fried potatoes, fried sweet potatoes, string beans, taro cake, green peppers, steamed bun rolls, pressed tofu, chicken hearts, chicken buttoms, hash browns, etc., as long as all the ingredients are already prepared.

學生 C： 既然一樣是要準備食材，不如賣滷味吧。熱的滷味只要將食材放入鍋內用滷汁滷完後撈起，加入調味料、酸菜等配料後就可以給客人直接食用了。

Since we are going to prepare foods, how about selling pot-stewed food then? We just need to cook all the food in the marinade, pick it up when it's fully cooked, then add seasonings, pickled cabbage and other ingredients. People can eat it when it's done.

學生 D： 可是聽說別班已經有人要賣真空包裝的常溫滷味了，這樣會不會重複啊！？

But I heard that one of the classes is going to sell packed pot-stewed food. It's going be the same!?

學生 E： 我覺得可以賣蚵仔煎，作法很簡單，先用平底鍋把油燒熱，放上蚵仔、攪拌後的雞蛋、茼蒿菜或小白菜再淋上太白粉芡水，蚵仔熟時裝起來淋上特製醬料即可。

I think we can sell oyster omelette. It's very easy to make. All you need to do is to heat oil with a frying pan, then put oysters, eggs, tongho leaves, Chinese white cabbage (Bok-choy), and pour the mik of cornstarch and water over the ingredients, then top it with sauce.

學生 D： 或是賣肉圓，肉圓是以地瓜粉、太白粉等材料作成的小吃，內餡多為豬肉或其他配料。雖然聽起來很麻煩，但我們不必自己動手做肉圓，只要批好材料過來，再以油加溫（並非炸）或蒸就可以了，醬料則是準備甜與鹹兩種，再加上少許蒜泥、香菜。

Or we can sell Taiwanese meatballs. Taiwanese meatballs are a snack made with sweet potato starch, cornstarch and other materials, of which are usually pork or other fillings. Although it sounds like a lot of troubles, we don't have to make it by ourselves. We only need to order the Taiwanese meatballs and heat them up with oil (not fried) or steam. We can also prepare two kinds of sauce, sweet and salty, with a bit of garlic and coriander.

班長 A：　各位同學的提議都很好，不過這些中式小吃在調理上都要用到油炸或是高溫，在安全上會有疑慮，是否有其他建議呢？

Each of you has a very good proposal. However, these Chinese snacks are to be fried in high temperature, and there will be safety concerns. Are there other suggestions?

學生 B：　賣麻糬如何？材料只需要準備糯米和花生粉、糖粉等，再找木杵或石臼來現場表演搗麻糬，既可以招攬客人又簡單方便。

How about selling mochis? We only need to prepare glutinous rice, peanut powder, powdered sugar, etc., and then find a wood mortar or stone mortar to have a live performance of pounding mochis. It's convenient and easy to attract customers.

班長 A：　我覺得是個不錯的提議，大家來舉手表決吧！

I think it's a pretty good suggestion. Let's vote by a show of hands.

飲食小百科 文化大不同
Differences in Cultures

 筷子文化
The Chopsticks Culture

中國 China

　　筷子是世界公認為中國古老的發明，自隋唐開始，筷子傳入朝鮮半島及日本、越南等國後，筷子也隨前往國外定居的華人和中國餐館走向世界各地。美國哈佛大學人類學系主任張光道於報上發表論文寫道：「中國烹調的特點是把食品切成小塊，用碗盛著，就無需用刀叉切食，需要的是將小片食物從碗中送進嘴裡，於是筷子應運而生。中國最古老的用筷大約出現在西元前 1200 年。顯然，叉子來到西方人的餐桌上，比筷子遲了好幾百年。」

　　The world recognizes chopsticks as an ancient invention from China. After chopsticks spread to the Korea Peninsula, Japan, Vietnam and other countries, they also settled with the overseas Chinese and Chinese restaurants around the world. The chair of the Anthropology Department of Harvard University, Guangdao Zhang, wrote in a report that "the characteristic of Chinese cuisine is to cut the food into small pieces and put them in a bowl, so we don't need to cut the food with a knife and fork. The chopsticks are to put small pieces of food in the mouth from the bowl, so here is where the chopsticks are from. The oldest chopsticks appeared in China about 1200 BC. Apparently, forks appeared on Westerners' tables several hundred years later than chopsticks."

日本 Japan

　　中日用筷文化雖然同根同源，但由於兩國飲食習慣的不同，筷子傳到日本後逐漸變短，原來的平頭筷開始漸漸變成尖頭。據說這是由於日本人喜愛

生魚片，為了便於戳起或夾起薄薄的魚肉而改良的。還有一種說法是，將筷子削尖，使它同時具有筷子和叉子的功能。

Although the chopsticks culture between China and Japan had the same root, due to the different dietary between the two countries. In Japan, they shorten the sizes of chopsticks, and made the pointed side from flat to pointy in order to poke and pick up the thin raw fish slice. Others say that sharpened chopsticks can also function as forks.

韓國 Korea

韓國用筷與中國和日本不同之處是筷子和湯匙同時運用。筷子夾菜；湯匙舀飯。其實這是中國先秦的古老習俗，當中國的飲食文化傳到朝鮮之後，他們一直嚴格遵守著筷匙分工明確的習俗，即使後來中國的用筷文化最終只需用筷，朝鮮仍保留古風至今。韓國用筷還有一個特徵就是一律使用金屬筷，以扁體為多。有一種說法是朝鮮半島冬季寒冷，常常冷到零下四十度。使用金屬筷夾熱菜可以傳熱，使手部感到溫暖。至於是否符合史實，仍有待專家做進一步探討。此外，韓國的筷子之所以較短，是因為他們多在地坑上用餐，因為桌子矮小，夾菜方便，也避免碰到同桌人，因此筷子不需太長。

The difference of using chopsticks between Korea, China and Japan is that Koreans use chopsticks and spoon at the same time. Chopsticks for picking the food up, spoon for scooping the rice out. Actually, it is an ancient pre-Qin Chinese custom. When the Chinese food culture spread to Korea, it has been strictly compliance with clear division of using chopsticks and spoons. Even though the Chinese chopsticks culture finally simplified to use chopsticks only, people in the Korean Peninsula still retains the tradition today. Also, most chopsticks in Korea are flat, metal chopsticks. It is said that due to the Korean Peninsula's temperatures can go as low as negative 40℃ in winter, people use metal chopsticks to pick the hot dishes up, and the heat will warm the hands as well. Whether it is a fact or not, this issue needs further research by experts. Moreover, the reason why Korean chopsticks are shorter is because people dine in undersized tables, so it is easier to pick the food up and also avoid hitting other people in the same table. That is why chopsticks do not need to be too long.

菜餚的故事 你知道嗎？
Stories About Food

肉圓的誕生 The Origin of Taiwanese Meatballs

相傳肉圓是在北斗地區的寺廟擔任文筆生的范萬居先生所創。當時北斗地區發生水災，范萬居將地瓜曬乾、磨成粉後揉成糰狀再煮熟給災民食用，當時內餡並未包肉。肉圓後來經過改良，加入豬肉、筍子等配料，逐漸發展成現今為人所熟知的肉圓，並且流傳到台灣各地，成為今天我們所之到的肉圓。

It is believed that Taiwanese meatballs were first prepared in the Beidou township's temple of Taiwan by a translator named Wanju Fan. When Beidou had a flood disaster, Wanju Fan dried the sweet potatoes, grounded them into powder, then prepared it for the victims. At the time, they were not stuffed with meat. Later, people improved Taiwanese meatballs by stuffing pork, bamboo and other ingredients inside, evolving into today's Taiwanese meatballs. It eventually spread to the rest of Taiwan, and became the meatballs we know today.

鄭成功的發明 Koxinga's Invention

民間傳聞在西元一六六一年時，荷蘭軍隊占領台南，鄭成功從鹿耳門率兵攻入，意欲收復失土。鄭軍勢如破竹大敗荷軍，荷軍在一怒之下便把米糧

全都藏匿起來。鄭軍在缺糧之下急中生智，索性就地取材，將台灣特產蚵仔、番薯粉混合加水和一和煎成餅吃，想不到竟流傳後世，成了風靡全台灣的小吃－蚵仔煎。

There was a popular rumor that in 1661 AD, when Tainan was occupied by Dutch troops and Koxinga was trying to reclaim it. He successfully defeated the Dutch, but the Dutch troops were hiding all the rice. Koxinga suddenly thought a solution. He simply took local products to make oyster omelets by mixing oysters and sweet potato starch together. He didn't expect this dish would pass down to posterity and become a popular snack in Taiwan - oyster omelets.

實用會話 聊天必備
Useful Phrases

 一位台灣人與外國朋友站在鹹酥雞攤位前。
A Taiwanese and a foreign friend are standing in front of a fried salty chicken vendor.

我們買一些鹹酥雞回我家邊聊天邊吃吧！
Let's buy some fried salty chicken and have some chat in my place!

好啊！一靠近攤位就有一股好香的味道，真讓人難以抗拒。
Ok! There is an incense smell when we approach to the vendor. It's really hard to resist.

聽說外國人不吃內臟類的料理，那除了一定要吃的鹹酥雞之外，我就幫你挑些蔬菜、豆干、甜不辣讓你吃吃看吧！

I heard that foreigners don't eat guts. Besides fried salty chicken, I will also choose some vegetables, pressed tofu and tempura for you to taste.

好啊，這幾天到台灣來，我覺得台灣的美食好對我的胃口，尤其是小吃，不但到處都有非常方便，而且有甜有鹹、每種都各有不同的特色，我回美國一定會懷念的。

Ok, I enjoyed the dishes a lot these days in Taiwan, especially snacks. They are not only everywhere, but also very convenient. From sweet to salty, each of them has their own characteristics. I certainly will miss them when I'm back in America.

身為台灣人，我也覺得有這麼多種類的小吃很幸福呢！對了，你敢吃辣和九層塔嗎？

As a Taiwanese, I also feel the happiness of having this many types of snacks! By the way, do you eat spicy and Asian basil?

一點點辣沒問題，倒是我沒吃過九層塔，是一種香料嗎？

A little bit spicy is fine, but I haven't tried the Asian basil before. Is that a kind of spice?

對，其實九層塔就是義式料理經常出現的羅勒，外國朋友應該可以接受，你看，老闆現在放進鍋裡炸的就是九層塔。

Yes, Asian basil is actually basil leaves which usually show in Italian cuisine. It's fine for most of foreigners. Look, the boss is putting the basil leaves into the pan to fry now.

哇，好香啊！其實台灣小吃在製作上的講究程度一點也不輸給餐廳裡的料理呢！

Wow, it smells so good! In fact, the attention on Taiwanese snacks is not less than any dish in a restaurant!

對呀，台灣小吃兼具了美味與便利，平常下午餓了，或是晚上想吃個消夜，家附近都看的到鹹酥雞或滷味，說到這裡，害我突然也好想來點滷味喔！對面就有滷味攤，我們也去買點滷味回家吃吧！

Yeah, Taiwanese snacks are delicious and convenient. Usually if you are hungry in the afternoon or want to have some snacks at midnight, there will be always vendors selling fried salty chicken or pot-stewed food. Talking about this, I suddenly want to have some pot-stewed food too. Just in front of here there is a pot-stewed food vendor. Let's go buy some pot-stewed food too!

好用句型 點餐必會
Sentence Patterns

（位置選擇相關）

1. We would like to sit in a booth.
   我們想訂一間包廂。
   booth：（餐廳等的）雅座

   會這句更加分 They sat in a corner booth away from other diners.
   他們坐在角落的雅座，遠離其他客人。

2. How about sitting at the bar? 請問您願意坐在吧檯嗎？
   bar：酒吧

   會這句更加分 There are several bars on this street.
   這條街上有好幾家酒吧。

239

3. Q: Do you have a corner table for six?

請問你們有 6 個人、靠角落的位置嗎？

A: Sorry, we only have a table for two right now. Would you like to take it?

抱歉，我們現在只剩下 2 人座的了，請問要嗎？

corner：角落、偏僻處

👍會這句更加分 The fire extinguisher belongs in the corner.

滅火器應該放在角落。

4. Q: Could we have a table next to the window?

我們可以坐靠窗的位置嗎？

A: I am sorry. Our window tables are all taken.

抱歉，我們靠窗的位置都被訂走了。

take：佔領

👍會這句更加分 Sorry, our rooms were all taken tonight.

不好意思，我們今晚的房間都被訂走了。

5. Q: Could we sit in the non-smoking area?

我們想訂禁菸區的位置。

A: The non-smoking area is full right now. Do you want to go ahead and sit in the smoking section?

目前禁菸區都已經客滿了，請問你們想稍等一下還是坐在吸菸區呢？

area：區域

👍會這句更加分 There is a parking area in front of terminal 1.

航廈一前面有一處停車場。

6. Please let me know when a table is ready.

有位子空出來的時候請通知我。

ready：現成的、準備好的

👍會這句更加分 Your table is ready. Please come with me.

您的位子空出來了，請跟我來。

7. Q: How long do we have to wait for a table?

請問我們需要等多久才有位置？

A: About 20 minutes. We have quite a long line/queue at the moment.

大約要二十分鐘，目前還有很多客人在排隊。

queue：隊伍、行列

👍 會這句更加分　Wc were at the tail of the ticket window.

我們排在售票亭的最尾端。

4.3
日式點心大集合
Japanese Snacks

Talking About Food In English

創業夥伴 B： 這次去了趟日本研究當地的特色小點心，我們就來討論要在夜市裡擺攤賣甚麼吧！

I went to Japan to do research on local Japanese specialty snacks this time. Let's discuss about what do we want to sell in the night market!

創業夥伴 A： 我覺得日本關西的章魚燒好美味，可惜在台灣的各大夜市都已經買的到了。不如來賣「明石燒」你覺得如何？

Unfortunately, in Taiwan each large night market has people selling takoyaki from Kansai, even though I think it's very delicious. What do you think about selling "akashiyaki?"

創業夥伴 B： 啊，你是說章魚燒的祖先、在日本稱為「玉子燒」的明石燒嗎？我記得作法是用蛋白蒸成軟嫩的圓形糕狀，搭配高湯食用，目前在台灣來說很少見，應該有市場，但是蛋的比例佔得比較多，成本也會相對比較昂貴喔。

Ah, you mean akashiyaki, ancestors of takoyaki, also known as "Tamagoyaki" in Japan? I remember akashiyaki is made with steamed custard, topped with soup stock. It's quite rare in Taiwan, and there is a potential market.

However, it would be more expensive, because we need more eggs for it.

創業夥伴 A： 我覺得可樂餅也不錯，將馬鈴薯煮軟弄成泥狀，與配料以 1：1 的比例混合後揉成圓餅，沾上蛋汁和麵包粉再油炸，做法不難。配料則可以有多種樣式，如絞肉、海鮮、蔬菜、咖哩等。另外我們還可以考慮關東煮。

I think croquettes are also good as well. Boil potatoes into soft and mashed it up, mix the ingredients in a ratio of 1:1, and then fry them with soaked eggs and bread crumbs. The method is not difficult. There is a variety of ingredients and styles, such as ground meat, seafood, vegetables, curry, etc. In addition, we can also consider oden.

創業夥伴 B： 關東煮？這在臺灣已經十分流行了，大家都知道它俗稱「黑輪」，在便利商店就可以買的到。

Oden? It has become very popular in Taiwan. It is commonly known as "heilun." You also can buy it at the convenience store.

創業夥伴 A： 不過你忘了一點，實際上台灣的關東煮大部分已不是我們在日本吃到的原始口味，且在放置的材料上也有相當的差異性。如果我們可以使用日本正統的關東煮食材的話，一定可以獨樹一格。

But you forget one thing. In fact, most of the oden we eat in Taiwan are different fro the original flavor of Japan, and the ingredients are also very different.

創業夥伴 B： 我倒是對「今川燒」念念不忘。今川燒在台灣常稱為紅豆餅 (Custard pancake)或車輪餅，外皮以麵粉、雞蛋與砂糖製成，中間夾有內館，以紅豆館、菜豆館、毛豆館與卡士達奶

油等傳統甜餡為主。近年來也發展出許多新式的口味，如巧克力、抹茶等，更流行加入麻糬或起司增添口感。

I am actually quite obsessive about "Imagawayaki." Imagawayaki, often named custard pancake in Taiwan, stuffs from red bean paste, bean paste, soybean stuffing to other traditional sweet custard cream filling. Many new flavors are developed in these years, such as chocolate, Matcha, etc., and it's even more popular to add mochi or cheese for increasing the taste.

創業夥伴 A： 可是這與台灣的紅豆餅有甚麼不一樣？

But what is the difference with Taiwanese custard pancake?

創業夥伴 B： 今川燒在日本是屬於高級的和菓子，餅皮製作過程不加水稀釋，所以比起台灣紅豆餅更加扎實，奶香也更濃郁。

Imagawayaki is a high class Wagashi in Japan. The process of making crust is not diluted with water, so Taiwanese custard pancake is more solid, richer and its milk is more aromatic.

創業夥伴 A： 我們先來試做看看吧！

Let's try to make it first!

飲食小百科 文化大不同
Differences in Cultures

今川燒
Imagawayaki

在日本，今川燒隨著地區不同而有不同的稱呼。在關東被稱為「今川燒き」或「二重燒き」，在關西與九州地區則稱為「回転燒き」，另外還有「大判燒き」、「太鼓燒き」、「太鼓饅頭」等不同的稱呼。而做成鯛魚的形狀則是大家常聽到的「鯛魚燒」。

In Japan, Imagawayaki has different names depending on the areas. It is called 今川燒き(magawayaki) or 二重燒き(Nijū-yaki) in Kanto; in Kansai and Kyushu is called 回転燒き(Kaiten-yaki); other names are 大判燒き (Ōhan-yaki), 太鼓燒き(Taiko-yaki)", and 太鼓饅頭 (Taiko manjū). Taiyaki is the way we often hear, made in the shape of bream.

日本今川燒的甜味口感來自當地的上白糖，而台灣紅豆餅大多是使用台灣的紅糖或白糖，也有部分使用冰糖。

The sweetness of Japanese Imagawayaki taste is from the local caster sugar, Taiwanese custard pancake mostly uses brown or white sugar, and some of them also use crystal sugar.

日本今川燒與其他和菓子一樣，都只有甜的餡料，大多為紅豆與白豆．紅豆餅的餡料以紅豆、卡士達奶油、芋頭、花生、地瓜、芝麻為主。也因餡料以豆類等蛋奶素食材製成，不像台灣紅豆餅有甜、鹹、葷、素等多樣化選擇。在日本是見不到像台灣紅豆餅一樣的鹹餡口味，如蘿蔔乾、蘿蔔絲、鮪魚、高麗菜、咖哩、酸菜等。

Imagawayaki is the same as other Wagashi, only filled with sweets,

which mostly are red beans and pea beans. Custard pancake's filling base are red beans, custard cream, taro, peanuts, sweet potatoes and sesame. Due to the fillings are made with beans and other vegetarian ingredients, it is not like Taiwanese custard pancake, which has a wide range of choices (sweet, salty, meat, vegetarian, etc.). In Japan, it is impossible to see a pancake similar to Taiwanese custard pancake filled with salty flavors, such as dried radish, dried radish slices, tuna, cabbage, curry, sauerkraut, etc.

可樂餅 Croquette

可樂餅是日本的家常菜之一，據説起源自法國料理當中的炸肉餅（croquette）。法國的炸肉餅是以魚肉、雞肉等絞肉混合而成的油炸物，亦有使用搗碎的馬鈴薯並裹上麵包粉後油炸。

Croquette is one of Japan's homemade food, originated from French cuisine croquette. French croquette is fried with the mixture of fish, chicken and other ground meat, and it can also be fried with mashed potatoes with wrapped bread crumb.

另外在荷蘭也有一道叫作 kroket 的料理，不只使用白醬、也有使用馬鈴薯，因此據説也可能是可樂餅的起源。

There is also a dish called "kroket" in the Netherlands, which not only uses cream sauce, but also potato. Therefore, it may be the origin of croquette.

關東煮 Oden

據説關東煮源自於「味噌田樂」，是用水將豆腐或蒟蒻煮熟，再以味噌調味後食用的鄉土料理。

It is said that oden derived from "Misodengaku," a local dish cooked with tofu or konnyaku in boiled water and then flavored with miso.

關東各地製作關東煮的方法不盡相同。不過跟一般的火鍋料理不同，關東煮製作簡便，材料可以隨時放進湯裏煮，因此在冬天的時候格外受到歡迎。在日本，關東煮可以在便利商店或者路邊攤買到。

The methods of production of oden vary around Kanto. Different from the average hot pot cuisine, oden is simple and convenient, and materials can also be put in the soup to cook anytime. Consequently, it is popular especially in winter time. In Japan, oden can be purchased at convenience stores or street vendors.

關東煮近幾年在中國大陸也相當風行，亦可在便利商店和商業餐飲區內買到。口味和用料同樣與正宗的關東煮有所差異，在中國大陸的羅森便利商店所賣的關東煮當中，最受歡迎的 3 種口味分別為貢丸、魚豆腐和蘭花豆腐乾。

Oden has become quite popular in recent years in China, and also can be purchased at convenience stores and commercial catering areas. The tastes and materials are different from authentic oden. The three most popular kinds of oden in Mainland China's Lawson convenience store are pork meatball, fish tofu, and aburaage.

菜餚的故事　你知道嗎？
Stories About Food

章魚燒 Takoyaki

　　章魚燒在日本已有 70 多年的歷史，是日本民間流傳已久的風味小吃，據說章魚燒的祖先是明石燒，是用蛋白蒸成的軟嫩圓形食物。1933 年，大阪會津屋的創始人遠藤留吉在明石燒裡面加了牛肉、蒟蒻和醬油販賣，但有客人不滿地說：「明石燒可是有加章魚的耶！」1935 年，遠藤留吉開始使用章魚作為主原料，並在麵糊裡加入調味，如此煎出的章魚燒大受人們的歡迎，很快地就從大阪被推廣到日本全國。

　　Takoyaki has more than 70 years of history in Japan. It has a tradition in Japanese snacks for a long time. It is said that Takoyaki's ancestor is akashiyaki, which is made with steamed custard, topped with soup stock. In 1993, Osaka, the founder of Japanese restaurant "Aizuya," Tomekichi Endo, filled it with beef, konnyaku and soy sauce, but there was a dissatisfied guest that said: "Akashiyaki is filled with octopus!" Tomekichi Endo started to use octopus as main ingredient and mixed the flavor in the paste in 1935, Takoyaki became very popular among the people. Soon it spread from Kanto region to other areas in Japan.

　　鯛魚燒其實是由今川燒演變而來的，名稱由來為江戶時代中期的安永年間 (1772 年～1781 年)，因為在神田的今川橋開始販賣這種圓餅形狀裡面包紅豆的小點心，故如此命名。而後「浪花家總本店」有感於一般市井小民吃不起昂貴的鯛魚，於是特地將今川燒的圓餅形狀改為鯛魚的形狀，就成了我們常聽到的鯛魚燒。

　　Taiyaki actually evolved from Imagawayaki. Imagawayaki began to be sold near the Kanda Imagawabashi bridge during the An'ei years (1772 -

1781), in the Edo period. The name of Imagawayaki originated from this time. Then, "Langhuajia restaurant" helped the common people in the streets who cannot afford expensive snapper by specifically making the shape of bream from the Imagawayaki's round shape. This is the taiyaki that we often hear today.

實用會話 聊天必備
Useful Phrases

媽媽，我聞到好香的味道喔！那是甚麼？
Mom, what smells so good?

那是祭典上在賣的章魚燒啊！
That's the takoyaki selling at the festival.

我餓了，可以吃章魚燒嗎？
I'm hungry. Can I eat takoyaki?

當然可以啊！今天帶你來參加祭典，就是想帶你來吃小吃的。我們待會看到想吃的都買一份分著吃，從頭吃到最後一攤好不好？
Of course you can. It's for you to have some snacks while attending the ceremonies today. We'll share the food from the first stand to the last. You can buy whatever you want to eat, ok?

耶！太棒了！
Yeah! That's great!

來，章魚燒好囉！小心燙！
Here! Here is the takoyaki. Be careful. It's hot!

呼，外面吹涼了裡面還是好燙喔！
Ou... it gets cold outside, but it's still hot inside!

有沒有燙傷舌頭？
Did you burn your tongue?

我沒事。我只吃了一顆，剩下的都給妳，接下來
我想吃今川燒。
I'm fine. I just ate one. The rest are for you. I want
to eat Imagawayaki next.

你這孩子，真不知道是孝順還是浪費！？才剛吃
完鹹的，甜的今川燒等最後再回來買吧。
I don't know if you are really filial or you are just
wasting food!? You just had something salty. We'll
come back to buy the sweet imagawayaki in the
end.

那我要吃可樂餅跟關東煮。
I want to eat croquette and oden then.

好，不過別忘了留一點肚子給今川燒喔。
Ok, but don't forget to save some stomach for imagawayaki.

一定要在這裡吃完嗎？我們可以買回家順便分給爸爸吃啊！
Do we have to finish here? I can buy it back home and share it with dad!

好用句型 點餐必會
Sentence Patterns

1. **What are your specialties?** 請問你們的招牌是甚麼？
   specialties：特製品、特產
   會這句更加分 Octopus is a local specialty here. 章魚是這裡的特產。

2. **What do you recommend in this season?** 請問在這個季節裡你推薦甚麼？
   season：季節
   會這句更加分 It was the high season for strawberries. 現在正是草莓盛產的季節。

3. **What do you recommend for unique food?** 請問你們有甚麼推薦的罕見食材？
   unique：獨特的

251

👍 **會這句更加分** There was something unique about the 3D movies. 這些 3D 電影有其獨特之處。

4. Do you have a seasonal beer? 請問你們有季節限定的啤酒嗎？

　 seasonal：季節性的

👍 **會這句更加分** The demand for ice creams is very seasonal. 對於冰淇淋的需求是非常季節性的。

5. Can I leave my order to you for $100 per person? 可以請你幫我們搭配每人 50 美元的餐點嗎？

6. What is the most reasonable course? 請問最便宜的套餐是甚麼？

　 reasonable：合理的、價錢不高的

👍 **會這句更加分** The government claimed that oil price is "fair and reasonable." 政府宣稱石油的價格「公平且合理」。

　 course：套餐

👍 **會這句更加分** Can I take a course for just one? 請問我一個人也可以點套餐嗎？

7. I'd like to have the same order that person sitting next to us is having. 我們想要點跟隔壁桌的人同樣的餐點。

　 person：人

👍 **會這句更加分** Don't judge a person by his appearance. 不要用外表來評斷一個人。

NOTES

主食 Main Course

甜點 Desserts

飲料 Beverages

點心 Snacks

4.4
義式點心大集合
Italian Snacks

Talking About Food In English

披薩店師傅：員工用餐時間到了，今天我們自己做披薩來吃吧！

Time for staff meal. Let's make our own pizza today!

披薩店學徒：謝謝師傅，我從進披薩店開始就一直在學習揉麵團，真的好想吃披薩喔！

Thanks, master. I always wanted to learn how to knead dough since I got in the pizzeria. I love pizza so much!

披薩店師傅：你桿一片麵皮給我，剛好可以順便驗收你學習的成果。

Roll a piece of dough for me, so I can test your learning result.

披薩店學徒：好的。師傅，這樣可以嗎？

Okay. Is it fine, master?

披薩店師傅：還不錯，為了獎勵你，我們今天就把所有義式材料都放上去，做成特製的豪華披薩吧！

Not bad! To reward you, let's put all the Italian ingredients on top and make a special luxury pizza!

披薩店學徒：太棒了！我一直很想吃吃看這些食材。

Awesome! I always wanted to try these ingredients.

披薩店師傅：這是莎樂美腸（Salami），又稱為「義大利香腸」，是歐洲一種風乾的豬肉香腸，可以直接搭配紅酒食用，常見於歐美國家的超市、肉食店，是一般家庭的日常肉類來源之一。莎樂美腸較為流行的國家包括義大利、匈牙利、德國、西班牙等。這個則是帕爾瑪火腿（Prosciutto di Parma），出產於義大利，一般是切成薄片生食。可和義大利麵包，蘆筍、青豆和氣泡酒一起吃。與其他火腿相比，帕爾瑪火腿放的鹽較少，而且正宗的帕爾瑪火腿只用海鹽。

This is salami, also named Italian sausage. It's one kind of sausage from dried pork, and can directly match with red wine. It's common in western' supermarkets and butchers, and it's one of the daily meats for most families. Salami is very popular in Italy, Hungary, Germany, Spain, etc. There is also Prosciutto di Parma from Italy. It can normally be cut into slices and eaten directly. It can match with Italian bread, asparagus, green peas and sparkling wine. Compared with other hams, Prosciutto di Parma uses less salt and the authentic Prosciutto di Parma only uses sea salt.

披薩店學徒：光這兩樣就好豐盛喔！

These two are bountiful enough!

披薩店師傅：帕馬森起司（英：Parmesan 義：Parmigiano-Reggiano）是種硬質的起司，喜好乳酪者稱這種起司為乳酪之王。Parmigiano-Reggiano 一名有註冊商標，在義大利有專門的政府部門控制其製造及銷售。沒有達到標準的乳酪不能稱為帕馬森起司，而且只能餵豬，這些吃乳酪的豬也就是帕爾瑪火腿的來源。莫札瑞拉起司（Mozzarella）俗稱水牛起司，是源自義大利南部的淡起司。最初是以水牛奶為主原料，但

現在大部分已經改用牛奶製作了。莫札瑞拉起司冷吃的話，與生番茄切片搭配起來非常可口。加熱食用的話，質地柔軟的莫札瑞拉起司會於烤箱內慢慢融化於食物裡。用這兩種起司來做披薩最棒了。

Parmesan (English: Parmesan, Italian: Parmigiano-Reggiano) is one kind of hard cheese. The people who love cheese call this kind of cheese the king of cheeses. Parmesan has a registered trademark, only specialists from Italian government can control its production and sales. It cannot be named parmesan if it does not reach the standard, and Prosciutto di Parma comes from pigs feed only with disqualified cheese. Mozzarella, commonly referred to as buffalo cheese, is a light cheese from southern Italy. Buffalo milk was originally the main ingredient, but now most of them are using cow's milk. Mozzarella matches with tomato and can be a very delicious cold dish. Mozzarella is soft, it will be melted if you hit it in the oven. These two cheeses are the best for pizza.

飲食小百科 文化大不同
Differences in Cultures

莎樂美香腸 Salami

在歐洲有上千種莎樂美腸，其中最受歡迎的包括義大利的米蘭莎樂美（Salami Milano），匈牙利的冬季莎樂美（Winter Salami）等等。在歐洲許多國家的莎樂美腸都習慣以產地命名，例如米蘭莎樂美和匈牙利莎樂美。由此可知在歐洲有各種具有不同特色的莎樂美腸。有些莎樂美經大蒜調製，有些則是在調味料中加入辣椒粉末或咖哩，如匈牙利的皮克莎樂美（PICK salami）。

There are thousands of salami in Europe. The most popular are Salami Milano from Italy and Winter Salami from Hungary. They used to be named salami because of the original habitat in many European countries, for example, Salami Milano and Hungarian salami. Some salami are prepared with garlic and some of them seasoned with paprika or curry, as PICK salami.

莎樂美腸的製作方法大致不脫以下關鍵步驟：將豬肉的瘦肉和肥肉按一定比例打碎、混合、灌腸，在乾燥室經過發酵，用鹽、胡椒、酒、辣椒粉等調料醃製入味，再經過一個月至數個月的風乾後，就可以切成薄片或者整塊銷售。莎樂美腸無需加熱可以直接食用。

There are some key points of its general production process: smash both lean and fat porkwith certain percentage, mingle them together and make it like sausages. After fermentation in the drying room, salt, pepper, alcohol, paprika, etc. are added to improve the taste. After months of air drying, it can be sold either in slices or as the whole. People can eat salami without heating.

起司 Cheese

　　各國的起司有不同的做法和吃法，起司配餅乾是西方人充飢解饞的選擇，起司與葡萄酒則是法式主餐之後、甜食之前的一道料理。義大利料理亦離不開起司，不論是做義大利麵食或披薩都需要用到起司。希臘人用生菜、橄欖和起司做涼拌。傳統的瑞士起司火鍋（fondue）更是當地冬季的暖胃美食。

Every country has different methods of producing cheese and different cheeses. Cheese cookies are one of the preferred snacks for Westerners, being cheese and wine a French dish after the main course and before the dessert. Italian cuisine can't even live without cheese, pasta or pizza. Greeks use lettuce, olives and cheese to make a tossed salad. The traditional Swiss cheese fondue is a typical cuisine in winter time.

菜餚的故事 你知道嗎？
Stories About Food

　　相傳起司是源於阿拉伯。約在六千年前，阿拉伯人將牛奶和羊奶放入皮革器皿中，繫在駱駝身上欲作為旅途中解渴之用。未料到經過漫長且酷熱的旅程之後，奶類產生變化。在艷陽高照的沙漠上顛簸行走數小時，袋內的羊奶已經分為兩層，一層透明狀的乳清及白塊凝脂。原來皮革器皿中含有具有凝乳成分的酵素，加上旅途顛簸搖盪及太陽的高溫照射，奶類隨之發酵，形成半固體狀態，於是最初的起司就這樣誕生了。

Allegedly, cheese is from the Arab. About 6000 years ago, Arabs put cow's and goat's milk into a leather utensil for drinking in a journey. During a long and extremely hot journey, the milk began to change. The milk in the utensil separated into two parts after a sunny day walking several hours in the desert- a transparent whey and a white congealed fat. As the leather utensil had enzymes chemical elements of curd and also due to the heat of the bumpy journey, the milk fermented and became semisolid, followed by the very first cheese.

實用會話 聊天必備
Useful Phrases

媽媽，我肚子餓了，有沒有甚麼小點心可以吃？
Mom, I'm hungry. Do we have any snacks?

我看看，冰箱裡有一些起司和吐司，我們可以把起司放在吐司上面用烤箱烤。
Let me see. There is some cheese and toast in the fridge. We can make cheese toasts in the oven.

我可以直接吃起司嗎？
Can I eat cheese directly?

不行，光吃起司太鹹了。
No, it's too salty if you just eat cheese.

那我可以用小餅乾夾著起司吃嗎？我看電視上的義大利料理節目他們都是這麼吃的。
Can I take cookies and put cheese in between? I saw that in Italian cooking programs on TV.

既然要這樣吃的話，不如媽媽去切一些番茄切片，再看看有沒有火腿可以夾。
Since you want to eat it this way, how about I go cut some slices of tomato and see if there is any ham to put in between.

好啊！聽起來好棒！
Okay! Sounds great!

番茄切好囉！不過可惜火腿用完了，但家裡還有鮪魚罐頭，我想這樣搭配起來一定也不錯！
Tomato is ready, but we run out of ham. However, we still have tuna cans at home. I think they can match pretty well!

小餅乾夾番茄、起司和鮪魚，看起來色彩繽紛又可愛，而且好好吃喔！
Cookies with tomato, cheese and tuna filling. It looks so colorful, also lovely and very delicious!

我也沒想到這樣的組合竟然這麼好吃耶！下次家裡有客人來可以用這個招待他們。
I couldn't imagine they will be such a perfect match! Next time we can make this to entertain our guests at home.

而且做法好簡單，以後我肚子餓了也可以自己弄來吃，謝謝媽媽。

And it's very easy to prepare. Next time if I'm hungry, I can also prepare it for myself. Thanks, mom.

好用句型 [點餐必會]
Sentence Patterns

1. What kind of cheese is this？ 請問這是什麼口味的起司？
   chooco˙起司
   會這句更加分 There Is some cheese and some bread on the table.˙桌上有一些起司和麵包。

2. This glass/fork is dirty. Could you bring us another one? 這個坡璃杯／叉子有點髒，可以幫我們換一個嗎？
   dirty：髒的
   會這句更加分 Do not get your new shirt dirty! 別把你的新襯衫弄髒了！

3. At what time do you serve dinner? 請問晚餐是幾點供應？
   serve：供應
   會這句更加分 Do you serve vegetarian with buffets? 請問你們的自助餐有供應素食嗎？

4. How long do we need to wait for takeout? 請問外帶要等多久？
   takeout：外帶
   會這句更加分 I don't want to eat takeout on my birthday. 我不想在生日那天吃外帶的菜。

5. I'm starving. Let's hurry up and order. 我餓壞了,我們趕快點餐吧！

　　starving：餓的

　👍 會這句更加分　I am so starving that I can eat a cow. 我餓到可以吃下一頭牛。

6. May I have the check, please? 可以給我帳單嗎，謝謝。

　　check：帳單、發票

　👍 會這句更加分　When Mom saw the check she nearly passed out. 當媽媽看到帳單時幾乎昏了過去。

7. I have to avoid food containing fat/salt/sugar. 我必須避免含有油脂／鹽份／糖份的食物。

　　avoid：避免

　👍 會這句更加分　He wanted to avoid meeting his ex-girlfriend. 他想避免見到自己的前女友。

NOTES

4.5
港式點心大集合
Hong Kong Snacks

用英文聊美食 聊天必備
Talking About Food In English

朋友 A： 熬夜讀書一整晚，現在天都快亮了，肚子好餓喔！我們去吃早餐好不好？

I had been staying up all night studying, and dawn is coming now. I'm so hungry. How about going to have some breakfast?

朋友 B： 好啊，你想吃甚麼？

Ok, what do you want to eat?

朋友 A： 我突然好想吃口味重、味道濃郁的東西喔！有沒有甚麼早餐是淋了醬汁之後更好吃的？

I suddenly want to eat food which tastes heavy and strong! Is there any breakfast taste better after pour the sauce?

朋友 B： 蘿蔔糕（Radish cake）怎麼樣？淋上醬油膏超對味！

How about radish cake? It tastes great with soy sauce on it!

朋友 A： 對，就是這類的早餐！小籠包、燒賣也不錯，本身包的餡料就很好吃，搭配沾醬更棒！

Yes, that's the kind of breakfast! Xiaolongbao, Shumai are pretty good. The filling itself is very tasty. The sauce makes it even better!

朋友 B： 我們香港還有一種叫做拉腸粉（粵語簡稱拉腸或腸粉）的食物，外皮是使用米漿作成的，內餡一般是以碎肉、魚片、鮮蝦仁等，吃的時候搭配芝麻、甜醬、辣醬等，也是一絕！

There is one kind of food we have in Hong Kong named rice noodle rolls (in Cantonese referred to as steamed rice roll or shahe fen). The crust is made with rice milk, generally the stuffing was based on ground meat, fish fillet, shelled fresh shrimp, etc., matched with sesame, sweet sauce, chili sauce, etc. It tastes perfect too!

朋友 A： 在香港會吃腸粉當早餐嗎？

Can you eat rice noodle rolls as breakfast in Hong Kong？

朋友 B： 當然囉！在香港，腸粉是傳統粥店裡常見的早餐食品，還有在腸粉裡面包油條的吃法。

Of course. Rice noodle rolls are a common breakfast in the traditional porridge stores. There is another way to eat them, as fried bread stick rolls inside the rice noodle rolls.

朋友 A： 說到香港的小點心，我覺得最經典的就是叉燒包了！好吃的叉燒包裡面有肥瘦適中的叉燒肉，叉燒包蒸好之後稍微裂開露出裡面的紅色叉燒餡料，發出陣陣鹹甜的香味，越想我的肚子越餓！走，我們趕快去吃早餐吧。

Talking about snacks in Hong Kong, I think the most classic is the Cha siu bao! The tasty Cha siu bao inside has moderate Cantonese barbecue-pork, after steamed the Cha siu bao slightly exposing of the cracked inside of the red fillings of Cha siu, transpire the savory fragrance of sweet and salty. I'm more hungry after thinking on it! Go! Let's hurry to have some breakfast!

朋友 B： 等等，我知道學校附近有一間新開的早餐店，上次經過有注意到菜單裡面有叉燒三明治，不知道是不是叉燒包裡的那種叉燒？

Wait. I know there is a new breakfast shop near our school. I noticed there is cha siu sandwich in their menu last time I passed by. I don't know if it's the Cha siu that we are talking about.

朋友 A： 先上網查一下好了，以免白跑一趟。

Let's check on the Internet first, to avoid going there for nothing.

朋友 B： 好，我馬上查。有了… 看來是加在日式拉麵裡面那種滷過的叉燒…。

Ok, I'll check it right the way. There is... it looks like the Cha siu have been marinated by adding in the Japanese ramen…

朋友 A： 好可惜…。咦，不過這家店有好多種類的三明治喔，你看，醬汁還可以任意搭配耶！走，我們去吃吃看吧！

What a pity… well, however, this store has many kinds of sandwiches. Look! You can also choose any combination of sauces! Let's go and try it.

飲食小百科 文化大不同
Differences in Cultures

三明治 Sandwiches

在印度，三明治多是素食主義者食用，他們會製作素食的三明治。

In India, sandwiches are mostly vegetarian food, they make vegetarian sandwiches.

在英國，特別是北部，三明治十分常見並且不拘製作形式。三明治材料包括新鮮現煎的培根和奶油。所謂的 BLT 三明治，便是指培根（Bacon）、生菜（Lettuce）和番茄（Tomato）這三種餡料。

In the United Kingdom, particularly in the North, sandwiches are very common and are produced in different forms. Sandwich materials include freshly fried bacon and butter. The so-called BLT sandwich has three fillings-bacon, lettuce and tomato.

在美國，三明治會搭配薯條作為配菜。

In the United States, sandwiches will match with french fries as a side dish.

在香港，三明治稱為「三文治」，是茶餐廳的必備食品。香港的三明治通常以白麵包製成，最常見的三明治餡料有：煎雞蛋（蛋治）、火腿（腿治）、熟牛肉（牛治）等。

In Hong Kong, sandwich is called "sanwenzhi," which is an essential food for tea restaurants. Sandwiches in Hong Kong are usually made with white bread. The most common sandwich fillings are: fried eggs, ham, cooked beef and some other filling.

在澳門，三明治也是茶餐廳的必備食品。除了一般的餡料之外，也會融合葡萄牙人喜愛的辣椒橄欖油沙丁魚作成辣魚三明治（辣魚多），是除了豬排包之外的另一項澳門特色美食。

In Macau, sandwiches are also an essential food for tea restaurants. They combine Portuguese's favorite, sardines in spicy olive oil, to make spicy sardines sandwich. It's one of Macau's specialties, besides pork chop bun.

在台灣，三明治是西式早餐店必備的餐點，一份三明治加一杯紅茶是台灣人常見的早餐組合，有豬排三明治、雞排三明治、總匯三明治等各種搭配，與傳統西式三明治並不相同。三明治在台灣的便利商店也買的到。

In Taiwan, sandwiches are a basic meal in Western breakfast shops. A sandwich and a cup of black tea is a common breakfast combination for Taiwanese. There are pork chop sandwiches, fried chicken breast sandwiches, club sandwich and others, which are different from the traditional Western sandwiches. Sandwiches can also be bought in the convenience stores in Taiwan.

蘿蔔糕 Radish Cake

傳統粵式茶樓的蘿蔔糕一般分為蒸和煎兩種做法。蒸煮好的蘿蔔糕加上醬油調味，而煎蘿蔔糕則是將已蒸煮好的蘿蔔糕切成塊，放在少量的油中煎至表面金黃色即成，還可以選擇搭配甜醬、芝麻醬或辣醬作調味。

Traditional Cantonese restaurants radish cake is generally divided into two kinds, steamed and fried. Steamed radish cake is dipped with soy sauce. You may also cut steamed radish cake into pieces and fried them until it appears golden yellow. Sweet, sesame or chili sauces can be choosen for seasoning.

而新加坡、馬來西亞的「菜頭粿」通常以炒蘿蔔糕的方法為主。做法則是將已蒸煮好的蘿蔔糕切成小塊，再和甜醬油、蔥花、雞蛋、蒜粒等一併放進油鍋中炒熱而成。近年，一些新興的粵式茶樓亦同時加入這種炒蘿蔔糕作為點心。

The main method of "fried radish cake" in Singapore and Malaysia is usually pan-fried radish cake. The method is to cut the steamed radish cake into small pieces, then use pan fry it with sweet soy sauce, chopped green onions, eggs, garlic, etc. In recent years, some new Cantonese restaurants also add this kind of fried radish cake as dessert.

台灣的客家蘿蔔糕簡單、沒有太多的添加物，以蘿蔔的味道為主角。作法是將在來米泡水後去水磨漿，添加燜煮過的蘿蔔絲，經調味後蒸熟。可以沾醬油、桔子醬等調味料食用。

Taiwan's Hakka radish cake makes the radish flavor the protagonist, which is simple and without many additives. The method is to grind the indica rice after soaked it in water and add stewed shredded turnip, then steam after seasoning. It can be dipped with soy sauce, orange sauce and other seasoning.

菜餚的故事 你知道嗎？
Stories About Food

三明治－懶人的發明物 Sandwich - a Lazy Invention

據說於十八世紀時，英國有一位嗜賭如命的約翰·孟塔古，第四代三明治伯爵（John Montagu, 4th Earl of Sandwich），每當他手拿撲克牌就欲罷不能，非打到筋疲力盡為止。這位伯爵連離桌用餐都覺得浪費時間，便要

僕人把麵包和肉、蔬菜等擺在賭桌旁，方便他隨時取食。他也懶得使用刀叉，索性將肉和蔬菜夾在兩片麵包當中，一手抓著吃，以便另外一隻手還可以繼續打牌。伯爵的朋友品嚐過後也大聲叫好，這種食物由於製作簡單、便於攜帶且變化無窮，很快就流傳開來。後來，人們便拿三明治伯爵的名字「Sandwich」作這個食物的名稱。三明治伯爵大概從沒想過，自己的名字會隨著食物流傳下來吧。不過，嚴格説起來，三明治不能算是三明治伯爵發明的，因為早在古羅馬就有類似的食物記載。

It is said that in the 18th century, John Montagu, 4th Earl of Sandwich, who had a passion for gambling. Whenever he had the cards on his hand, he wouldn't stop until he felt completely exhausted. He didn't even want to spend time on dining while he was gambling. He asked the servant to put bread, meat and vegetables next to the gambling table, so he can eat them easily. He also didn't want to use knife and fork, so he simply held the meat and vegetables with two slices of bread, using one hand to eat, the other hand to continue playing cards. Earl's friends also applauded after tasting the food. Due to its simple production, easy to carry and endless variations, it spread very quickly. Later, people took the name from Earl of Sandwich to call the food "Sandwich." Earl of Sandwich probably never thought that his name would be handed down by food. However, strictly talking, sandwich can't be regarded as an invention of Earl, because there were similar kinds of food documented as early as Ancient Rome.

實用會話 聊天必備
Useful Phrases

請給我一份三明治。
I would like to have a sandwich, please.

我們有火腿、鮪魚、雞蛋沙拉、培根、熟牛肉和
豬排三明治，請問您要哪一種呢？
We have ham, tuna, egg salad, bacon, cooked
beef and pork chop sandwiches. Which kind of
sandwich would you like to have?

哪一種賣的最好？
Which one sells the best?

熟牛肉和豬排三明治是我們的招牌商品，其他幾
種也都很暢銷。
Our signature products are cooked beef and pork
chop sandwiches. Other kinds are also very
popular as well.

那我來一份豬排三明治好了。吐司不要烤太焦。
I would like to have a pork chop sandwich. Be
sure not to overbake the toast.

好的，請問生菜都要加嗎？
Ok. Would you like to add all raw vegetables?

 你們有加哪幾種生菜？
Which kind of raw vegetables do you have?

今天有萵苣、番茄、洋蔥和小黃瓜。
There are lettuce, tomato, onion and cucumber today.

 我不要小黃瓜，其他都加。
I want all, except for cucumber.

好的，請問醬料要番茄醬、美乃滋或是黃芥末醬呢？
Ok, which kind of sauce would you like to add, ketchup, mayonnaise or mustard sauce?

 妳推薦哪一種？
Which one do you prefer?

我個人覺得豬排三明治搭配美乃滋不錯。
I personally think that mayonnaise matches with pork chop sandwich.

好，那就聽妳的。對了，可以多幫我灑一點胡椒粉嗎？

Ok, I will listen to you. By the way, can you spray more pepper for me?

沒問題。先生，這是您的豬排三明治，祝您有個愉快的一天，期待您再次光臨。

No problem sir. Here is your pork chop sandwich. Wish you a pleasant day and looking forward to seeing you again.

好用句型 點餐必會
Sentence Patterns

1. Can I have a Tuna on whole wheat bread, please? 我想要一份全麥麵包夾鮪魚三明治，謝謝。

   tuna：鮪魚

   👍會這句更加分 Try some tuna sashimi. It's delicious. 試試看鮪魚生魚片，很好吃喔！

2. Can I have some more lettuce, please? 我可以加多一點萵苣嗎？謝謝。

   lettuce：萵苣

   👍會這句更加分 My grandmother grew some lettuce in her garden. 我的祖母在菜園裡種了一些萵苣。

3. Can I have extra cheese, please? 我可以多要一點起司嗎，謝謝。

   extra：額外的

會這句更加分 These were extra supplies in case they should be needed.
這些額外的備用品是為了以防不時之需。

4. Do you have a plain meal? 請問你們有口味清淡一點的餐點嗎？

plain：清淡的、平淡的

會這句更加分 This is the recipes for the people who like their food plain.
這是給希望食物口味清淡的人的食譜。

5. Is it the right amount for one person? 請問這樣的份量一個人吃得完嗎？

amount：量

會這句更加分 Mayor's assistant has a large amount of E-mail to answer
every day. 市長的助理每天都有大量的電子郵件要回覆。

6. How many pieces in one order? 請問一份裡面有幾片／塊？

piece：片、部分

會這句更加分 The boy gave me a piece of chocolate. 那個小男孩給我一塊
巧克力。

7. What's the garnish? 請問配菜是甚麼？

garnish：為增加色香味而添加的配菜；裝飾物

會這句更加分 The cook garnished the cake with strawberries. 那位廚師為
蛋糕裝飾上草莓。

NOTES

4.6
泰式點心攤
Thai Snacks

朋友 A： 上次去你家玩，你媽媽招待我們吃的甜點好好吃喔！我到現在還念念不忘！

Last time we went to play at your house. The dessert made by your mother was very delicious! I still miss them.

朋友 B： 你是說炸香蕉嗎？

You mean fried banana?

朋友 A： 對，就是那個。外皮炸的又酥又香，裡面包的香蕉口感綿密又帶點微酸，還有濃濃的椰子香味撲鼻而來，那滋味真是難以忘懷。

Yes, that's the one. The skin was crisp and smells wonderful. The stuffing inside tasted creamy and a little bit sour. Also the strong coconut fragrance greeted me. That taste is really hard to forgot.

朋友 B： 炸香蕉是泰國道地的特色小點心，只要將香蕉切塊再裹上麵糊油炸就可以了，很簡單。

Fried bananas are authentic Thai snacks. You only need to cut bananas into pieces and then wrap them in butter to fry. Very simple.

朋友 A： 平常她也會做泰式點心給你吃嗎？

Does she usually prepare Thai desserts for you as well?

朋友 B： 嗯，還滿常的。我家餐桌上每天都可以吃到泰式料理，假日她有空的時候就會做甜點給我們吃。

Uhm... pretty often. We have Thai food on the dinner table in my family every day. She will make dessert for us if she has free time on holiday.

朋友 A： 好羨慕你有一位來自泰國的媽媽喔！你會跟你媽媽學習怎麼做嗎？

I envy you for having a mother from Thailand! Will you learn how to make those desserts with your mom?

朋友 B： 比較複雜的料理我不會，不過一些簡單的小點心我已經學起來了，像是青木瓜沙拉。

Not the complex ones, but I have learned some of simple snacks, such as green papaya salad.

朋友 A： 那個我知道，酸辣的泰式醬汁配上口感爽脆的青木瓜絲，非常開胃。

I know that. The Thai sauce which taste hot and sour accompanied by crisp taste of green papaya silk. It is very appetizing.

朋友 B： 我媽媽教我做的還會放入花生、蝦米、檸檬、大蒜、辣椒、魚露等等，搭配泰國米線吃也很好吃！

My mother taught me to add peanuts, dried shrimp, lemon, garlic, chili, fish sauce, etc. It's also delicious to match with Thai noodles!

朋友 A： 我越聽越餓了啦！可以現在就跑去府上打擾嗎？

I'm getting hungry listening to you! Can I go to your house for some food now?

朋友 B： 我媽媽現在不在家，不過你要來的話我倒是可以準備一些泰式小點心給你吃。

My mom isn't at home now, but I can prepare some Thai snacks for you if you want to come.

朋友 A： 耶！太棒了！那你會做月亮蝦餅嗎？

Yeah! That's great! Do you know how to make shrimp pancake?

朋友 B： 我媽媽說月亮蝦餅其實不是源自於泰國，而是來自於台灣。

My mom says that shrimp pancake is actually not derived from Thailand, but Taiwan.

朋友 A： 甚麼！？我不相信？

What!? I can't believe it!

朋友 B： 是真的！月亮蝦餅的由來已不可考，不過據泰國觀光局表示，泰國從來沒有「月亮蝦餅」這道菜，而是台灣人綜合緬甸菜、越南菜，加上台灣口味研發而成，是從台灣紅回泰國的泰國菜，對許多泰國人來說也感到很不可思議！

It's true! The origin of the shrimp pancake can't be proved, but according to the Ministry of Tourism of Thailand, Thailand never had a dish named "shrimp pancake." Taiwanese research and development integrated Burmese, Vietnamese and Taiwanese flavors. It's the dish that got famous in Taiwan, then spread back to Thailand. Many Thai people feel amazed too!

朋友 A： 那你還會做甚麼小點心？

Which kind of snacks can you make then?

朋友 **B**： 我做馬加魚餅和沙嗲給你吃吧！

I can make mackerel cake and satay for you!

飲食小百科 文化大不同
Differences in Cultures

沙嗲 Satay

沙嗲據說是爪哇攤販根據印度的卡博串所發明的。沙嗲從爪哇跨越海峽傳遍荷屬東印度諸群島，不同島嶼上的居民製作出各式各樣的沙嗲食譜，到了 19 世紀末期，沙嗲已經傳到鄰近的印尼、新加坡和泰國。荷屬東印度群島的馬來人長程移民將沙嗲傳到南非，成了 sosatie。

Allegedly, satay was invented by a Java vendor based on the Kebab from India. Satay spread from Java to all the Dutch East Indies islands, different kinds of satay recipes were produced by residents from different islands. In the late 19th century, satay spread to neighboring Indonesia, Singapore and Thailand. The Malays of the Dutch East Indies who emigrated far away spread satay to South Africa, becoming "sosatie."

沙嗲是在泰國很受歡迎的大眾美食。由於泰國在國際上大量推廣泰國美食，幾乎全球所有的泰國餐廳都可以吃到沙嗲，比印尼美食還要早吸引世界烹飪界的注意，因此國際上普遍誤以為沙嗲的起源地是泰國，殊不知正確的起源地其實是印尼。

Satay is a very popular delicatessen in Thai cuisine. Thailand does a lot of promotion of Thai cuisine and satay can be found in almost all the Thai restaurants in the world, which even attract attention earlier than the

Indonesian restaurants in the culinary community in the world. The international community generally mistaken satay originated in Thailand. In fact, it originated in Indonesia.

沙嗲在荷蘭被稱為 saté 或 sateh，已經完全融入荷蘭當地的日常菜餚，在小吃店和超市隨處可見。荷蘭的印尼餐廳會供應加了甜醬油的山羊肉沙嗲（satehkambing）、附花生沾醬的豬肉或雞肉沙嗲。沙嗲搭配沙拉和炸薯條在酒吧或小餐館裡極受歡迎。

In the Netherlands, satay is called saté or sateh, which has been fully integrated into Dutch local daily dishes, and also can be found everywhere in the snack bars and supermarkets. Dutch Indonesian restaurants will supply the satehkambing by adding sweet soy sauce, accompanying pork or chicken satay with peanut sauce. Satay with salad and french fries is extremely popular in bars or small restaurants.

在新加坡，常見的沙嗲類型有雞肉沙嗲（Satay Ayam）、牛肉沙嗲（Satay Lembu）、羊肉沙嗲（Satay Kambing）、牛腸沙嗲（Satay Perut）以及牛肚沙嗲（Satay Babat）。新加坡的國家航空公司，新加坡航空公司使用沙嗲作為頭等艙和商務艙乘客的開胃菜。

In Singapore, common types of satay are Satay Ayam, Satay Lembu, Satay Kambing, Satay Perut and Satay Babat. Singapore's national airline uses satay as an appetizer for the first and business class passengers.

馬來西亞各地都有被稱為馬來沙嗲（Sate）的沙嗲，在餐館、街頭與夜市的小販都有販賣。雖然流行的通常是牛肉沙嗲和雞肉沙嗲，但在馬來西亞的不同地區已經逐漸開發出當地獨創的沙嗲。

Malaysia's satay (Sate) came throughout the Malay, who sell it in restaurants, streets and night market vendors. However, the popular satay is usually beef satay and chicken, but in different areas of Malaysia has been gradually developed a unique local satay.

除了穆斯林馬來人的清真沙嗲，馬來西亞的華裔也吃豬肉沙嗲。

Except for the halal satay for Malaysian Muslim, Malaysian Chinese can also eat pork satay.

菜餚的故事　你知道嗎？
Stories About Food

在歐美的神話故事中常可見到「羅勒」的蹤跡。在古羅馬時期，羅勒被稱為 basilescus，源自噴火龍 basilescus 之意，傳說胸前必須佩帶著羅勒才能解除魔咒、擊敗噴火怪獸。也因此在歐美的民俗療法中會以羅勒作為蛇毒或蜘蛛毒的解藥。據傳耶穌基督復活之後，在他的墓穴旁長滿了羅勒，因此東正教祭典使用的聖水都是以羅勒調製而成。羅勒在希臘文中代表著皇室或國王，據稱當時在宗教祭典上祝賀希臘國王的香油即為羅勒精油所製成，因而羅勒又被稱為「國王的藥草」。而在羅馬尼亞，羅勒代表的意涵較為浪漫，當男孩接受少女所送的羅勒枝條，表示他們已經正式訂婚。在印度，羅勒則被視為神聖的植物，當在法庭上發誓的時候必須以它發誓。在印度也認為配戴羅勒葉片可以避邪。

In Europe and America's fairy tales, it often can be seen the trail of "basil." In Ancient Rome times, basil was known as "basilescus," from the Charizard "basilescus," that in the legend must had worn the basil in the chest for lifting the curse to beat the Charizard. Therefore, an old remedy in Europe consists in using basil as an antidote to snake venom or spider venom. It is said that after the resurrection of Jesus Christ, there was basil

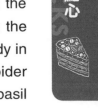

covering his grave, so holy water of Orthodox ceremonies are blended basil water. Basil represents the royal family or the king in Greek. It is said that sesame oil in religious ceremonies is made with basil oil to commemorate the king of Greece. Due to this reason, basil is also referred to as "the king of herbs." In Romania, representative implications of basil are more romantic. When a girl accepts basil branches from a boy, it means that they are officially engaged. In India, basil is considered to be a sacred plant, which have to swear to it in the court. In India, people also believe that wearing basil blades can avoid evil spirits.

實用會話 聊天必備
Useful Phrases

陳先生，好幾天沒看到你出現了。
Mr. Chen, I didn't see you for several days.

是啊，前幾天加班比較晚，我就沒過來用餐了。
Yeah, a couple of days ago I had to work overtime quite late, so I didn't come to dine.

上班族真是辛苦了！今天要吃甚麼？
Being an office worker is really hard. What would you like to have today?

老樣子！你也知道，我一直是你們的忠實顧客。
Same old! As you know, I've always being your royal customer.

謝謝啦！都這麼熟了，我們最近也決定推出月亮蝦餅，要不要吃？我免費招待！
Thanks. Since we are so familiar, we decided to launch shrimp pancake recently. Would you like to try it? My treat!

好啊！不過我一直想不透，這月亮蝦餅為什麼要加「月亮」兩個字呢？
Ok! But I can't figure out why shrimp pancake has to add "moon" this word?

據說是蝦餅在還沒有下鍋油炸之前，一整片白白圓圓的，像極了滿月，所以才稱為月亮蝦餅。
It is said that because before deep-frying the shrimp pancake. The whole shrimp cake is round and white and looks like the full moon, so it is called shrimp pancake.

原來如此。
I see.

其實這道菜色早在十多年前就有了，直到近五年才變的火紅，身為泰式餐廳當然要跟進一下。
In fact, this dish appeared as early as ten years ago. It has become famous in the last five years. As a Thai restaurant of course we have to follow up.

不過我看其他餐廳賣的月亮蝦餅，在上桌前都會先切成像披薩那樣一片一片的，再將尖的部分朝外擺設，這樣比較方便取用。
But I see some restaurants cut it like a piece of pizza before bringing it on the table and then display the tipping portion outward. This way will be more convenient.

好，我會改進！
Ok, I will do it!

好用句型 點餐必會
Sentence Patterns

1. Could you take a picture of our family with the food?
   請問可以幫我們全家跟餐點拍張照嗎？
   picture：照片、圖畫

   👍會這句更加分 She pasted the pictures that she took on the wall.
   她把她拍的照片貼在牆上。

2. I don't think we ordered this dessert. Can you recalculate it?

我不認為我有點甜點，可以請你重新計算一次嗎？

recalculate：重新計算

👍會這句更加分 We can recalculate the rate if it is necessary.

如果有需要，我們可以再重新計算一次費用。

3. Can I pay the food with credit card and pay the tips with cash?

請問我可以刷卡付食物的錢然後用現金付小費嗎？

cash：現金

👍會這句更加分 How much cash on hand to buy a house?

手頭上要有多少現金才能買房子？

4. Can you break the 100USD into 5 of 20 USD to get a change?

請問你可以幫我把 100 塊美金找開成 5 張 20 塊嗎？

break：兌鈔

👍會這句更加分 Where can I break money when I'm in the airport?

請問我在機場的時候可以去哪裡換鈔？

5. Can you call a cab and tell me when the cab is here?

請問你可以幫我叫計程車並通知我車到了嗎？

cab：計程車

👍會這句更加分 The college student called a cab for the old man.

那位大學生幫老人叫了一輛計程車。

6. I'd like to come back to this restaurant. Do you have any business cards?

我還想再回來這家餐廳用餐，請問你們有名片嗎？

business：商業、公務

👍會這句更加分 My husband has to go to Japan on business next week.

我先生下週必須到日本出差。

7. I found a tiny hair in the food. I'd like to cancel this order and have a check.

我在餐點裡發現了一根毛髮，我想要取消所有的餐點並結帳。

tiny：極小的

會這句更加分 Look the tiny nose of that cat! It's so cute.

看看那隻貓的小鼻子！真是可愛。

NOTES

Learn Smart! 033

美食英語
Let's Talk about Gourmet in English!

作　　者	伍羚芝、倍斯特編輯部
發 行 人	周瑞德
企劃編輯	倍斯特編輯部
執行編輯	劉俞青
特約編輯	焦家洵
英文翻譯	林采薇
封面設計	高鍾琪
內文排版	菩薩蠻數位文化有限公司
校　　對	徐瑞璞 陳欣慧

印　　製	世和印製企業有限公司
初　　版	2014 年 5 月
出　　版	倍斯特出版事業有限公司
電　　話	（02）2351-2007
傳　　真	（02）2351-0887
地　　址	100 台北市中正區福州街 1 號 10 樓之 2
E m a i l	best.books.service@gmail.com
定　　價	新台幣 329 元

港澳地區總經銷　泛華發行代理有限公司

地　　址	香港筲箕灣東旺道 3 號星島新聞集團大廈 3 樓
電　　話	（852）2798-2323
傳　　真	（852）2796-5471

國家圖書館出版品預行編目(CIP)資料

美食英語 / 伍羚芝, 倍斯特編輯部著. -- 初版. -- 臺
北市：倍斯特, 2014.05
　　面；　公分
　ISBN 978-986-90331-5-2(平裝)

　1. 英語 2. 會話

805.188　　　　　　　　　　　　103007720